living FAST

ADRIENNE GIORDANO

STEELE RIDGE
www.SteeleRidgeSeries.com

Print Edition, October 2016, ISBN: 978-1-944898-08-3
For more information contact: adrienneg@adriennegiordano.com

BOOKS AVAILABLE BY CO-AUTHORS OF THE STEELE RIDGE SERIES

BOOKS AVAILABLE BY TRACEY DEVLYN

NEXUS SERIES
Historical romantic suspense
A Lady's Revenge
Checkmate, My Lord
A Lady's Secret Weapon
Latymer
Shev

BONES & GEMSTONES SERIES
Historical romantic mystery
Night Storm

TEA TIME SHORTS & NOVELLAS
Sweet historical romance
His Secret Desire

Books available by Kelsey Browning

PROPHECY OF LOVE SERIES
Sexy contemporary romance
A Love to Last
A Passion to Pursue

TEXAS NIGHTS SERIES
Sexy contemporary romance
Personal Assets
Running the Red Light
Problems in Paradise
Designed for Love

BY INVITATION ONLY SERIES
Sexy contemporary romance
Amazed by You

THE GRANNY SERIES w/NANCY NAIGLE
Southern cozy mysteries
In For a Penny
Fit to Be Tied
In High Cotton
Under the Gun

JENNY & TEAGUE NOVELLAS
Contemporary romance
Always on My Mind
Come a Little Closer

living FAST

ADRIENNE GIORDANO

CHAPTER ONE

EVERYTHING WAS GOING TO HELL.

Fast.

Reid stood on the back end of his mother's property and stared out at acres upon acres of open land while his youngest brother, Jonah, rattled on about…something. Jonah's mouth was moving and words were definitely coming out, but by the time they got to Reid's ears everything morphed to a muddled *rowr, rowr, rowr.*

"Wait." Reid shook his head to clear the fog. "Slow down. What I think you're telling me is that you want *me* to oversee building some kind of law enforcement training center? Here? In Mom's backyard?"

In the distance, the bright May sunshine reflected off the windows of the large empty building the town had intended to be a state-of-the-art sports complex.

The Baby Billionaire waved one hand at enough open space for a man to get lost in. "You can use the building already available from the defunct sports complex. And it's not exactly Mom's backyard. I gave her the house, but she doesn't care what we do with the rest of the twenty thousand acres." Jonah flashed a grin. "I'm giving you seven of them."

Whoa. Giving him? Nobody gave Reid Steele

anything. He worked for every damned dime he earned. And what the hell did he know about building a training center for cops?

From the age of sixteen, he'd set his goals around becoming a Green Beret. The tip of the spear. The baddest of the bad. He wanted it all. And got it. At least until he jumped off the back of a truck eight months ago and blew out his knee.

All that work, the studying of foreign cultures and the accents and languages, work that he loved and shared and occasionally bitched about with the guys in his unit, was gone now. All of it.

Poof.

Gone.

He drew a deep breath and scratched a sudden itch on the side of his face. "Dude, this isn't my thing. I'm boots on the ground. What do I know about zoning regulations and all the bureaucratic bullshit that'll come with developing a training center?"

Jonah faced him, his hazel eyes direct. "We'll figure it out. All I know is I got a boatload of money wrapped up in this place and we need to revitalize it. I see this as a family operation. Last I checked, you were part of the family."

Oh, leave it to Jonah to play that card. Reid held his finger up. "No one told you to use your own money to bail the town out of a bad deal. You made that decision yourself. And even if I knew anything about building a training center, maybe this isn't in my plan. You already did this to Grif, you're not railroading me into giving up my life. That's bullshit."

Freaking Jonah.

Baby Billionaire made a grunting noise low in his throat, looked out over the property he now owned, and after a few seconds turned back to him. "Let's take a minute here. Before we wind up bloody."

Because, yeah, that had been known to happen with the Steele brothers. As much as they all loved each other, none of them had a problem throwing hands to settle an argument.

"Maybe I came at this wrong," Jonah continued. "I don't expect you to give up your life or your plans, *whatever* they might be."

Freaking Jonah. He knew Reid was at loose ends trying to figure out his next career.

One for a washed-up Green Beret.

And the occasional firearms safety lessons he'd been giving at one of the local ranges to bring in some money wouldn't cut it.

Dammit.

"My thought," Jonah said, "is that you oversee the development of a facility where law enforcement agencies can send their officers for training. A privately owned police academy, if you will. Once it's done, you can go off and do whatever it is you're planning. Think of it as a temporary gig. You sure as hell have the skills for it. Who would know better than you what a facility like this would need?"

Reid looked out over the tall grass and shrubs. All that open land a prime location for a facility like the one he'd been trained on. In actuality, it might be fun. If he didn't have to deal with bullshit paperwork and being stuck in the small town he'd left at eighteen. Back then he'd wanted to experience the world. And he'd done it. Loved it, too. And he sure as shit didn't expect to give up that exploring at the age of thirty.

Again he scratched his cheek and tried to ignore his brother's stare. "I don't know; I'll think about it."

Jonah sighed. "What if I pay you? Think of yourself as some hotshot consultant. Consultants get paid big bucks for shit like this."

And now his little brother expected to *pay* him.

As.

If.

He'd sooner cut out his own eye than take Jonah's

money. The kid worked hard for that fortune and shouldn't be giving it away.

"My ass. I'm not taking your money. We're family. My only issue is that I don't want to be tied down."

Tied down and obsessing over his current circumstances. Something he despised. For years, he'd thrived on military life. The ability to serve. To make a damned difference. Now he didn't know where the hell he fit.

So he'd come home to regroup and figure out how to become whole again. Swapped out his BDUs for jeans and T-shirts and wound up in the middle of his calculating baby brother's plan to reenergize Steele Ridge.

"Who said you're tied down? Is this about the job in Georgia? Did they make you an offer?"

Two days earlier he'd flown to the land of peaches for a look-see at a private security operation interested in hiring former military guys for some overseas contract work. Thirty minutes into the interview, they'd offered him a job. But the damned knee. Could it hold up?

And did he really want to be doing private contract work?

"Yeah, they made an offer."

"So you're leaving?"

Was he? Who the hell knew? Reid shrugged. "I don't know if it's the right fit."

"Then do the build-out while you're waiting for whatever is the right fit. It's not like you have a plan otherwise."

Well, that was part of the problem, wasn't it? He didn't have a plan. Except to not be in Steele Ridge permanently. He'd been offered a job that might satisfy his craving for action and allow him to utilize his skills, yet...what?

He didn't know. He was great at blowing shit up and could sell a dog off a meat truck, but he wasn't a nine-to-fiver. No way.

"If I had a plan, would I be whining?"

Jonah snorted. "You're not whining. You might be pissed at me, but you're not whining. Just do this. It's a total no-brainer for you."

Reid bit down hard enough to send a shot of pain through his jaw. He did *not* want to be saddled with this monster. A project like this would be huge. A helluva challenge, which Reid loved, but the red tape? Enormous.

Goddamned Jonah.

But, hell, he didn't have anything else to do and in truth, he was bored out of his skull. Reid glanced down at his knee, where the dull throb reminded him he might need an ibuprofen soon. He redirected his thoughts, vying for more time without medication. Each day he'd been stretching it out a little further. The goal was zero ibuprofen and he'd just dropped from five to four. Definitely on his way.

He focused on the building in the distance, let the tweeting birds and warm sun settle his mind.

A training center.

With his experience, he could probably do it.

What the hell else do I have to do?

"All right," he said.

"You'll do it?"

"I'm not dealing with paperwork or red tape. I'll do the hands-on stuff while I'm deciding if I want this job in Georgia." He poked his finger at Jonah. "But I'm pissed at you. Just so you know."

After agreeing to Jonah's request, Reid hauled ass into town. What he needed now was a beer and a bitch session and when it came to bitch sessions, big brother Grif always made it worthwhile.

Reid pulled into a parking spot in front of La Belle Style and sat behind the wheel of his truck staring at the window display. A fancy boutique.

In Steele Ridge.

Everything.

Going.

To hell.

What did the Ridge need a place like that for? Nobody here wore that edgy New York stuff.

He glanced in the rearview, spotted Grif coming out of the old Murchison building across the street where he kept an office. Perfect. Just the guy he'd come looking for.

The sun spilled across the dash, heating up the interior, stealing his air and making his head pound— *trapped*—reminding him how he'd felt for the past months, since coming back to the Ridge. He yanked the door handle and kicked the door open, sucking in much-needed oxygen.

Grif knocked on the passenger side and Reid hit the window button. "The Baby Billionaire." he said. "Do you care if I kill him? I mean, he's screwing us up. I'll make it quick. Painless even."

Grif let out a sigh. "You can't kill him. I already tried. He's too stubborn to die."

The two of them shared a laugh, more out of frustration that Jonah, their little brother/video-game tycoon/billionaire and general pain in the ass had more or less set a bomb off in their lives.

Grif, older brother number two, understood all too well what it felt like to have his existence throttled by Jonah.

Needing to move, Reid slid his .45 from the holster mounted under his steering column, secured it at his waist, and hopped out of the sweet F-150 it'd taken five years to save his army pennies for. All that saving and he'd barely driven the damned thing in the two years he'd owned it.

Welcome home, kid.

The afternoon sun continued to beat down, glowing hot, for May in North Carolina anyway, and he tipped his head back, let the warmth wash over him.

He needed to relax. Just let the fickle universe do its

thing, and stop obsessing about what he was supposed to do with his life.

Because one thing was for sure. Special Forces was out.

On the other side of the truck, Grif adjusted the sleeves of his pretty-boy dress shirt. Reid glanced down at his jeans, biker boots, and T-shirt and snorted. It wouldn't be the first difference between him and Grif.

He leaned his elbows on the hood, spotted a minuscule ding that needed repair. He'd get to that later. "Here's the thing I don't understand."

Grif laughed. "You mean there's only one?"

No shit there. "Give me ten seconds and I'll give you a few more. But, for now, what I don't understand is how Jonah-the-runt thinks he's gonna turn our shit upside down with rebuilding this town. Now he wants a training center built. And dummy me, I agreed to it. All he has to do is write a fucking check. You and me? Total life change."

At this point, Grif had probably taken the bigger hit on that one because he had a client list, based in California, he was trying to manage from the East Coast.

And that was in addition to being the Jonah-appointed city manager of the newly minted Steele Ridge.

Reid? His blown-out knee had ended his Army career so he was in the wind anyway. Still, he didn't like Jonah telling him how to live his life.

A quack—literally—disrupted his mental rant and Reid turned.

Oh, come on. Now this?

A mama duck led her troop of ducklings across Main Street. The lack of cars eliminated the possibility of a traffic jam and if some asshole teenager came barreling through town, forget it. Lights out for the duckies.

And Reid wasn't letting that happen. "No way," Reid said, marching into the street where, yep, a car whipped the turn on Main.

Oh, jeez. This was worse than an asshole teenager.

Crazy Mrs. Royce in her giant '85 Lincoln Continental. Not only was she half deaf, she was blind as a bat and meaner than a pissed-off grizzly. And her driving? Please. Everyone in town hauled ass when she got behind the wheel. No one was safe—never mind a bunch of ducklings—with Mrs. Royce on the road.

In the middle of the street, he held his hand up in the classic stop signal and hoped to hell that giant Lincoln didn't make him a pancake.

Mrs. Royce kept coming and Reid looked back at the ducks, the mama now squawking, bitching at him for getting too close.

"Hey," he said. "Don't yell at me. You're the one walking your babies across the street. Where are *your* protective instincts?"

The knocking of the Continental's ancient engine drew closer.

Please let her see me in the street.

"Reid," Mr. Perkins said from the sidewalk, "did someone hit you with a pipe? That woman'll run your ass over."

He could see the obit now. *Green Beret killed saving ducklings.*

Shit.

What a way to go out.

For added presence, he held up his other hand, started waving his arms, but the Lincoln rocked along, bearing down on him.

In all the ways he'd almost died, this one was a total disappointment.

"Stop!" he hollered.

With only ten yards to spare, Mrs. Royce slammed on her brakes, bringing the land yacht to a lurching halt.

Mrs. R. stuck her head out the open driver's window. "Reid Steele! What in God's name are you doing?"

Seriously? She didn't see the ducks?

He pointed at the still-bitching mama duck. "Ducks,

Mrs. Royce. I'm trying to get them across the street."

The woman tipped her head down, then swung it left as she watched the mama and babies waddle along.

Unbelievable.

Behind him, another car beeped, sending mama duck into another hormonal rage.

And, hello? This was the Ridge, where the hell were these people going in such a hurry?

Reid angled back, spotted the Peterlin kid's truck. That kid. He was the one who tried to get Evie's pants off her in the eleventh grade. And didn't that bring a fresh bout of anger racing to the surface.

Back then Britt had handled the situation by cleaning his shotgun on the front porch whenever the kid showed up.

The subtle approach.

Reid? He'd have shoved the horny bastard against a wall and showed him exactly where he could put his hands on their baby sister. Which, pretty much, came down to the top of her head.

"Relax," he said to the Peterlin kid. "She's almost across and you'll be on your way."

"I'm busy, Reid!" Mrs. Royce yelled.

At least one of them was. Mrs. Royce's role of being the crazy lady in town at least gave her a legacy to leave behind. Which was a whole lot more than Reid could say about himself.

Mama and her babies marched up the handicapped ramp on the opposite side of the street and made their way down the sidewalk. Reid stepped back, waved the cars through and headed back to his truck where Grif hit him with a caustic grin.

"Saving the day again. You just can't help yourself."

"Fuck off. I wasn't about to watch those ducklings get plastered. Now I need a beer. You coming with me or am I getting drunk alone?"

"I can't. Sorry. Meeting with the mayor."

As the newly appointed city manager of Steele Ridge,

part of Grif's responsibilities included keeping the mayor and council members from blowing the wad of cash Jonah had ponied up to save the town from bankruptcy. It also meant Grif was busier than a one-legged man in a kicking contest.

Out of the corner of his eye, Reid spotted a flash of blue. Coming out of the boutique—*hiya, sweet thing*—was a dark-haired woman wearing a tight dress the color of a perfect summer sky. He'd seen her at Mom's birthday party a few months ago and she'd nabbed his very horny attention then, too.

She faced the front window and scanned its contents. And that rear view? Holy hell, Reid's lungs might have collapsed.

God, that ass.

He swiveled his head back to Grif, slid his sunglasses down his nose and jerked his head toward the store.

"Wicked hot," he said, keeping his voice low enough where the sweet thing wouldn't hear him.

He might be a pig, but he wasn't that much of a pig.

Grif rolled his eyes. "Forget it. That's Brynne. She's young and you're an animal."

"How young we talking?"

Big brother laughed. "Twenty-four, I think. You don't remember her?"

"Should I?"

"She's April's little sister."

Reid did a double-take. No way. "*That's* April's sister?"

"Yeah. Evie said she hasn't changed back to her maiden name yet. My guess is she likes the sound of Whitfield better than Snodder."

No wonder Reid hadn't recognized the name. "Didn't she used to be…" He waved one hand. "What's the word?"

"Plain? Chunky?"

Dang, that sounded harsh. But, yeah, compared to Homecoming Queen April, Brynne had been the ordinary one.

Like other things around this town, a *lot* had changed.

"Forget it, Reid. Evie fills in at the store when Brynne's shorthanded and they're friends. Do us all a favor and stay clear."

Twenty-four. He could handle that. In spite of his foul mood, Reid ripped off a grin. "But I'm bored and Jonah pissed me off."

And he knew Grif could sympathize. Here they were, brothers roped into helping to revitalize the Ridge because *Jonah* did his thing and managed to save the town from bankruptcy. Now, in a truly let-me-shove-this-up-your-ass flash of brilliance on their kid brother's part, the Steele family had their name on the town.

Reid looked across the hood at Grif and held up his thumb. "Boredom." His index finger went next. "Anger. Not a good combination for me. Throws my chakras all out of whack."

At that Grif burst out laughing. "What the hell are you talking about? Chakras."

"I don't know. One of the guys in my unit used to say that all the time. 'Dude, your chakras are blocked.'"

He always meant to look that up and had never done it. Now it seemed he had the time. And who knew, maybe this chakra thing could eventually get him out of being chained to Steele Ridge.

Grif pointed to the truck bed. "What's in those boxes?"

Heh, heh, heh. *The boxes.* He'd just picked those babies up from the post office because they wouldn't deliver them without a signature and nobody had been home at the house.

Until he had a look at the contents of said boxes, he wasn't sharing. No sir.

"Nothing. Just some shit I ordered."

A siren wailed and the two of them spotted Maggie, their cousin and Steele Ridge's top cop, screaming out of the sheriff's office parking lot, lights flashing on her cruiser. She honked as she roared by and Reid rolled his lip out, felt a stab of jealousy because his favorite cousin apparently had some action to tend to.

Even if it was Steele Ridge action and probably amounted to a nine-year-old breaking a neighbor's window.

Grif's phone rang and big brother stared at the screen a sec, clearly deciding whether to swipe it away.

"It's the mayor. I'm late for this meeting. You good?"

Ha. Now that was a loaded question.

He glanced back at the sidewalk where the sweet thing with the world's best ass headed toward the Triple B. Maybe he'd kill two birds with one stone here. Drown his anger while admiring the insanely attractive ass of the she's-not-*that*-young Brynne.

"I'm gonna grab a beer. See if I can find someone to keep me company."

"Oh, boy," Grif said. "You got that hound dog look. I'm telling you, don't do it. She's a nice girl and I don't need you getting one of the business owners in a snit."

Reid laughed, then flipped his middle finger up. "Piss. Off."

Brynne walked into the bar side of the Triple B— Blues, Brews, and Books—and scanned the tables. The lunch rush had long past thinned out and the early dinner folks had started to wander in, but only a few tables and a couple of barstools were occupied.

For years this space had been the town café, but since taking over the lease, Randi, the new owner, had converted the storefront between Brynne's shop and the bar into a coffee shop and Little Free Library.

"Hey, girl," Randi said from her spot behind the bar.

She wore her dark blond hair back today and her green eyes sparkled, leaving Brynne, as usual, entranced and more than a little jealous over Randi's ability to be beautiful while wearing a graphic T-shirt and minimal makeup.

How was that even fair when Brynne spent ninety minutes on hair and makeup?

Randi wiped her hands on a rag and leaned into the bar. "You're not usually here in the middle of the afternoon. Everything okay?"

"Yep. Meeting Nelson for a few minutes."

"Ah."

Nelson, her childhood friend, had been a constant in her life, and lately had been helping her rebuild that life after her husband decided to dump her for his skinny, fair-haired intern. Men, in Brynne's opinion, were the enemy. Well, all men but Nelson. Nelson, in many ways, had saved her. For that she'd love him—in a completely platonic way—forever. No question.

"Hey," she said to Randi, "stop by later. A new shipment came in last night. There's a red miniskirt you might like."

"Ooh, I love when you get new stuff."

Brynne had spent all morning sorting through the shipment from the designer, an up-and-coming genius she'd met when she'd been living up north and attended New York Fashion Week.

Her marriage and life in New York were over, but she'd learned a lot while there and made some great contacts with newbie designers.

So she'd ordered a few things from Gilian's spring line to shake things up in Steele Ridge.

If only she could pull off that little crotch-length number herself, life would be grand.

Miniskirts didn't always play nice with women built like her. Women with *curves*.

And cellulite. And a giant rear. Still, maybe she'd try it on to see.

Something drew Randi's gaze and Brynne glanced over her shoulder to find Reid Steele, the most perfectly chiseled hunk of man she might have ever set eyes on, entering the Triple B. Reid had gone to school with her sister and even back then he was a hottie. Now, he'd been back in town for a few months, since his stint with the Army ended. Between the dark hair and muscles, a Reid sighting sent every female hormone in town fluttering.

Brynne's included. Except she only wanted to look. Looking was harmless. Looking didn't require the gutting, soul-sucking, emotional annihilation of relationships.

Besides, she'd sworn off men for the next five years.

Particularly ones like Reid. From the time she was ten and Reid sixteen, she'd been watching her older sister roll through boys while Reid did just as much rolling with the girls.

In the backseat of his car.

At least that's what Brynne had heard. And looking at him? All that swagger and cool confidence, she didn't doubt it.

"Ladies," he said as he strode toward them and settled onto the bar stool next to Brynne.

"Hi, Reid," she said. "Nice work with the ducks."

He slid off his sunglasses and his deep blue eyes—stormy ocean—zoomed in on her, traveled over her face, settling on her lips, and the usual nagging insecurity poked at her. Stupid ex-husband. They'd met as sophomores in college after she'd come so far in slaying her childhood demons. College had been paradise. Newly confident and shedding weight, little by little, Brynne had enjoyed freedom from her insecurities and then...New York, where her kind, amiable Kurt turned into an aggressive and highly critical up-and-comer. He scrutinized her appearance daily, sometimes hourly, until she was afraid to leave the house without his appraisal.

At least until he dumped her.

She lifted her fingers to her lips. The lipstick. She'd tried a new shade today, hadn't liked it and rubbed it off. Maybe she'd gotten some on her face.

No. She'd checked. Five times. She dropped her hand,

forced herself to be still. To not step back or run from the blast of Reid Steele's focused attention. The man was so darned intense. Totally unnerving.

"Thanks," he said. "Always ready to please a woman in distress."

At that, Brynne snorted and Randi mockingly fanned herself. Such a man.

"What can I get you, Reid?" Randi asked.

He snagged the menu from the holder on the bar. "I'll have a beer to start. Whatever's on tap. And you know I'm digging your Gouda burger. I'll have one of those, too. Medium rare."

"You got it."

Randi set a beer in front of him and wandered off to the kitchen, leaving Brynne alone with the hunk of all hunks. Great. What would they, the chubby girl and the beefcake, possibly have to talk about?

He pushed his sunglasses and keys off to the side and swiveled to her, once again storming her with all his attention. Fighting the urge to make herself smaller, she threw her shoulders back and sucked in her stomach.

"So," he said, "I...uh...need a gift for Evie."

Evie. Yay. Neutral ground. Plus, Brynne loved Evie. She only got to see her on weekends since she was away at school, but even with their four-year age difference, they'd immediately clicked when Evie started working at the shop.

If Brynne remembered correctly, Miss Evie had a birthday coming up.

"I was in your shop the other day," Reid said. "You weren't there."

"I have part-timers that help out."

"I couldn't figure out what to get her, but I'll tell ya, it smelled good in there."

"It's potpourri," Brynne said. "Made by a friend with neroli oil. If customers like it, I'll start carrying it in the store."

"My mom goes for all that stuff."

Ah. Potential sale already. "I'll give you some to take to her. She can be my test case."

She set her purse on the bar, snatched her iPad out and tapped at the screen. "I have Evie's wish list in my customer file."

"Her wish list?"

"Yes. If customers see something they like, they tell me and I add it to their file. Kind of like a bridal registry."

Reid scrunched his face. "A what?"

How cute was he? She entered Evie's name into her customer file and...yep. Birthday next month.

Beside her, Reid shifted and she glanced back to see his insanely haunting eyes sliding down her body, landing, if her guess was correct, on her butt.

She bolted upright, casually angling sideways and hiding the ginormous continent known as her rear. The one her ex-husband insisted would get smaller if she lowered her fat intake.

Forget him. She cleared her throat, drawing Reid's gaze back to her face. "You must be getting ahead of your shopping."

The comment was met with silence. And a straight-faced look of bewilderment.

"Uh, getting ahead?"

What was she missing here? She rolled one hand. "Evie. Her birthday is next month."

"Shit," Reid said.

Oh, my. "I thought that's what you needed a gift for."

His lips quirked and he ran his hand over his face before hitting her with the full-wattage I-am-*the*-man smile that had probably taken out half the female population on the Eastern seaboard.

"Busted me," he said.

"Sorry?"

"I...uh...saw you outside. Wanted to say hello."

Well, that was neighborly, but, really, she didn't even know him. Sure, she knew of him, everyone in this town knew the Steeles. But he certainly didn't know her and didn't need to go out of his way to say hello.

She cocked her head and the corner of his mouth lifted. "I used Evie as an excuse. To talk to you."

Okay. What was she supposed to say to that?

"Alrighty," he said. "I've definitely lost my touch because I'm hitting on you and you don't even know it."

Hitting on her? The man who induced flash-mob panty drops was hitting on *her*? Even if men weren't the scum of the earth, who'd have guessed Reid Steele, master of the orgasm—if the rumors were true—would even notice her.

Not plain-old Brynne. Her normal truckload of makeup and big hair helped, but she still couldn't compete with her sister's natural beauty and sculpted bones.

A flaming ball of heat rushed up her throat and she whirled away before her face flooded with color. "Um." She stuffed the iPad back into her purse. "There's a bracelet Evie wants. They're like bangles, but they have different charms you can add."

"Bangles?"

Without looking at him, she held her wrist up. "This. Sterling silver. How much did you want to spend?"

"Whatever. If that's what she wants."

"Yep," she chirped. "That's what she wants. You can keep buying her charms." Still refusing to look at him—*five-year plan, five-year plan, five-year plan*—she tapped a note into her phone. "I can set one aside for you when I go back to the store. Shall I wrap it for you?"

Reid dug into the back pocket of his jeans, and his T-shirt stretched across his chest and—wow—the guy was ripped.

And then ripped some more.

Total man candy.

He slapped his wallet on the bar. "Wrapping it would be good. How much?"

"Eighty-five. Plus tax."

His eyes widened. "Holy hell, my sister thinks all her brothers are billionaires. Let's bill that to Jonah."

She stared back at him, mute. Dear God, what was wrong with her? He'd made that damned crack about hitting on her and now she was totally thrown.

Reid let out a huffing laugh. "I'm going down in flames here. Brynne, I'm kidding. It's a running joke in my family. Bill everything to Jonah." He waved it away. "Never mind. I don't have that much cash on me. I'll stop in and you can run my card. That work?"

She put her phone back into her purse, went to move the purse to a stool, knocked over the cup of straws Randi had on the edge of the bar, and decided she wanted to die right then.

They both reached for the cup, their fingers tangling together and—wow, he had awesome hands. A little rough at the fingertips and work-hardened and enough to make a girl's skin go hot.

She snapped her hand back.

Reid righted the cup and replaced the straws that had spilled out.

"Thank you."

"Brynne?"

"Yes?"

"Do I make you nervous or something?"

Ha! Nervous. If he only knew. He was a nice guy. Everything she'd heard about him said so. A good guy who didn't mind helping out a neighbor. Fixing a lawnmower, changing a tire, shoveling a driveway, whatever.

Yes, he had a reputation as a player, but so what? According to the gossipmongers, he never misled anyone. He simply liked sex. Most men did. She'd learned that the hard way.

But since he'd walked into the bar, he'd been respectful—aside from staring at her rear, of course—and now he'd asked her a question. One he deserved an answer to.

She met his gaze, let those eyes of his scrape the crud off something she'd tried so hard to bury.

"Not nervous," she said. "I'm just..." She flapped her arms.

"What?"

"Terrified."

CHAPTER TWO

TERRIFIED? WHAT IN HELL DID that mean?

Now he was the one cocking his head. This conversation had definitely flown above him. He paused for a second, took note of the Luke Bryan song playing on the ancient jukebox. "What does that mean?" He sniffed his pits. "Do I smell bad?"

Finally, the sweet thing smiled and it lit up her entirely over-made-up face. He'd never understand why pretty women plastered all that crap on their faces. And the hair? Jeez, she had enough spray on there to withstand a hurricane. But, he'd admit, it fell into a nice long swoop over her shoulders that must have taken some time to get right.

The whole deal fired his engines on all kinds of levels. Pure sex. And hot. And sweet.

She shook her adorable head, looked down at her feet. "No. You don't smell."

Just then, Cherlyn Marstin cruised by, overheard Brynne's comment and broke out laughing. Great. Back in the day, he and Cherlyn had hooked up for a minute before he'd gone off to college in search of anything bigger than the Ridge. It wasn't that he disliked his hometown. He enjoyed the comforts of it, the sameness that came with coming home and knowing everyone and their business.

But he'd craved something more. Something that would force him to stretch his mind and let him grow.

How ironic that all that growing landed his butt right back home, in the Triple B, falling back on his old tricks of trying to get laid.

The Luke Bryan song ended, making room for Little Big Town, and Reid moved closer to Brynne. Close enough to get a whiff of her perfume. Something sultry. Vanilla maybe? Almonds? He didn't know. He liked it, though.

"I don't want to make you uncomfortable," he said. "I'm sorry."

"It's not you. I'm...I'm divorced. About six months ago."

Ah, crap. Grif could have mentioned that. Information, when dealing with women, was key. If he'd known about the divorce, maybe he'd have handled this differently. Not been so, what? Aggressive?

He nodded. "I see. So because you're divorced, I make you nervous."

She grinned at him again and holy crap, she was cute. "I've sworn off men. For five years."

"That's a long time."

Still with her head down, she nodded.

Okay. Enough. He lifted his hand, set one finger under her chin and tipped her head up. "I'm up here, sweet thing. And I'm guessing this guy must have shredded you."

"Something like that."

"Damn near ruined you for all the rest of us schmucks. If you ask me—" he laughed at himself, "—hell, even if you don't ask, I'll tell you. I think it would suck if you let one guy take you out of commission for five years. I mean, that right there, that's a crime against men."

Her mouth dropped open. "A crime against..."

Oh, yeah. That got her going. A flyer on his part, but it got a reaction out of her. Now he had to argue it.

Which, considering the ridiculous factor, might be a challenge.

But that never stopped him. "I mean, think about it. Never mind you having to be celibate for five years." He threw his hand over his heart. "Sweet baby Jesus, save me. Who are you punishing? You get divorced and we men think"—he waved his arms—"woo-hoo, she's available. And then you go and swear off men and we're like boo-hiss. I'm telling you, it's a crime against men. In fact, I'm going down to Maggie's office and I'm telling her. Mags loves me, she'll arrest you. No kidding."

Brynne's eyebrows came together, her lips slightly puckered. Dumbstruck.

That crime against men line was a flipping flash of genius. But if she didn't get the humor in it?

Fucked.

And not in the way he wanted to be.

She continued to stare at him. Time for a tension buster. He smacked his hands together. "I'll leave you with that thought. Give you some time to mull it over. I'm not going anywhere and since you own a business here in town, you're not either."

The corner of her lush mouth lifted. "You know, you talk a lot."

"Yeah. I'm told. My mother always tells me I don't know when to shut up. She doesn't mean it, though."

"Actually, she probably does."

Well, look at that, Brynne *did* have a sense of humor. He tweaked her nose. "Good one. I like it. I like it a lot."

Above the bar, a television was tuned to the local news station. The sound had been muted and subtitles scrolled the bottom as a peppy blond anchor's lips moved. Apparently an Asheville teenager had smoked some kind of synthetic hallucinogen, had a stroke, and died. A twisted version of an overdose.

Reid shook his head, thankful once again that Evie had four pain-in-the-ass older brothers running herd on her. At twenty—their resident *oops* sibling—she wasn't even legal drinking age and he harassed her night and day about staying away from alcohol.

And drugs.

Chances were she drank while at school. He couldn't control that. What he *could* do was scare the hell out of her and make sure she understood that a pretty, incapacitated college coed was a prime target for a gang rape.

After all, what were big brothers for if not to terrify their younger sisters into staying sober?

"Excuse me one second. I need to harass my little sister." He picked up his phone, searched for the news station's link on the teenager's death and texted it to her. Couldn't hurt.

Randi appeared and slid his burger and a mountain of fries in front of him. "Here you go. Anything else?"

"Nope. Smells great."

With that, she took off again and Reid went back to Brynne. "Can I stop at the store for the bracelet after I eat?"

"Sure. That's fine. I'll toss some of the potpourri in a bag for you to give to your mom."

"Excellent. Thank you. And I get another opportunity to talk you out of this crimes-against-men campaign you have going on."

She dipped her head again and the upper curve of her perfect cheeks fired red. So damn sweet.

What made him do it, he wasn't sure, but he leaned in, got another whiff of that amazing scent she wore, and kissed her on the cheek. The heat from her face poured right into him. "You're cute, Brynne. Even if you decide to break my heart and not go out with me, I'm glad we talked. You make me smile. I haven't done a whole lot of that lately."

"Hey," Nelson said. "Sorry I'm late. I went to the shop, but Jules said you were here."

Brynne swung away from Reid and faced Nelson. He wore khakis and a white T under an unbuttoned striped shirt.

Going somewhere.

Otherwise, this late in the day, he'd be in shorts and flip-flops.

"Hey, you," she said. "No problem."

Reid eyeballed Nelson, then held out his hand. "Reid Steele."

Right. Introductions. "Sorry," Brynne said. "Reid, this is my friend Nelson. Nelson, Reid."

Hellos and handshakes were exchanged and Nelson cleared his throat. Clearing his throat? Really? What was that about?

He jerked his thumb to one of the tables. "Sorry to steal her."

"No problem."

Nelson broke away and Reid focused on her for a few long seconds. Ignoring the inclination to curl her shoulders, she stood tall. "I'll hold the bracelet for you."

"Thanks." He jerked his chin to the table Nelson had walked off to. "I don't want to hold you up."

"Yep." She turned to walk away, but stopped and looked back. "It was nice talking to you."

That got her another panty-dropper smile and instead of whirling away, running from all that male heat, she let herself smile back.

Flirting. Brynne style.

It was a start. A scary one, considering she'd sworn off men.

She made her way to Nelson, wondering what the heck had gotten into him. He'd practically told Reid to buzz off. Totally rude and totally out of character for her normally über-friendly buddy. She reached the table and he pulled a chair out for her. As she sat, she zeroed in on his puffy eyes, pale skin, and unkempt blond hair. Working too hard.

"You look tired."

Which might explain his rude behavior.

"A little." He waited for her to settle in, then sat in the seat across from him. "Watch out for Reid Steele."

Brynne waved off Nelson's protectiveness. "He needed a gift suggestion for Evie's birthday."

"And to screw you?"

Brynne pondered that one and gave the two sides of her brain—the man-hater side versus the they're-not-all-bad side—a second to battle it out. Those sides had been at war these past few months, each trying to convince the other to switch.

As yet, there hadn't been a clear winner. Brynne still smarted from the rejection by her jerk of a husband, but each day her mood grew marginally brighter and her heart less stony.

The recovery from the absolute bombing of her self-esteem lagged behind.

Which might explain why, rather than agreeing with Nelson, who grew up with her and knew Reid's reputation as well as anyone else in town, she chose to reserve judgment on Reid's intentions.

After all, reputations built in Steele Ridge weren't easy to tear down. Just ask her sister.

But Reid had been...nice. In a backward sort of way.

"He seems okay to me. It wasn't like he was all over me. Not smarmy."

Except for that staring-at-my-ass thing.

That might have been a little smarmy.

What did it matter? If she shot him down, he wouldn't have trouble finding another willing and warm female. Heck, even if she didn't shoot him down, he'd probably find someone else. Wasn't this her own little nightmare? He terrified her, but the idea of him turning those amazing eyes on another woman didn't appeal either.

Lonely.

That's all she was.

Lonely and ruined by a rotten ex-husband. Enter

Nelson. Since she'd left Kurt, Nelson had become her de facto rent-a-husband. She was more than capable of handling clogged sinks and loose screws, but the big stuff that required muscle? Nelson handled that.

"Anyway," she said, "what's up? I didn't expect to see you until tomorrow."

For their Friday night date. Nelson was living life as a bachelor and they'd been seeing more of each other as a result.

Brynne didn't mind. It gave her male company and a night out of Steele Ridge.

"I...um..." He turned back to the door, waved at it. "I have to go out of town. For work. Figured I'd come by and let you know."

A waitress swung by, took their drink order, and left menus. Already knowing she wanted a garden salad with grilled chicken, she set the menu aside. Although Reid's Gouda burger sure looked good.

She shoved the menu away another inch. "When do you leave?"

"Tonight."

"Tonight? Wow. Is it an emergency?"

Although, what kind of an emergency an insurance salesman could have, she wasn't sure.

He shook his head. "Emergency?"

"Yes. That you're leaving so fast."

Nelson shifted sideways, half facing her and half facing the door. "No. No emergency. It's a conference. The guy that was scheduled to go got sick. I'm taking his place."

Ah. That made sense. "Well, I hope it's someplace fun."

Nelson stared at her and she snapped her fingers in front of his face. "Buddy, you in there? Maybe you need to get some sleep tonight instead of going on this trip."

"I'm sorry." He whirled his finger next to his head. "A lot on the brain. Anyway, figured I'd come by and see you before I went. Since I'm bailing on you for tomorrow."

His phone went off and he stood to dig it out of his pocket and read the text. "Ah, damn."

"What?"

"I need to go."

Go? Was he kidding? First he was late and now he was leaving? Without an explanation? She held out her hands. "We're about to order."

"I know. I'm sorry. It's this damned trip. I have to leave tonight and now I just got a text that I have something else to do for work before I leave."

Being a business owner, she understood the plight of a career-minded person. For some, work never left them. Or they never left work.

Either way, she knew his dedication and as much as she wanted him to stay, she'd let him go.

That's what friends did. They understood. She pushed herself up from the table and wrapped him in a backslapping hug. "It's all right. But you're stressed. Seriously, you need to take it easy."

"I know. I know."

He brought his arms around her, held her for a second and squeezed. Now that was definitely weird. They didn't do snuggly hugs.

Not usually.

She leaned back and studied him. "You're sure you're okay? Something feels off."

He snorted. "I'm fine. Really. Just a lot going on."

"Can I help?"

"I wish you could. But, no. After this trip, I'll be fine." He tugged on the end of her hair. "Don't worry."

"If you say so. Now go. Beat it. You have things to do. Call me tomorrow. Let me know you got there okay. And get some sleep!"

"Will do."

As Nelson strode from the B, Brynne made eye contact with Reid, who still sat at the bar nursing what looked like the same beer.

He held his hands out. "What happened?"

"He had to leave. A last-minute business trip." She slung her purse over her shoulder. "I'm heading back to the shop."

"Now, see, if I'd just waited a few minutes to eat, I could have tried to convince you to let me buy you dinner."

Ha. Good one. "Reid Steele," she said. "Slayer of women."

And let's not forget master of the orgasm.

"Well, don't get crazy. I'm good, but not that good."

Brynne burst out laughing. Couldn't help it. Perhaps, with all his other talents, Reid was a mind reader. "Five years," she said.

"Seriously? We're back to crimes against men?"

She poked his rock-hard biceps. "You're funny, Reid."

"Funny enough for you to sit here and keep me company?"

"In five years, maybe. Right now, I'm leaving."

He hopped off the stool, pulled some bills from his wallet and dropped them on the bar. "I'll come with you and grab the bracelet."

She glanced back to the cash. "Do you need to wait for change?"

"Nah. I'm good."

A 30 percent tip. At least. He sure was good.

Outside, the waning afternoon sun spilled shadows along Main Street and Brynne spotted Nelson approaching his car two doors down, in front of her shop. He stopped and checked his phone again as they headed that way. What was going on with that phone that was so important?

She shook it off and looked back at Reid standing beside her, towering over her, even in her five-inch heels. The hem of his T-shirt caught on the grip of his sidearm, something that, in the South, didn't surprise her. Particularly from a former military man. "You were in the Army, right?"

She knew the answer. Sure did. But she wouldn't admit it. Admitting it might imply interest on more than a friendly level, and with her whole dedication to swearing off men—even if they did look like Reid Steele—she wasn't going there.

"Yeah. Blew out my knee and my tour was up. Rather than be a desk jockey, I came home. Now I'm figuring out what's next."

A desk jockey. Not exactly a glowing endorsement for a job. "Was that hard? Coming home?"

He met her gaze, held it for a few long seconds and the answer was there. Right there, between them in a mutual understanding of just how hard it was to return to this tiny town, with all the gossipmongers and nosy neighbors, after trying to strike out on his own.

"Immensely. But it's old news."

Didn't seem like old news. Seemed like it still bugged him. But he obviously didn't want to discuss it, something she understood all too well, considering everyone's fascination with her husband dumping her.

So she'd give Reid a break, something she'd hoped for when first moving back, and not push him. "Change is hard. You'll figure it out. Give yourself time."

"I had a job offer the other day."

"See, there you go."

He flashed a smile. "I'm not sure I want it. The company is based in Georgia, but the job is overseas. Security work."

Ah. He'd be leaving again. Even more reason not to let him woo her into dating. One thing she didn't need was a man leaving her. Even if it was for a job. "Would you like that?"

He shrugged. "Probably. But I don't know if my *knee* would like it."

Bang.

Brynne froze. Was that...?

Bang, bang.

An engine roared and she swung toward the street where a black SUV stormed down Main.

A huge force plowed into her, shoving her toward the

front of a car and then down. Momentum snapped her head back and—*ooff*—she hit the ground. Her ribcage connected with concrete and a burst of air rushed out. Her chest seized and her head spun and…*no air.*

"Stay down," Reid said.

Reid. On top of her. His massive body smothering her. He'd put his hands on top of her head, shielding her from the gunfire and *no, no, no.* Who the heck was shooting off a gun on Main Street? Probably some wild teenager looking to get the adults riled up. Idiot kids. The sheriff would have a fit.

But when had that ever happened? The locals knew to keep their shooting confined to safe areas.

Which meant…

Gunfire.

Someone was not shooting up Main Street and she was not going to die on a sidewalk. She began to shiver, her body systematically shutting down as fear took hold.

"Reid? What's…hap…happening?"

"You're okay," he said. "You're out of the line of fire. Stay right here. Don't move. I'll see what's happening."

Someone shrieked, a high-pitched wail—young—that knifed through Reid. His body, as usual, reacted all at once and blood rushed. His limbs shook and he forced his breathing to a normal rhythm.

Go time.

He hopped to his feet and ripped his .45 from his holster. He stayed low, protected by cars on either side of him in case the shooter was still on Main, but he'd seen that SUV fly around the corner just as he pushed Brynne to the ground. Jeep. Black. Older model.

He peered around the back of a vehicle, scanned right, then left, searching for anyone else who might be firing or walking or running.

But the street and sidewalks were empty. Across the street, Mrs. Hobbs had ducked between two cars and was on her cell phone. Probably calling 911.

Good.

One thing down.

The street had gone quiet. No more screams, no traffic noise, no sirens. Just…nothing. Had the shooter been tackled by someone?

"They turned off Main and raced down Buckner," someone shouted. "Went north! Shooter was still in the car."

Goddamn. Whoever it was, they were gone now. No chance to catch them unless Mags or one of the deputies could intercept.

Reid took the chance and stood up, .45 still at the ready as he stepped into the street and—holy shit.

Nelson.

Brynne's friend lay sprawled in the street right behind what Reid assumed was his car. A fucking drive-by shooting in the middle of Steele Ridge. Blood poured from the guy's chest and Reid rushed over, reholstered his weapon and dropped to his knees to check for a pulse.

Nothing. Shit.

"Someone make sure an ambulance is on the way!"

An ambulance?

Reid's warning to stay down looped in Brynne's mind. But if people were hurt she could help. She levered up to her knees, drew a quick breath, and concentrated on helping the injured.

She needed to *do* something. She peeped around the side of the car and glanced across the street, where Mrs. Hobbs was talking on her phone. The woman made eye contact and pointed at her phone.

Help.

Brynne crawled to the edge of the car's bumper and still on all fours, dug her fingertips into the concrete as questions paralyzed her.

What happened? Who fired?

How could this be happening?

In Steele Ridge.

"Brynne!"

Reid's voice. She pushed herself up, scrambling to her shaky limbs and slipping. She fell, her right knee banging hard, but she popped up again, ran between the two cars parked at the curb and found Reid on the other side giving CPR to...

"Nelson!"

She let out a small squeak, the panic ripping free, and she gasped as blood poured from the middle of her closest friend's chest.

This couldn't be happening. Couldn't be. Even in New York she hadn't seen anything like this.

She landed next to him, her brain still trying to lock in and form coherent thoughts. She had to help. Had to. "What can I do? I learned CPR in school."

"Mouth-to-mouth. I'm on compression twenty-five. At thirty, give two rescue breaths."

A siren came alive, but it wasn't close enough. The firehouse was on the west edge of town.

Reid stopped. "Now!"

She pinched Nelson's nose shut, sealed her mouth over his, and gave two breaths.

"Good," Reid said. "Now me again."

Brynne sat up, silently counting each compression as Reid worked. Blood seeped between his fingers and the metallic smell permeated the air.

Mrs. Hobbs bolted toward them. "I called nine-one-one!"

If the woman had been walking along the sidewalk, maybe she saw something. "Did you see the shooter?"

"No. Just an SUV. Black. They drove right by." Mrs. Hobbs knelt beside Brynne. "What can I do?"

"I don't know," Brynne said. "Maybe elevate his feet?"

God, she didn't know. She stared down at her unconscious friend and panic erupted again, making her skin buzz. The distant siren came closer and she peered over her shoulder, watching for the ambulance. *Please, hurry. Please.*

"Brynne," Reid said, "two more breaths."

She did as she was told and Reid continued CPR. She let out a gasping sob, her shoulders bowing in as she drew air through her nose, took in that nasty metallic odor, on him, on her, everywhere.

Pull it together.

She pushed her shoulders back and focused on her friend, on him not dying.

Please, don't die.

"Hang on, Nelson. Help is on the way."

CHAPTER THREE

IN THE MIDDLE OF MAIN Street, blue, red, and white swirling lights of the ambulance and two police cruisers bounced off the buildings and lit up the darkening street. The cruisers sat crosswise, stretched across Main, and Reid glanced down at Brynne. After the shooting, Randi had rushed outside and now stood with her arm slung over Brynne's shoulder.

Brynne's bloodshot eyes and the black streaks of eye makeup trailing down her face weren't the worst of it. Not by a long shot.

Blood stained her hands and cheeks and the formerly dynamite blue dress. The blood and the black streaks were the only color against her ashen skin, and she stared at him with a zoned-out look—vacancy—that he'd seen enough to know shock had set in.

A pop went off in his chest and he flinched, recalling the first time he'd felt that pop after one of his army buddies got a leg blown off by a roadside bomb. *She's okay.* Unharmed, but dealing with emotional trauma. Not wanting to spook her, he shoved his hands in his pockets. Shock did weird things to people. If he touched her, it might snap whatever control she clung to.

So, yeah, he'd keep his hands to himself.

For now.

Down the sidewalk, in front of the Mad Batter bakery

where the daily message on the sidewalk board screamed "Seize the day, eat a cookie," a small group of folks were barricaded by one of Maggie's deputies. Do-Right, they called him.

Reid couldn't see beyond the ambulance and the people milling around, but saw enough to know two paramedics tended to Nelson. Miracle of all miracles, Reid and Brynne had managed to get a pulse on the guy and now the two medics stood, raised the gurney, and wheeled it to the ambulance.

He faced Brynne and waited for her foggy brain to track that he wanted her attention. She blinked once. Then again and—bam—the haze in her eyes evaporated. *There you go.* "Brynne, are you okay?"

One of the paramedics counted three and Reid angled back, spotted them hoisting the gurney into the ambulance.

Damn. Shit like this was bad enough on a battlefield. In the middle of town? With innocent civilians? It chapped his ass.

He took a small step sideways, blocking Brynne's view of the ambulance. "The deputies will want to talk to you."

She nodded, but had she even heard him? Definitely in shock. Total space zombie right now. He slid a look to Randi, and she hitched her eyebrows up in the universal *holy crap, this is nuts* way.

He brought his attention back to Brynne, who kept her gaze plastered to the center of his chest, just staring.

"Brynne," he said, keeping his voice low and even. "Honey, did you see the shooter?"

Something in Brynne's head *snick, snick, snicked* as Reid and his massive body blocked her view.

He'd asked her a question. Hadn't he? Something

about the shooter. Shooter. Shooter. Shooter. But she continued to stare at the defined valley between his pecs where the fabric of his T-shirt curved over that exact spot where Nelson's chest hemorrhaged.

Ohmygod.

Finally, she raised her gaze. Reid's mouth moved again, his lips forming words that came to her as one long *whum.* She shook her head.

"What?"

He said something to Randi and she lifted her arm from Brynne's shoulder, taking all her comforting closeness with her.

"Wait," Brynne said. *Come back.*

"Water," Reid said. "She's getting you some."

Water.

Huh. "Okay."

But damn, why did Randi have to go? For a few seconds there, with Randi hovering, she felt...protected. Against her thoughts, against Nelson bleeding on the street. Against the disgusting, smelly blood smeared all over her.

Now? Gone. And it all rushed back. The shots, the sirens, the panic.

"No." She balled her hands so tightly her nails pressed painfully into her palms.

Moving fast, Reid wrapped his giant hands around her skull and dragged her forward, into his chest. He held her there and the musky scent of his soap overrode the nasty metallic odor of Nelson's blood. And, oh, a man hadn't held her this way since her husband.

She wrapped her arms around his waist and squeezed. Just held on because—God—what had happened?

"You're okay." Reid ran his hands down her back, gently stroking. "Don't breathe too fast. You'll hyperventilate. You're in shock. Totally normal."

Nothing about this felt normal. How could it? She rolled her head back and forth against his chest. The guy must spend hours in the gym. And what a crazy thought right now. Coping mechanism. Right? That's all. She wasn't a bad person.

Was she?

"Is he dead?"

"I...uh...don't think so. They're taking him to the hospital. We probably saved his life."

He lifted one of his hands away. "Thanks," he said to someone and Brynne looked up, took in his strong jaw and blue eyes and dark hair.

Superman.

That's who he looked like. Lord, she really must be in shock if she was suddenly seeing superheroes.

"Randi brought you water," he said. "Take a drink."

He stepped back, unscrewed the cap on a drippy water bottle and handed it to her. A shot of cold condensation shot through her palm, an oddly relaxing sensation that focused her. "Thank you."

"Ah, honey," Randi said, "I'm so sorry you went through this."

Pressure built behind Brynne's eyes and in her throat and all the controlled emotion—the horror—whipped back at her, banged at her, trying to burst free. She squeezed her eyes shut and—*I'm going to lose it.*

"Brynne, look at me."

Reid's voice had an edge now. All the cooing softness vanishing.

"Don't hold it in," he said. "Believe me, it won't help you. You've just seen some of the worst shit a person can. You wanna scream, do it. Cry? Have at it. I don't care. Neither does Randi. Tear this whole goddamned block apart if you have to, but don't shove all that garbage away. You bottle it up and it'll eat you alive."

Of all people, he could relate. *It's normal.*

The pressure in her throat eased and she brought the bottle up. Glugged half of it. So good. Who knew?

He tapped the bottle. "Take it easy. Not so fast."

Thankful for the gift of friends, she took one last gulp. Here were two people, one who knew her and one who didn't, but they'd taken the time to help her. And not make her feel like a crazy person.

She held the water up. "Thank you. Both of you."

A door slammed from the street and a siren blared. One of the deputies pulling away.

The ambulance was gone. In her fuzzy state, she'd missed them taking Nelson away.

"I have to go," she said. "To the hospital. I need my keys."

Randi shook her head. "No way. You can't drive."

"His parents live out of state. He can't be alone."

Gently, Reid touched her arm. "The sheriff'll want to talk to you."

"They can talk to me at the hospital. My friend needs me."

Because, shock or no shock, she knew he'd lost a lot of blood. If he died, she didn't want him to do it alone, in a hospital, surrounded by strangers.

Asshat that he was, the extremely male part of Reid wanted to know exactly what Brynne's relationship with this guy was.

What the hell was wrong with him? A couple of conversations and all of a sudden he was all up in her business—or wanting to be anyway.

A man had been shot; what the fuck did it matter what her relationship with him was? Friends or lovers, she had a need to be with him.

"I agree with Randi," he said. "You can't drive." A tight-lipped, mutinous glare took over her face and Reid held his hands up. "Before you go apeshit on me, how about one of us drives you to the hospital?"

"I can do that," Randi said. "Not a problem."

"Excellent." Reid tag-teamed Randi's attempt to avoid an argument. "You take her and I'll talk to

Maggie. They'll be looking for her. I'll tell her to head over to the hospital. That work?"

Brynne was already on the move, striding toward the entrance to her store. "Sure. Fine. I need to tell Jules to close up and go home. I'll meet you right in front here in two minutes."

"I'll get the car."

Brynne disappeared into the store and Reid faced Randi. "Try to keep her calm. I think she's in shock."

"She sure is. When you were talking to Deputy Blaine I couldn't get anything out of her." Randi closed her eyes for a second. "This is unbelievable. She's been friends with him forever. Who'd have imagined this could happen?"

Not in Steele Ridge anyway. Reid let out a long breath and gestured to the road. "You'd better get your car. She'll be out here and ready to go. Let's not get her riled up."

He didn't know what a riled-up Brynne presented like and that was a problem when trying to help her deal with tragedy.

With the guys in his unit, he'd known exactly what to expect. Who got quiet, who threw things, who got verbal and chattered on endlessly, rehashing every element of the op—they all had a thing, a way to cope, they employed.

Reid? His was music. Tuning out with his iPod, grabbing a guitar, whatever, music helped him channel the anger and grief.

Randi headed toward the Triple B and Reid stood for a second, hands on hips, surveying the controlled chaos in the street and his sheriff cousin ordering bystanders to break it up.

Reid strode toward Maggie and stopped just outside the barricade. "Mags, I need a minute."

She looked over at him, angling back without turning, clearly deciding whether he was being nosy or actually wanted something.

"It's important," he said.

That got her moving. His family knew when to take him seriously. She headed over, her long legs moving fast, her blond ponytail bobbing with each step.

Maggie was all legs. Not thin, not fat. Athletic. From the time they were kids, she'd been into sports and still worked at staying fit. She might be ten pounds heavier these days, but it was all muscle.

She stopped on the other side of the barricade. "What's up?"

"Brynne may have seen something. I was with her, but my head was turned. All I saw was the SUV."

"Do you think she saw the shooter?"

"I don't know. She's zoned out. She's friends with the guy who got shot."

"I know," Mags said. "I see them around. Where's Brynne now?"

"Hospital. He doesn't have family nearby. She wants to be there for him. How'd it look?"

Maggie gestured to the blood-soaked street. "Not good. He lost a lot of blood."

In the fading sunlight, the dark red stain on the street glowed. The human body held somewhere in the vicinity of a gallon and a half of blood.

By the looks of it, a gallon of it had spilled.

Next steps. "If you need to talk to her, I think she'll be at the hospital awhile. But listen, she's wrecked right now. Total zombie."

"Poor girl. I don't blame her."

"You need anything from me? Can I help?"

"I wish you could. But no. This scene is already contaminated with all the first responders trampling through it. Tomorrow you're gonna buy me a beer, though."

"You got it, cuz."

"Sheriff!" one of the deputies yelled. "Need ya."

"Go," Reid said. "Do some good in this mess."

He watched his cousin head into the fray of an active

investigation and once again mourned the loss of the rush that came with action.

Inside, sick fuck that he was, he burned with envy. Eight months ago, he'd been the one in the fray, constantly throwing himself in danger and getting off on every second of it.

Now? Nothing. Did he have a hero complex? Absolutely. So what? He'd long ago given up denying it. He knew things about himself. The soft spot for puppies—and apparently baby ducks—and the even bigger soft spot for his loved ones.

Or really, anyone deserving of protection.

He knew that.

Now, standing on the sidelines and about to embark on a pity job from his billionaire baby brother, well, he knew that sucked.

Brynne sat in the surgical waiting area, spacing out in front of the television. A rerun of a sitcom about a blended family. She'd never been a big television person, but she suddenly understood the therapeutic value of sitting around, completely focused on the lives of the characters. Particularly their problems and embarrassing moments.

And not her own.

Ninety minutes she'd been here. The last thirty of it alone because Randi's cook had sliced open his hand and needed a trip to the hospital himself and someone had to deal with the kitchen at the Triple B. Brynne had shooed Randi out the door, telling her she'd call with an update.

Except for the bloody dress she still wore because she'd forgotten to grab something clean to change into, being alone wasn't a big deal. At least she'd had a chance to wash the blood off her hands and face.

She'd spent so much time solo in New York, where

the only family she'd had was her cheating husband who was always "working," that being by herself didn't faze her anymore.

It was simply a state of being.

"Hey."

In the doorway stood Reid, all six foot plus of him, still in his jeans but wearing a clean T-shirt that wasn't tight yet clung to him enough to indicate the hardness underneath.

He moved toward her, his long strides confident and more graceful than any man his size should be able to pull off.

Her chest hammered. Of course it did. Looking at him would make any woman react, but she suspected her reaction—at the moment—had more to do with the presence of someone who'd turned into a hero in front of her.

Commanding. That was Reid.

She sat up a little and held his gaze. "Hi."

He dropped into the chair next to her and shoved a small paper bag her way. "Protein bars. Randi said you hadn't eaten. Figured you weren't hungry, but you should get something in your system. Keep your sugar up."

She took the bag and he set his hands on his thighs, tapped his fingers.

Whoever Reid Steele was, regardless of the gossip around town about his cocky, know-it-all attitude, he'd been kind to her.

"What are you doing here?"

"I called Randi for an update. She said she had an emergency." He shrugged. "I didn't want you to be here by yourself."

In case Nelson died.

He didn't say it. Didn't need to. They both knew it could happen.

"Thank you," she said. "I was going to call my dad, but...I don't know. He'd have questions and I don't have answers and I'm strung out and just the thought of that conversation wore me out."

"I get that. Believe me. I've had a few of those conversations recently. You just want everyone to be quiet and stop chattering at you."

"Something like that."

"Can I get you anything? Coffee?"

"No. Thanks. They should be updating us soon."

His gaze drifted to the television and he watched for a few seconds before turning back to her. Oh, this man. Too...too...what? She didn't know. He was just...a lot. The size of him, the intensity, the brutal honesty, and the mouth that sometimes let loose with inappropriate things.

"I talked to Maggie," he said. "They're dealing with the scene, but they're gonna need to talk to you."

Brynne nodded. "That's fine. Whenever they want. I didn't see much, but if I can help..."

"You wanna talk about it?"

Not in the least. Bad enough she'd have to tell the sheriff, she didn't want to be repeating it over and over again. Reliving it.

She shook her head. "Not yet. Is that silly? I know I'll have to talk about it. Probably a lot. Sitting quietly feels like the calm before the storm."

"And you don't want to ruin it."

Exactly. She angled toward him, crossed one leg over the other. "Thank you."

"For what?"

"Understanding. Most people would pressure me. I'm going to talk about it. I will. And I heard what you said before, about not keeping it bottled up. I just can't do it yet."

"I know."

He knew. Two simple little words that carried so much weight. Yes, the big ape of a guy had a way with her. An understanding. She liked him. Liked the way he didn't make her feel...stupid. Or foolish.

Or less.

And where did that come from? *Less?* How incredibly pathetic.

Stress probably. Thinking too much about her own life as Nelson fought for his. It happened, she supposed, when faced with mortality.

Reid slouched down, rested his head against the back of the chair, and focused on the television.

"This is a good show," he said. "Evie made me watch it with her last week. She's such a goof. She was at school and called me. We watched it together on the phone."

Not only did he understand what she was going through, he humored his sister and sat on the phone with her while watching television. What man did that?

She curled her fingers around the armrest, holding tight as a vision of her imploding five-year plan took hold.

"She gets lonely," Brynne said.

His eyebrows hitched up. "Evie? No way."

"Yeah. She likes school, but she misses her family. Why do you think she comes home so much?"

"Huh. Good to know. I guess I'll have to drop in on her more."

"Oh, great. Now she'll be mad at me."

"Why?"

"You know why. How about three weeks ago when you showed up and threw her study partner out of her dorm room."

She'd heard all about it from Evie, who'd called to complain about her obnoxious brother.

But Reid was all smiles. "Man, that was great. I had to toss him. It was a guy. And he looked suspicious. Like he wanted more than a study buddy."

Brynne smacked his shoulder. "News for you, big guy. He was a study buddy. Nothing going on. Except that he's helping her bring up her C average in chemistry. And you scared him off."

"Shit. Seriously?"

"Seriously. She wanted to murder you."

He went back to the television. "Eh. Wouldn't be the first time. I could have helped her with the chemistry. I was honors chemistry. And then I had four years of it in college. For fun. And really, she shouldn't have horndog college guys in her room. She's asking for trouble."

Protective brothers. Having only one sister, Brynne couldn't fathom it. "She's a big girl now. This isn't my business, but she's my friend and maybe showing her you trust her judgment will make her feel good. It'll score big points and she won't get mad at you."

Still watching television, he twisted his lips. "Okay."

"Okay?"

"Yes. I'll try that. Thank you." He looked down at her hand still resting on his shoulder and waggled his eyebrows. "Keep that up and this horndog guy will get the wrong idea."

Men. Total pigs. "You know you're a pig, right?"

"I know a lot of things. Like what I want when I see it. But we're not gonna talk about that now. I'm easing you into it."

Easing her into it. Funny. "As long as it fits into my five-year plan, that's fine."

"Pfft. Five years. I bet I can do it in three."

Ha. So typical and yet not. When she'd offered her opinion on Evie, he'd simply accepted it and didn't try to convince her why it had to be his way.

"You surprise me," she said.

"Is that good?"

"So far, it is. I'm sure it's no shock to you, but you have a reputation in town."

"The rumors of my whoring around this town are wildly exaggerated. First of all, there aren't that many women here for me to rack up those kinds of numbers. Second, if I'd banged that many females, by now my body would be riddled with infectious diseases or my dick would have fallen off. I can assure you, neither of those is a problem. Believe it."

"Oops." An older woman stood in the doorway, her lips curled in, trying to hide a laugh.

"Crap," Reid said. "Sorry, ma'am. Didn't see you there. That was…bad."

If Brynne had the energy to laugh, she would have. Someday, maybe.

The woman held up her hand. "No problem. Although this sounds like a fun conversation to eavesdrop on."

Color flooded Reid's face and something inside Brynne's chest snapped. Total puzzle. One second a cocky player and the next a contrite teenager who'd gotten busted talking dirty.

The woman left and Brynne turned sideways, grabbing a handful of his shirt. "I'm having a moment," she said. "Half horrified because, no, you did *not* just say that to me in front of a stranger and half entertained because, yes, you did actually say it and you have the decency to be embarrassed."

Reid glanced down at the front of his T-shirt still curled in her hand and pointed. "That right there? Tugging on my shirt? Seriously hot. But I apologize if I embarrassed you. I'm a dumbass."

"You're not a dumbass." She grinned at him. "Mostly."

"Nice!" he said. "But back to the original topic of my reputation. It's exaggerated, but I'm used to it. Most of the time, it doesn't bother me."

She let go of his shirt, smoothed the fabric. "Most of the time?"

"Yep. Right now it bothers me." He met her gaze. "I care what you think and I definitely want to obliterate that five-year plan."

"You're persistent for sure."

The waiting room door whooshed open and in strode a doctor wearing green scrubs and a surgical cap. He scanned the room, found Reid and Brynne the only ones in there and approached. He moved quickly and she took that as a good sign. No impending disaster. No walking slow and putting off giving them the bad news.

At least in her mind.

Brynne straightened up, readying for the news. Whatever it might be. Because now that he'd gotten closer with his stoic doctor-face, she couldn't tell what he might say.

"Ms. Whitfield?"

She raised her hand. "That's me."

"You're here for Nelson Marsh?"

"Yes, sir."

Next to her, Reid rose from his seat, but Brynne couldn't move. Stuck. Glued to the chair. The doctor squatted in front of her. "He's out of surgery."

"He's alive?"

"He is."

She collapsed back in the chair, relief weighing her down, forcing her shoulders to droop.

"The bullet penetrated his lung. We removed the damaged part of the lung and he's in recovery now."

"Can I see him?"

"Not yet. We're leaving him sedated overnight. We have him on a vent to help with breathing. We'll try to remove that tomorrow morning and evaluate him."

"Will he...survive?"

"He made it through the surgery. Always a good sign. Barring any complications, he should recover, but it's still early yet. We need to get him off the vent and breathing on his own. You won't be able to see him tonight. I'd suggest going home and getting some rest."

"I understand. Thank you."

The doctor left her with Reid and she dropped her chin to her chest.

Reid sat next to her, set his hand on her knee and stroked it with his thumb, and the repetitive motion settled her.

"That's good news," he said. "Surviving the surgery was step one. Don't let the vent freak you out. It's common. Takes the stress off the body by doing the work for it."

"I know. I'm just…relieved." She dug her phone from her purse. "I need to call his parents. Let them know. They couldn't get a flight out so they're driving."

"While you do that, I'll pull my truck around and pick you up out front. I'll call Maggie and see if they need to talk to you tonight or not. Then we'll go to your place and grab you some clothes."

"Clothes?"

"You're not staying alone tonight. I'll take you wherever you want to go, but you're not staying alone."

CHAPTER FOUR

REID PARKED IN THE ALLEY behind La Belle Style near the outside stairs that led to her second-floor apartment. He hopped out and whipped Brynne's door open. It took a second for her to situate herself—the tight dress and heels weren't helping—and maneuver out of the truck. He'd either need a stepstool or she'd have to rethink her clothing choices.

Although, watching her and that amazing ass was worth box office admission.

"Who knew I needed to be an Olympic gymnast to get out of your truck?"

Reid laughed. "You need help?"

"Over my dead body."

Eee-doggies. The independent sort. How he loved that.

Under the glare of the street lamp, she grabbed her purse and dug out her keys.

Reid scanned the alley. The backs of stores and dumpsters lined both sides. Hiding places. After so many years of military life and the constant need for vigilance, he tended to be hyperalert to those things.

"Is there an entrance to your apartment from inside the building?"

"No. But I don't usually walk through the alley at night. I come through the store, out this back door, and then up the stairs. I mean, I still have to be out here for a minute to get upstairs, but it's better than walking down the alley."

"I'll talk to Grif. We've gotta do better on the lighting. It's a safety hazard."

"I'd appreciate that. Thank you."

"My last name is on this town. We need to make sure it's safe."

He gestured to the stairs leading to her apartment. "I'll walk you up, but I'll wait outside. Give you some privacy."

"It's all right, you can come in. After what you did for me tonight, I'm not leaving you outside."

"Suit yourself." He grinned. "I won't peek while you're packing your underwear."

That earned him a scoff. "Lord! You are a beast, Reid. Or a pervert. Not sure which. Maybe both."

"Hey, I'm a guy." He leaned in, got right next to her ear. "We say shit like that."

She gripped the front of his shirt again, crumpled it in her hand, and he straightened, looked down at her as she stared up at him, her gaze locked on to his in the shadowed alley.

Bam.

She kissed him. Just lifted herself onto tiptoes and hit him with it.

Hello, Brynnie. And good-bye five-year plan.

If he had anything to say about it.

He slid his hands to her waist, pulled her closer and deepened the kiss, added a little tongue. Not too much. Just enough to show her he could be patient. And that he knew, without a doubt, what he was doing.

Letting go of his shirt, she placed her hands on his chest, sliding her fingers up to his shoulders where she held on to him and he pulled her even closer, enjoyed the feel of her tongue on his and...*Brynnie, Brynnie, Brynnie, I have plans for you.* Because, damn, that kiss rocked. *She* rocked. And whatever was happening between them, it gave him that high, that sense of being part of something special he'd been missing since leaving the military.

Slowly, she inched back, breaking the contact but watching him, her gaze moving all over his face and settling on his lips.

"So," he said, "I'm definitely up for more of that."

She sighed and dropped her forehead to his chest. "I'm exhausted and you're destroying my plan."

"Good, because that's *my* plan. I won't rush you, though. And, might I add, you kissed me first. I didn't initiate that."

She backed away, smiling. "I take full responsibility. I guess all the testosterone ravaged my mind."

"Whatever it is, you let me know when you're ready to try that again."

"I will." She slid out of his grasp, flipped that mane of hair over her shoulder. "Before we go up, I want to grab a couple of things in the shop. Randi has been eyeing a pair of earrings. I'd like to give them to her. And I need to give you the bracelet for Evie. Gosh, everyone has been so nice through this."

"Don't worry about the bracelet. We have time on that."

On the way from the hospital, Brynne had called Randi and asked if she could crash on her couch that night. In Reid's mind, it wasn't that big of a deal and didn't require a gift. What were friends for?

But Brynne? The smallest gestures seemed huge to her and that, mixed with the comment she'd made about not wanting any help getting out of the truck led him to think she was accustomed to managing on her own. Not surprising for a divorced woman, but she sure as shit hadn't been divorced that long.

He stood behind her, glancing around while she unlocked the door. In front of the building, Mags and her crew had finished their evidence collection and cleared out. All was quiet in town, but a single woman shouldn't be alone in dark alleys this time of night.

Most nights at this hour Reid would sneak one of his

mama's favorite Adirondacks off the porch—or the futon he'd found in the basement and confiscated for his newly acquired bunkhouse—and stargaze. Life in the military meant lots of nights away, hoofing along darkened streets or mountain ranges. As focused on his missions as he'd been programmed to be, he'd learned to appreciate a sky full of stars. Peace could be found in a sky blanketed with stars.

Always.

Brynne opened the door and he held it for her as she stepped into the darkened hall.

Really, she should leave a nightlight on or something. But nope, she walked straight down the hallway. In the pitch black. Was she kidding right now? Where the hell was the light switch?

"Uh, light switch?"

"It's at the end of the hall. On the other side of the door."

Oh, come on. "Seriously? You don't have a switch near the exit door?"

"No. My fault. I asked my landlord to add a door separating the shop from the hallway. Which left the light switch on the other side."

Cheap-ass Gus Pippen wouldn't spend the money to make sure his building was safe. Unfuckingbelievable.

And how was that Brynne's fault?

Either way, it had to change. Even if he had to do the wiring himself, she would get a switch by the back entrance.

They reached the door and Brynne stopped, her body frozen in front of him and the energy in the combined space shifted and charged.

And then it hit him.

Noise. She'd heard it too. On the other side of the door. What was it? His nervous system fired, that sweet little buzz that put him on alert.

"It ain't in the desk," a male voice said. "Shit. Where'd the fucker put it?"

Reid grasped Brynne's elbow, dragged her toward the back door. "Out." He kept his voice low, barely a whisper. "Right now." He yanked his keys from his pocket, shoved them at her. "Get in my truck and leave. Call nine-one-one."

At the door, she spun back. "You have to come with me."

"In a minute. Call nine-one-one. Now."

He gently nudged her into the alley and pulled her to the driver's side of the truck where he opened the door and boosted her up.

"Eeep," she said.

"Sorry. But you gotta move. Get out of here. Go get help."

He stepped back and waited for her to clear out. She reached the end of the alley and turned left, leaving Reid in the dark alley.

Now what?

He'd have to be a dumbass to bust in on these guys. Not knowing for sure how many were in there, what kind of weaponry they had, and just how reckless they were—considering they'd broken into a shop on a street that had been crawling with cops a few hours ago—he wasn't taking a chance they were rocket scientists and had a lick of sense.

Wait.

That's what he'd do. He'd lure them out. Ambush them. If he got lucky, he'd nab all of them.

And he had training. Fierce training.

In the close distance, a siren wailed. Brynne's 911 call getting traction.

Unless they were as deaf as they were stupid, the mopes inside would hear the siren and hopefully haul ass.

Through the back door.

Where Reid would bust their asses.

He scanned the area. Dumpster between Randi's bookstore and Brynne's shop. Potential hiding place. But the angle was wrong and the piss-poor street lamp would cause a shadow. Screw hiding.

He hustled to the building, positioned himself beside the back door, readied for the first guy to come through. Drawing air through his nose, he forced his body to a semi-relaxed state. Controlled his heart rate, kept his mind patient.

Wait.

At least two of them. That he knew of. There could have been a third or even a fourth who hadn't spoken.

Two guys Reid could take. Four? That might be a challenge. He inched his foot back, the heel of his boot coming to rest on something and he glanced down.

A hose.

Wound and stacked by his feet and connected to a faucet. Probably used by the building tenants to clean the alley's walkways. The sirens drew closer and inside he heard a door slam. The interior door.

He went for his weapon, still holstered at his waist and stopped.

Two guys.

Maybe.

And if they were armed? Jeez, that'd be a mess. Mags would kill him. Getting into a firefight now would totally send this sitch into FUBAR territory and he'd spend the rest of the night being grilled by his cousin and getting his beloved Sig Sauer confiscated.

He bent, grabbed the hose, and found the nozzle. Then he cranked the faucet open.

The doorknob rattled.

The door swung open and the first thug came through. *Whoosh!* Water fired from the nozzle and blasted thug number one's face. Hands up, blocking the spray, he turned away and Reid moved to thug number two. He too spun away and—*go*—Reid dropped the hose, threw a sidekick to the closest man's knee. The knee collapsed and the sound of cracking bone filled the alley as the man fell to the ground and howled.

Seeing his buddy on the ground, thug number one reeled back, swerved, and sprinted down the alley. Dammit. A runner.

And he couldn't chase him. He had the one guy on the ground and wasn't about to leave him and risk losing both of them.

And he sure as hell couldn't shoot the runner.

Crap.

He drew his weapon on thug number two. "Stay there, asshole. I'm not in the mood to get my favorite weapon confiscated tonight. That would really piss me off."

Brynne stood on the Main Street sidewalk with Sheriff Kingston—Maggie—and Reid while her shop was fingerprinted.

As much as she wanted to catch the two men who'd invaded her space, she had forty thousand dollars' worth of merchandise in there, some of it silk, and she dreaded the idea of black powder all over everything.

At first pass, she noted some jewelry gone from the front display and the day's cash from the drawer. Thankfully, due to the higher price points, most of her business was credit-card transactions, and the thieves had only gotten two hundred dollars. Still, two hundred dollars paid a few bills.

She locked her teeth together. Bastards.

First Nelson, then a robbery, now her inventory in jeopardy. Banner day. The only timesaving element here was that she'd given Maggie her statement on both the shooting and the break-in at once.

Another upside was that her parents weren't in town. Although someone—probably one of the town gossips—

had called her father, who'd immediately called her. Thankfully, they'd gone to visit some friends in Charlotte and were over two hours away. By the time they got back, she'd be tucked away at Randi's, avoiding the barrage of questions about Nelson and the break-in.

Reid waved a hand. "Mags, where are we on these guys?"

"Looks like they got in via the back door." She turned to Brynne. "Talk to your landlord about replacing that lock. A four-year-old could get past it."

Brynne nodded. "I've asked three times. This time, maybe he'll listen."

"I'll talk to him if you want," Mags said. "We sent the one Reid caught to the hospital. Then we'll process him and run him through the system. For now, he's not talking. We're fingerprinting and hopefully we'll get a hit on his partner."

Reid glanced at the shop, all lit up, the light spewing onto the street. "All her customers, the people in and out of there, that's gotta be a nightmare to lift prints."

"Could be worse. You said they were in the desk. We started there. You never know. We could get lucky. You didn't recognize them?"

"Nah. I didn't get a good enough look at the second guy. He's white. Brown hair. Hood-rat jeans hanging low on his ass."

Maggie jotted notes as Reid talked and Brynne stood there, doing nothing, feeling helpless. For many reasons.

She rubbed her hand over her forehead, pressed in on the center where an unrelenting pounding wore on her. Two ibuprofens hadn't done the trick. Between stress and fatigue, an entire bottle might not handle the job.

Reid looked over at her, even in the dark his blue eyes locking on to her. "Headache?"

"I'm fine. Tired."

"No doubt."

"Okay," Maggie said, "I think we're finished for now. Brynne, I'll call you when I have something." She flicked her pen toward the shop. "They should be wrapped up in another half hour. If you want to head upstairs, I can run the keys up to you. Heck, I can lock it up for you and run the keys back tomorrow if you'd like."

Small towns. In some ways, such a gift. An offer like that would never be made in the city. But here? Where she'd grown up, it was the neighborly thing to do.

"Oh, Maggie, thank you. Randi said I could stay with her tonight, so I'll just wait until y'all finish and I'll lock everything up."

"You look beat, Brynne. You've had a heck of a day."

Reid touched her arm. "Why don't I run you over to Randi's so you can settle in? I'll come back and get your keys."

"Absolutely not. You've done enough today. In fact, you should go and I'll get a ride to Randi's."

Maggie nodded. "I can run her over to Randi's. I have to be here anyway."

Reid shook his head. "Why should she stand here and wait?"

Maggie laughed. "Oh, boy. Here he goes. Stubborn as a constipated mule. And I know that look. He's bent on his plan. Brynne, save your energy and let him take you to Randi's."

"Thank you," Reid said.

Maggie shook her head, laughing a little. "Whatever, cuz."

She left them standing in the street alone, and Brynne poked his arm. "I'm not your responsibility. You don't have to do this."

"I know you're not my responsibility. And, yeah, I do. We don't know each other well. But we both grew up in this town and if this happened to Evie, I'd want—no— I'd expect someone to help her. Human decency." He hit her with one of his flashing grins. "So, shut up about it and get that fine little ass of yours into the truck. I'll drive you around back so you can grab some clothes from your place."

Fine *little* ass? Apparently, she'd been riding around with a blind man all night.

"Aside from the fact that you're totally inappropriate at times, you also have vision problems."

"Babe, my vision is twenty-twenty. Just had it checked."

She followed him to the truck, didn't complain when he opened the door for her, but then he grabbed her around the waist and boosted her into the passenger's seat.

"Yikes!" she said, grabbing on to his shoulders. "Holy smokes, soldier, I can still climb into a truck."

"Yeah, but it took you ten minutes to get out before. I just shaved nine and a half off."

Brynne's mouth dropped open just as he shut the door. Her mind circled around a snappy comeback. Nothing. Shoot. Fatigue had completely zapped her mental agility. Next time. She'd get him next time.

She looked over at the shop and then at the parking space just to the right of it where hours earlier, Nelson had almost died. She was still wearing the damned bloody dress. *I need a shower.* And a fire pit to burn her dress. After today, she never wanted to see it again. She rested her head back, fought a wave of tears clawing their way up her throat.

Breaking down here, in this truck, wouldn't do. No way. She'd get to Randi's, curl up under a blanket, and then she'd let loose.

In private.

Reid hopped into the driver's seat, jammed his key in the ignition, and glanced at her. "Not giving in yet, huh?"

"What?"

"You. You're about to pop off. I see it. You won't let it happen."

"Not yet. I will, though. When I lie down, it'll happen. I promise, Dr. Phil."

Reid snorted. "That'd be the day."

He rested one hand on the steering wheel, his gaze fixed on the shop.

"What?" she said again.

"Thinking."

"About?"

"A few things. Your security system for one. You don't use it or what?"

"At night I set it. Today, with all the chaos, I just locked up."

"From now on, every time you leave the store, you need to set it."

"I will. Our town isn't immune to crime, I guess."

Reid grunted. "In one day, the innocence was lost. Unbelievable." He shook his head, continued to study the front window with the mannequin and the killer red skirt.

"What else are you thinking about?"

"Your ex-husband."

"My…" She stopped. Lord, where did that come from? "You don't even know him. What brought that up?"

He shifted toward her, his big shoulders moving closer. "Hear me out on this one. Today you've been through two things that most don't experience in a lifetime." He held up a finger. "Your friend—your male friend—got shot soon after leaving your store." He held up a second finger. "And then that same store was broken into."

"What does that have to do with Kurt? My husband. *Ex*-husband."

"Is he jealous?"

"You think my ex-husband shot Nelson and then broke into my store?"

"Jealous men do stupid shit. They get vindictive. Maybe he doesn't like your relationship with Nelson. And maybe he's making you pay for it by terrorizing you."

"Ha. Good one. But I don't think so."

"Why?"

"Because he dumped me. For his twenty-two-year-old stick-thin intern. He, in fact, couldn't wait to get rid of me. Besides, I've been friends with Nelson forever. He never had an issue with it."

"Okay then, that leaves one thing."

"What's that?"

"We heard one of the burglars talking about checking the desk. They were looking for something. Something specific."

"Money probably."

"Then why not go straight to the register?"

Brynne sighed. She couldn't think right now. "I don't know."

"It just makes me wonder what they were looking for. And they were pretty friggin' specific, referring to someone as a *fucker*. Something tells me they weren't talking about you. If they were talking about you they'd have said *bitch*. Not *fucker*."

Her back went up. What was he getting at? "Then if they were looking for something, something I didn't put there, who did?"

"How about your friend Nelson?"

Brynne threw her hands up. "Oh, please. You're accusing someone I've known since middle school, someone I *love*, of hiding something in my shop?"

Mr. Arrogant shrugged, then pulled out of the parking space. "Why not? Don't you think it's an interesting coincidence? He was in your store before meeting you at the B. Then he gets caught in a random drive-by shooting—and when does that ever happen in our sleepy little town?—and right after, a couple of guys bust into your place. And, seriously, those guys showed up right after the cops left. They were waiting."

"Oh, my God. Just…" She put up both hands. "Please stop. I'm tired now. The man sells insurance. What could he possibly have put there?"

"I don't know. Maybe, when he wakes up, we need to ask him."

The man was barely alive and all they were talking about was a possible motive? "No way. He's like family to me and I'm not going to accuse him of putting my livelihood in jeopardy. Not without some kind of proof. If he came to me with an accusation like that, I'd be devastated. I won't do that to someone I love."

She turned and faced front, stared out the windshield at the pitch-black road leading out of town. Inside all that darkness, hidden from her, sat the mountain she could view from her bedroom window. Every morning she sat for a few minutes, staring at it, taking in nature's beauty and setting her mind right for the day.

She needed that view now.

Peaceful and calm, that view gave her faith in the world. Hope for beauty throughout the day.

And right now, she had little of either.

CHAPTER FIVE

DESPITE NOT GETTING HOME UNTIL two, Reid
was up by seven and wandering his mother's backyard
with a mug—his favorite with the American flag on it—
full of his mama's wicked strong pecan coffee. One thing
about his mother, she knew how to keep her boys happy.

Unlike Jonah, whom Reid was killing time waiting
on. His brother needed to get his skinny ass out of bed so
they could tour the property and figure out what needed
to go where for this training center.

And, yeah, it'd been Reid's idea to do it early. More to
irritate his little brother than anything, but now that
he'd gotten in so late, his plan bit him on his own ass.

What else was new?

Even so, the dawn sky had been amazing with bright
orange streaks thrown against the mountain. All these
years, no matter how desperate to escape he felt, the
mountain still drew him back. In all the places he'd been,
nothing compared to sunrise in the Ridge. He'd watched
that sunrise from the tiny porch of the bunkhouse just
down the dirt road that stretched around the property. The
bunkhouse, a leftover from Tupelo Hill's original owners
who'd built the tiny cabin for farm workers, offered much-
needed privacy, so Reid had claimed it as his own.

"Reid Sullivan Steele," his mom called from the back
door, "what are you doing?"

He turned and grinned. Sure as shit, without him asking, he knew she'd already gotten eggs, ham, and grits started for him.

Like he said, their mother knew how to keep her boys happy.

"I'm waiting for your baby boy to get his butt out of bed so we can figure out where to put a firing range. I guess I got nothing better to do than wait on him."

Truth of it was, he *didn't* have anything better to do. But his mom and Jonah didn't need to know that.

Get a life, man.

Mom shook her head and added an eye roll kicker. "You know this project excites you. Stop being stubborn. Besides, what else do you have on your schedule?"

Well, shit.

When he didn't respond, she laughed. "Come inside, my boy, and have breakfast. The shower is running so your brother is up. You have a few minutes to eat."

His mother moved away from the door just as his phone buzzed. Who the hell was texting so early? Had to be one of his army buddies from overseas.

Mags. And what was *she* doing up so early after the night she'd had? He tapped the message and read it. Was he awake? Unfortunately, yes.

He put his thumbs to work on a response.

Yeah. Waiting on Jonah. What's up?

Gotta talk to you. I'm coming by.

This had to be about last night or Mags wouldn't be rushing over here at seven in the damned morning.

Sure. Mama making brkfst.

He shoved his phone in his back pocket and headed inside where the aroma of grilling ham reminded him he hadn't eaten in over twelve hours.

He smacked a smooch on Mom's cheek and topped off both their coffees.

His mother had gone casual this morning in her favorite Levi's—and how cool was a mom wearing Levi's?—and a V-neck shirt. Her silver-streaked dark hair was still wet on the ends from her shower and the familiar smell of that perfumey soap she'd used since he was a kid reminded him of simpler times. Ah, to be fifteen again.

"You know," she said. "It wouldn't kill you to give Jonah a break on this training center. I think it'll be an excellent project for you while you're deciding if you're going to break my heart and take the job in Georgia. And who knows? It might lead to other work."

Guh. One thing he didn't want to do on four hours of sleep was deal with a guilt trip while having the what-are-you-doing-with-your-life talk with his mom.

Eight months ago, he'd had it all figured out. Career military. That was him. Special Forces was brutal and with the savagery he'd seen, the emotional drain could make a man crazy.

At times it had.

Nightmares, panic attacks, paranoia. All of it plaguing him at one time or another. He'd managed, even allowing himself to give in to the misery once in a while because he was a firm believer in the old adage about the only way to the other side was through it.

So, yeah, he'd let the pain in and then he got busy acknowledging it. Acknowledging it meant not losing his mind.

And when he didn't think he was losing his damned mind, he got off on the work.

Fighting for the greater good.

Corny?

Probably. But he was a believer. A proud American who saw the world as a place that could be better.

Now, without that beret on his head, he wasn't sure who he was. All he knew was that he had to get out of tiny Steele Ridge and make a life for himself.

Again.

Ready to steer his mother off topic, he swung to the other side of the giant farm table and dropped into the chair facing the stove. "Mags is coming by."

"So early?"

"Yeah. She just texted. Needs to talk to me about something."

Mom moved to the fridge to get more eggs. For Mags's sake, he hoped she was hungry. Even if she wasn't, she'd know enough to eat and save herself from the puppy eyes Mom would level on her.

Outside, a car door slammed and a minute later, the thunk of boots landed on the porch.

In came Mags, and based on the number of wrinkles in her shirt, it'd seen more than a full shift. His cousin was a freak for pressed uniforms.

Dark circles ringed the bottom of her eyes, and her hairband had given up the fight, letting a few wisps free.

Reid held his coffee cup up. "Grab a mug. You look beat. Slept any?"

"Hi, Aunt Joanie." She set her hand on Mom's shoulder and kissed her cheek. "Sorry to crash in, but I'm starved."

"Don't you apologize. Just sit your fanny down and take a load off. You know I love cooking for y'all. I missed this when my boys were scattered all over."

Welcome to the party, Queen of Guilt.

After pouring coffee, Mags slid him a sideways glance and sank into the chair next to him.

"I don't know how you military boys pull all-nighters," she said. "I'm fried."

Reid shrugged. "You get used to it. Plus, you had an unusual night. A shooting and a robbery. When the fu…"

Mom swung back, pointed the spatula.

No swearing. At least not around his mother. Another thing he had to adjust to in civilian life. Fucking miserable. He smacked his lips together. "Uh, when has that ever happened?"

"Not as long as I've lived here. Aunt Joanie, pretend you're not hearing this conversation."

"Did you say something, sweetheart?"

Mags grinned at her and as itchy as he was to run from his hometown and make a new life for himself, being in this room with two of his favorite women? Couldn't beat that.

He slugged more coffee, praying the caffeine would kick in any time now and even out his pissy mood. His cousin obviously had something on her mind and he'd need all cylinders for it.

By the way she looked, the exhaustion lying on her like wet cement, she would have gone home for some sleep if it hadn't been important. "What's up?"

She set her mug down, fiddled with the handle. Stalling.

"Mags, come on, it's me. Spit it out."

Her eyes shifted toward Mom, who shoveled eggs into a bowl. With him staying in the bunkhouse, Mom didn't necessarily know his comings and goings and he hadn't had a chance to fill her in on last night's activities yet.

"Brynne," Mags said.

"What about her?"

"How well do you know her?"

A steaming bowl of ham and eggs hit the table. Next came the grits and then Mom turned back to wait on some toast she'd popped in. "She's a sweet girl," Mom said.

"Aunt Joanie! You're not supposed to hear this."

Mom tossed her hands up. "Sorry. Forgot."

Holy crap. *Really?* Mags needed to chill. His mother wasn't deaf and she could absolutely keep a secret. Total vault. They all knew it.

"I know her a little," Reid said. "Not that well." Mom went to work buttering toast and Reid pointed at her. "I know you're listening. I also know the gossip mill has filled you in about the shooting and you probably know I was with her at the hospital last night."

Mom set the toast on the table. "You need to be careful. I know you can't help yourself, but don't throw yourself into danger."

"I'm fine, Mom."

"I heard Brynne's friend was the one shot. Right there on Main Street. What is happening around here?"

Over the rim of her mug, Mags eyed him. "So, that's the extent of your relationship with Brynne?"

"Yeah. I mean, I knew her sister back in the day. Before yesterday, I didn't realize who she was. Why?"

Mom cleared her throat and set all the pans in the sink. "I'll give you two privacy. Leave these dishes. I'll clean it up when you're through."

"Thanks, Mom. And tell Jonah to get his tail moving. Maybe remind him you don't reheat."

Reid dug into the eggs and passed the bowl to Mags. "What's your concern about Brynne?"

"I don't know. Something."

Alrighty then. Could she give him a tad more to go on? Knife and fork in hand, he held them out. "Seriously? That's what you're giving me?"

"I know it's not a lot. But Nelson gets shot coming out of the bar, after he'd been in her store, and then the store gets robbed. Seems a little off to me, no?"

Yes. He'd said as much to Brynne last night. "You think the shooting has something to do with her?"

"I keep coming back to her. She moves here and opens a boutique with fairly expensive items that—well, most twenty-four-year-olds don't have that kind of capital and all of a sudden I have two crimes around her."

Jonah wandered into the kitchen, his long, lean form moving at Jonah speed. That being slightly less than turtle. He wore torn jeans and a shirt that said Come to the Nerd Side. We have Pi.

"Hey, you," Mags said.

"Morning, Mags." He nodded at Reid. "Meathead."

Reid waved his fork. "Morning, dipshit."

Jonah, bless his sense of humor, laughed and headed straight for the coffee.

Mags finished off her eggs, then tapped the fork against her plate, her mind clearly on overload.

"I'll poke around," Reid said. "See if I can dig anything up."

She set her fork down, wiped her mouth and took her plate to the sink. "No. Thanks. I'll take care of it. I was just curious what you knew."

"He doesn't know shit," Jonah cracked, flipping him the bird before Reid could beat him to it.

Mags scraped the remaining food from her plate and set it in the dishwasher. "Ah, brotherly love. Time for me to go."

"And miss all the fun of Jonah and I killing each other?"

Mags dropped a kiss on Jonah's cheek. "Do me a favor. No homicides today. I kinda got my hands full."

Thirty minutes later, Reid hopped off one of the four-wheelers Jonah had bought to keep on the property and yanked off his helmet. No mystery why Jonah bought five ATVs. One for each of them. At least he'd remembered to include Evie in the fun, since the poor girl had hang-ups about being excluded from their male-dominated smackdowns.

But really, Reid couldn't bring himself to blast his baby sister with a slingshot. His brothers? Zero problem with that.

Jonah whipped up beside him, swinging the four-wheeler into a sharp turn.

"Keep that up, and you'll flip it."

Jonah removed his helmet, hooking it over the handlebars. He swung his leg over and stood beside Reid on a flipping gold mine of land to put a super-slick, kickass training center on. Behind them, just down the road, was the main building, empty except for a weight room, the walls painted and ready to go. They'd need furniture for the classrooms.

And instructors.

And students.

If nobody came, Jonah would lose his ass on a project like this.

Reid's stomach pitched and he shook his head. *Can't get hung up on that.* Jonah knew the risks. All Reid needed to do was help build it.

"I think," Reid said, "we could build something special here. It's gonna cost though. Big."

Jonah waved that off.

Of course he did.

"I don't care about the money."

"All right then. I researched other training centers in the area. If we build this one right and make it better than what's currently available, we'll get back our investment in the first year. Don't forget the economic boost it'll give the town. All those guys coming here to train will have to eat."

"And drink."

"And sleep," Reid said. "You thought about that at all?"

"What do you mean?"

Freaking civilians. Reid shook his head. "All we have in town are a couple of bed-and-breakfasts. Then there're the chain hotels on the interstate, I guess."

Jonah groaned. "I guess we build a barracks or something."

Great. Now they were adding housing to this project? Reid could handle the training center, but all he knew about barracks was the time he'd spent sleeping in them.

"Way out of my wheelhouse, dude."

"We'll worry about it later," Jonah said. "Figure out what we want for the center first and we'll talk to an architect about squeezing in a barracks somewhere."

Reid pointed to the northwest corner of the property. "Shooting range in the back. Way out of the way. We'll need to expand the weight room in the main building. Add some sleds and benches. More free weights. Out here, we put a driving track for emergency vehicle operation training. At least two miles. Multiple lanes. Hills, mock streets with structures, too."

"Hang on." Jonah whipped out his phone, punched the screen. "Let's record so we can put something on paper and see where it all lays out."

Reid looked out over the property again, formed a mental picture of what they'd need. "Explosives. Space for a demonstration range and post-blast investigation. A couple of houses for breaching techniques and for booby trap scenarios."

"Shit. We need to build *houses*?"

"Not actual houses, idiot, but structures we can use to simulate."

Jonah took that in, the full scope of this project hitting him.

"And," Reid said, "we haven't even discussed the shooting range specs yet. If you want to do this right, we're talking multiple ranges. Indoor and outdoor. I'd prefer forty firing points. More if the budget can stand it. Rifle range? At least, *least*, five hundred meters. Couple of shoot houses. And they should be two stories. Eh, one could be single story just for variety."

"More houses?"

Reid sighed. "Hey, you want it to be a world-class training center. Observation platform would help. And we'll need an armory for the weapons. Hold on to your ass on that one, pal, because that shit is expensive."

"Yeah, I figured that. Can you get us set up with all that stuff? I don't know where to buy that."

"No problem. I'll take care of it." He grinned. "I got a guy."

"No doubt."

Wow. They'd gotten through that exchange without an argument.

Maybe there'd be hope for this project yet.

Jonah waggled his phone. "Is that it?"

"Yeah. For now. Let's have an architect lay it out and see what it looks like. We'll tweak it as we go."

They headed back to the four-wheelers, taking their time because an out-of-work billionaire and a washed-up

Green Beret didn't necessarily have anyplace pressing to go.

Jonah swung his leg over his ATV. "What was Maggie doing here so early?"

"The shooting in front of La Belle Style last night."

"That is *so* fucked up."

That was one way to put it. "You know that dude? Nelson? He's younger than you, but he grew up here. You had to have gone to school with him."

Jonah shrugged. "I know who he is. Nothing special about him."

"What was he into?"

"No idea. He was just...there, you know. Not a jock, not a nerd. Nothing memorable. Why?"

Reid leaned on the seat of the four-wheeler, folded his arms, and took a long pull of crisp spring air. "Mags is right. Something's off. He walks out of Brynne's shop, goes to the Triple B, walks out again, and—bang—he gets popped. Then last night, I'm bringing Brynne home and there are two guys in the shop."

"You were there?"

"Yeah."

Reid took two minutes to bring Jonah up to speed.

"So," he said when he finished. "You tell me. Is it just a little fucked-up that someone tries to whack this guy and then a few hours later two thugs are in Brynne's place searching for something they think some 'fucker' put there? Am I right or am I right?"

Jonah smirked. God forbid he should agree that Reid was right about something. "Yeah. It's weird."

Huzzah! Another thing they'd agreed on. Two for two and nobody had gotten bloody. "Brynne tells me he sells insurance."

"You don't believe it?"

"Sure," Reid said. "Why not? Plenty of people sell insurance. I'm wondering what else he's into. Maybe he's banging some guy's wife and the husband decided to handle it his own way. Who the hell knows?"

Jonah stretched his fingers wide. "One way to find out."

"Lucky me that I have a brother who can hack into shit."

"Bet your ass. Whaddya want to know?"

Everything. "Anything that looks twisted, I guess."

Jonah shoved his helmet on his head. "Give me a couple days. I'll see what I can find."

"Thanks."

Reid grabbed his helmet as the earlier conversation with Maggie flashed in his mind, niggling at him. "Jonah?"

"Yeah?"

"Do me one more favor?"

"Sure, bro."

Good old Jonah. A pain in the ass, but he always stepped up. "See what you can find out about Brynne Whitfield."

CHAPTER SIX

AT TEN O'CLOCK SHARP, AFTER cleaning up the remaining fingerprint dust and removing any damaged merchandise, Brynne flipped the Open sign on the shop's door, shoved her key into the double-sided key lock, and...wait.

Her pulse did a little thump-thump. She was alone. Inside the store where last night two men had broken in. Looking for something they hadn't found. At least they hadn't found it before she and Reid discovered them.

And if they hadn't found it, someone might be back.

For the next few hours, she'd be here alone until her part-timer came in to help with the trickle of tourists who, thanks to Grif's efforts at revitalization, had begun stopping in on Friday evenings as they made their way into Asheville.

Being alone in the store after two men had broken in might not be her wisest choice. But businesses didn't make money with locked doors.

God, how had she never realized the danger in being in the shop alone?

Keeping a full-timer, in addition to herself, wouldn't work either. Her divorce settlement would only take her so far.

But this was Steele Ridge, where crime typically consisted of kids spray-painting buildings.

Being afraid in her own shop wouldn't work. She refused to accept that. No way. During her marriage, she'd spent too much time unsure of herself, questioning every darned thing and feeling weak. Now that she'd started building a decent life, on her own, she wouldn't lose the small ground she'd gained.

When it came down to it, she'd rather die than live the rest of her life in fear.

She flipped the lock.

Good girl.

She locked it again—*dammit*—and dropped her hand. *Come on, Brynne.*

"Hey," she said, "Nelson got shot in broad daylight. I'm entitled to be nervous."

Now she was talking to herself?

She shook her head, closed her eyes to regroup. "Broad daylight. Busy street. I can do this."

She opened her eyes—*eeep!*—and slapped her hand over her chest.

Reid stood on the other side of the door, his hulking muscles carving through a black T-shirt and between the shirt and his sudden appearance, her heart slammed.

He cocked his head. "You okay?" he asked through the door.

Hardly. The man shouldn't sneak up on people. She flipped the lock again and pulled the door open. "Morning. Sorry. I was…thinking."

He strode through and she let the door swing closed, eyeing the lock.

Reid jerked his thumb. "Don't leave your keys in the door."

"I know. Thanks, though. My mind is chaos today."

"And that surprises you?"

Brynne took that as a rhetorical question and didn't bother answering. "What are you doing here?"

"Jonah and I came into town to take care of some zoning crap."

When she'd visited the Triple B for coffee an hour earlier, she'd heard the rumors about Jonah asking Reid to build some kind of law enforcement center. She didn't necessarily believe half of what the town gossips said, but she'd heard enough to believe some of it might be true. "Training center?"

"Yeah. The Baby Billionaire wants to put a law enforcement training center on the Hill. I'm doing the build-out. I got seven thousand acres to play with."

"Wow. That's kinda cool."

Reid shrugged. "I guess. There's a shit-ton of paperwork involved, though, and pushing paper isn't exactly my strong suit."

Being a small business owner, she knew all about that. Marketing, payroll, taxes, insurance. All of it a full-time job on its own. One she'd learned on the fly with help from Randi. "I could help you."

What? She held up her hands. "Wait. No. Sorry. I shouldn't have said that."

"Why?"

"It's not my business."

At that, Reid laughed. "Honey, if I stayed out of everything that wasn't my business, I'd be in a mental ward dying from boredom. All you did was offer to help. I appreciate it. I might take you up on it, but I'm hoping Jonah or even Grif is gonna handle the red tape. We'll see. Right now, we gotta figure out where we're housing all the people Jonah thinks will flock here. Because, guess what? A few hundred law enforcement guys aren't gonna fit at the town's bed-and-breakfast."

"You'd need a hotel."

"Yeah. Or a barracks."

Brynne made an *ew* face. A barracks sounded so cold. "Would these people be bringing their families with them?"

"Ah, crap. Now families, too?"

"As a business owner, I'm thinking about tourism. While the spouse is in training, the other spouse and kids could come into town. And if that's the case, a barracks wouldn't be all that inviting."

Reid placed his hands on top of his head and winced. "This thing is huge. Seriously. Jonah has no idea. All I'm supposed to do is design the damned thing, but it's a monster."

"I don't think this is so awful. Some of the bigger hotel chains do franchises. Could y'all build a hotel on the property? That way families could come."

The big man dropped his hands, cocked his head and squinted. "Huh," he said. "I don't know."

"About?"

"The franchising." He whipped out his phone, shot off a text. "I'm dumping that one on Grif. But, honey, that's fricking brilliant. We'd get a hotel and wouldn't have to run it. This thing might not be as big a pain in the ass as I thought."

A low hum rippled in her chest. When had anyone ever told her she was brilliant?

He slid his phone into the back pocket of his jeans, reached up, and tickled her under the chin. "Thank you, Brynnie. You may have saved me from killing my kid brother."

Brynnie?

"Anyway," he said, "while I was in town, I figured I'd see how you were doing. Any word on your buddy?"

Nelson. He wanted to know about Nelson. She waved him to the loveseat behind the display table near the front of the room. "Sit."

Reid lowered himself to the chair, his big body taking up more of it than should be humanly possible. If she sat next to him...well...that would be mighty cozy and after the amazing kiss they'd shared the night before, her five-year plan would be leveled.

Instead, she sat on the arm of the loveseat and crossed her legs, hoping it would make her rear spread less. "I called the hospital this morning. He's still critical. His parents arrived this morning, so they're with him now."

"What did the docs say?"

"He's still on the vent, but they're hoping to take him off today. I guess if patients are on them too long they can develop pneumonia."

"Or blood clots."

Brynne nodded. "That's what the doctor told his parents."

"If a clot travels to his lung it could be dangerous."

"Nelson's mom said she'd update me later." She glanced around the shop. "So, I thought I'd open. Try and get back to my routine."

"Un-huh. That's a thought. If you're ready."

"I have to be ready. If the shop isn't open, I don't make a living."

"Well, yeah, but one day? I mean, yesterday was wild. Maybe you need a day to chill."

She sure did. But self-employed single women didn't have the luxury of days off. She needed to support herself.

"I'm fine. I called Maggie earlier. When I got back from Randi's, I went through my inventory again. There are some additional things missing."

"A lot?"

"Not really. A few small items. Some jewelry. Between the cash and jewelry, it was only about $500."

"They probably shoved everything in their pockets. If the guy we caught—"

"You caught. I didn't do anything."

"Whatever," he said. "If the guy we caught had it on him, Mags would have it all in evidence. Otherwise, the other guy probably has them."

"I'll check with her. My insurance should cover it. It just irritates me."

"Of course it does."

"And I still wonder what they were looking for."

He cocked his head. "You know my feelings on that."

"Nelson."

"Seems too convenient. But hey, it's your shop. Just

be ready. I can guarantee Mags will ask questions about him."

Oh, they'd already gotten that bit of nastiness out of the way. "She asked last night. When you were moving your truck."

"Ah. As soon as your boy Nelson is off that vent, Mags'll have questions for him, too."

Brynne shifted sideways a little, itched to slide into that tiny open spot next to Reid and maybe, just maybe, rest her head against his shoulder. What would be so bad about that? Taking comfort from a man willing to give it? At least as of yesterday when he'd flirted with her.

And what was wrong with her? Letting herself become dependent on a man had already burned her once—in a big way. Not happening. Especially not with this one. This one would slice her heart to pieces when he moved on.

But, wow, to see him naked would be a thrill. There, she'd admitted it. So what?

"It's crazy," Brynne said, not really sure if she was referring to her thoughts about Reid being naked or Nelson lying in a hospital bed. "I can't imagine Nelson doing something that made this happen. He's sweet and gentle. He has guilt when he breaks a dinner date."

"I guess he—and you—have nothing to be concerned about, then."

Reid left Brynne's shop and rather than move the truck, hoofed it to the sheriff's office just down the block at the intersection of Buckner and Main. Knowing Mags, she wouldn't pony up any info on an active case, but he wouldn't let that stop him from butting in.

He brought his focus to the Steele Ridge law

enforcement center, a one-story brick building that had to be a hundred years old. When Maggie had taken office, she'd massaged the budget and went to work on asbestos removal and repainting.

He pushed through the glass door and was greeted with homey beige walls and tiled floors that replaced peeling white paint and cracked laminate.

Shari, Maggie's assistant, sat at her desk, fielding a flurry of calls. She glanced up and hit a button on her phone.

"She saw you coming. Go on in."

Maggie's office window faced the center of town. If she was in her office, she saw everything. Including her pain-in-the-ass cousin making his way to her.

"Thanks, Shari."

She punched the button on the phone again and went back to her call.

"Forget it," Mags said before he even got to her office.

"What kind of greeting is that for your favorite cousin?"

"Nice try. I saw you leave Brynne's shop. I'm not telling you anything more than what I did this morning. It's an active investigation."

He dropped into one of the guest chairs. "You know I can help you. Make me a temporary deputy or something."

That made her smile. "Oh, *that* would be something."

They both laughed because, yeah, Reid as a deputy probably wasn't a great idea. He didn't have enough patience for the bullshit Mags and her deputies put up with in this town.

He'd be locking people up just for being stupid. Hell, they'd need an additional jail for all those arrests.

He needed a career, though.

He cleared his throat, fought to focus on his visit to Mags. "Anything new on Nelson?"

She pointed at him. "Two words. Active. Investigation."

"Mags, seriously, I can walk over to the Triple B and get a full update."

"Then I guess you'll have to do that. I'm not compromising this investigation. Now, if that's all you wanted, beat it. I love you, but I have work to do."

That wasn't all he wanted. He wanted to talk. Yep, he'd admit it to himself. A man—last he checked anyway—wanting to *talk*. Only he didn't know how to say that without sounding like a sissy.

His cousin sat back, studied him for a few seconds, then rested her hands in her lap. "I know that look. You need to vent. Or something. What's up?"

Once again, Mags had saved him from himself.

"Work."

"What about it?"

"Uh, my lack of it." He waved his hands. "I need a career. I mean, I have money saved and I've been picking up work giving firearms safety classes, but it's not gonna work long term. And, before you suggest it, I don't want to be a cop."

"Actually, I wasn't going to say that at all. I don't think law enforcement, per se, is right for you." She gave him a sarcastic grin. "You have trouble staying inside the lines."

Understatement of the century. Being a Green Beret meant improvising more times than not. Orders were orders, but in the field, if they needed a Plan B or C or M, they created one. As long as the orders were followed and the mission completed, he didn't worry too much about how they got there.

"What about this training center of Jonah's or the Georgia thing?"

"Georgia, I'm still thinking about. Could be good. I don't know if the knee would hold up with that. And the training center is only temporary. Once construction is complete, I'm done."

"Why?"

Reid craned his neck. What the hell was she asking?

"Did someone hit you in the head or something? Why, what? I'm supposed to help design and build it. But I'm not going to stick around to run it. I'd suck as a nine-to-fiver."

Mags let out a laugh. If he'd asked most women if they'd gotten hit in the head, he'd probably get smacked. Mags? She laughed. She might be part male. Maybe with Reid's suddenly female side and the whole wanting-to-talk thing, he and Mags combined might be the perfect human specimen.

"What's really bugging you?" she asked.

"I don't know."

"Yeah, you do. You just don't want to admit it. But guess what, cuz? I don't have all day, so I'm going to tell you what your problem is."

"Well, hell, Mags, you don't have to get pissy about it."

She poked her finger at him. "Your problem is you don't feel like part of a unit anymore. You thrived on that in the military. Now, being back home, you don't think you have a role to play."

Reid shifted in his seat and made a halfhearted attempt to shake his head.

"Don't even try it," she said. "You know I'm right."

"I'm not an admin guy. I'm boots on the ground. All that administrative crap. *Paperwork?* I'd put a bullet in my head."

Even if the idea appealed to him, the other issue, the bigger one, was more complicated. That sucker could tear his family apart.

He met her eyes, took a second to think about if he wanted to put it out there. If he said it, if he gave it up to the universe, it could happen.

Mags sat forward, rested her elbows on her desk. "You're worried about Jonah?"

Thank you. "Hell, yes. We'd kill each other."

On any given day, he and Jonah disagreed on random things. If Jonah said it was cold out, Reid would say it was hot. It wasn't that they disliked each other. They were…combative.

"Well," Mags said, "I'll give you that one, but as much as you drive each other crazy, I think you can make it work. Just set boundaries in the beginning."

The idea had merit, but he'd been wandering, exploring the world, for years. He liked it. The constant change and newness.

Being confined? Stuck in Steele Ridge? *Oof.*

Not so much.

He looked beyond Maggie's shoulder, out the window to Main Street, where a guy got shot in front of a store belonging to a woman he had an itch for.

Would Steele Ridge ever be enough?

He pushed out of his chair. "I'll think on it."

"You do that. In the meantime, stay out of my investigation."

Stay out of her investigation.

Good luck with that, cuz. Until the zoning permits for the training center were approved, Reid had been effectively placed in neutral.

Neutral. For him? Not a good place. Neutral made him antsy.

Restless.

And since his cousin hadn't given him any decent dirt on Nelson's case or the robbery at Brynne's store—all in one damned day—he'd go to the place he was sure to find intel.

The Triple B.

Gossip capital of Steele Ridge.

After hoofing back to the B, he pushed through the door of the coffee shop, found Randi pouring coffee.

"Hiya, Reid."

A few people stood in line, patiently waiting for Randi or her employee.

Forgoing the line—he'd come back when it died down—Reid headed to the doorway that connected the coffee shop to the bar next door.

The bar didn't start serving until later in the day, but the coffee shop's limited seating had raised a bunch of complaints, so Randi opened the door when they needed additional seating.

And in there, Reid knew, he'd find what he wanted. The Triple B at ten o'clock was a bona fide jackpot of information.

There he'd find all the bored, retired folks from town hashing out the latest rumors.

Case in point, Mr. Greene sitting at the bar, hovering over a bagel. The man had to be 110 by now, but still managed to get out of bed and come into town for a meal every day.

Reid waved hello to Mr. and Mrs. Trambly, another set of regulars who lived in the Ridge. He'd gone to school with their youngest son, Devin, but they'd lost touch years ago.

Most of the tables were empty, but Reid wasn't feeling it for a table today. Besides, Mr. Greene, resident chatterbox, was a supremely excellent starting point for digging up dirt.

He boosted onto the stool one over from Mr. Greene and set his elbows on the bar. Overhead, classic Travis Tritt streamed through the speakers about ten decibels below what it would be twelve hours from now. By then, wall-to-wall bodies and raised voices would destroy the peaceful quiet.

Randi stepped through the adjoining doorway carrying a carafe and topped off Mr. Greene's coffee. "Reid, you hungry?"

"Nah. Just coffee. But, who knows, if I sit here long enough, I might need some pie."

Who cared if it was still morning? Pie didn't have time constraints.

"Blueberry today."

His favorite. Of course. Might need two slices. Randi grabbed a mug from under the bar and poured his coffee while Reid turned to Mr. Greene.

"How's it going, Mr. Greene?"

"I woke up this morning. I can't complain."

After the day they'd seen in town yesterday, waking up definitely had its perks.

"I'd say you're right about that."

Mr. Greene took a healthy gulp of his coffee, his mottled hand shaking slightly. "I don't know what's happening in this world where a man ain't safe in his own town."

"Oh, Jacob," Mrs. Trambly said. "Don't be such a pessimist. We have no idea what was going on in that boy's life."

Reid swiveled another quarter turn to face Mrs. Trambly. "I thought it was a random shooting. God knows Maggie won't tell me anything."

Mrs. T set her fork down and peered at him over her bifocals. "Well, I don't know about all that. All I know is what Estelle told me."

Mrs. Trambly looked around, made sure no one was actively listening—in her dreams—and leaned over a little.

As if that would make a difference? Reid stifled a laugh. These people. Characters. Every one of 'em.

"*Estelle* lives two doors down from that boy. She told me the neighbors were all talking about it. And he had a friend that came over the other night and there was some yelling. Well, talking loud."

"Does the sheriff know that?"

Mrs. Trambly shrugged. "I suppose so."

Un-huh. Mags was definitely holding out on him.

Mr. Greene didn't bother turning around. "Don't keep us in suspense, Dolores. Did the neighbors see anything along with this so-called yelling?"

"I don't know," she said. "I never got clarification on that."

The old man grunted. "Then what good are you? Spreading this gossip when you don't know what's fact or fiction."

Ho-kay, folks. What they didn't need was a geriatric smackdown in the middle of the Triple B. Randi would kill him for inciting a riot.

"Eh," Reid said. "It's all speculation anyway. I guess we'll know when we know."

But that wouldn't keep him from taking a peek inside Nelson's house.

Reid headed to Nelson's and found a two-story farmhouse similar to every other one on the block. This eastern edge of town wasn't known for its wealth. What they had here was a mix of average blue-collar workers or entry-level white collar.

But the shiny green shutters on Nelson's place had obviously been recently painted and the roof shingles glistened under the late morning sun. All while the shingles on the surrounding homes were scraped bare by the elements.

New roof and freshly painted shutters.

Nelson, at the very least, had expendable income for home repairs.

"Yep, yep, yep," Reid said to himself. "We're gonna do a sneak and peek."

He swung around the corner, crossed the railroad tracks, and pulled into Barron's Park, a local hangout for stay-at-home moms entertaining the kidlets during the day. At night the Ridge's bored teenagers took over and Mags increased patrols because just breathing in that park could get you high. The locals liked to say the Ridge's entertainment choices included getting high, getting drunk, or getting pregnant.

Reid didn't exactly buy in to all that, but back in the day he liked to bring his girlfriend here to make out. Among other things. Hell, he'd lost his virginity under a giant oak tree.

Yeah. Good times.

He grabbed his lock-picking tools from the glove box. A guy like him never knew when he might need to pop a lock. He hopped out of the truck and tromped down the sidewalk.

At the corner, he veered right and scanned the quiet tree-lined street. Three houses down, a woman walked a German shepherd and—crap—he'd have to avoid suspicion and stay out of her sightline. Circle the block, try to cut through yards to get to Nelson's.

He shoved his hands in his front pockets and crossed the street. Just a guy out for a stroll.

Three minutes later, after hoofing halfway down the next block and doubling back through a couple of yards, he scaled Nelson's six-foot privacy fence—thank you very much—and swung over the top.

The fence gave him great cover for his lock-picking.

Had to love when a plan came together.

Especially his plans. Most times, his plans *didn't* come together. He had that kind of shitty luck. He never stressed over it. Why should he when the challenge of getting out of a jackpot was so much freaking fun?

He climbed the back porch, noted the wood sagging under his weight. The warped planks reinforced the lack of attention paid to the rear of the house. Old Nelson must have only kept up with the front for appearances.

The back door was solid wood and flanked by windows on either side. The shade on the right one hadn't been lowered to the frame, so Reid squatted and peeked through. Brynne had mentioned Nelson's parents were in town and considering his typical rotten luck, he didn't intend to break in and...*helloooo, 'rents.*

The slit between the window frame and the shade gave him a view of the kitchen on the other side and— whoa—every cabinet had been thrown open, their contents spilled on the counters and floor. An array of glass from broken plates, mugs, and glasses littered the floor.

Even the drawers were out and all the crap contained within tossed.

Ah, shit.

His nothing-goes-my-way streak was intact. Dammit. Someone had trumped his sneak and peek.

CHAPTER SEVEN

"SERIOUSLY," MAGS SAID. "YOU COMPLETELY ignored me telling you to stay out of my investigation?"

Reid leaned against Maggie's cruiser, the morning sun blaring down on him and bringing plenty of heat right along with her torpedo stare.

Oooh-eee, his cousin was pissed.

He crossed his arms, propped one foot on top of the other and hoped she'd go easy on him while they waited for Nelson's folks to show up and give consent to enter the house.

"I didn't *ignore* you."

Not much anyway.

"And don't say you heard me. I know you heard me, but you didn't listen because you left my office and came straight here."

Okay, well, that wasn't altogether true. He *had* made a stop in between. If he said it, Mags, family or not, would most likely whip out that Glock she carried and send him to his maker.

"Mags, you're right."

She cupped her hand behind her ear. "Excuse me? Repeat that, please."

"Hey, smart-ass, give it a rest. I'll admit when I've screwed up. In my defense, I was only looking. A peek in the windows. I saw the mess and figured I should call you. That's all."

She waved him off. "I know you. You were going in there. At least you had the good sense to look in the window first. I might have another crime scene here and you'd have trampled it. I swear, I could strangle you. Maybe I'll throw your butt in a cell for pissing me off."

In truth, he wouldn't blame her for either. Killing him or locking him up. He hadn't intended to get busted on this mission and a fairly hefty chunk of guilt damn near flattened him.

"I was—"

She whipped her finger at him. "Shut it. Not a word. You'll make it worse."

A white SUV turned onto the street and drove toward them at a speed slow enough that Jonah could beat it in a foot race.

Mags straightened. "This them?"

How the hell should he know?

He didn't answer. When it came to women being mad at him, he'd learned his best course of action was to keep his trap shut. Right now, she was steamed enough that anything he said would start a war.

The white SUV stopped in front of the house. An older man sat behind the wheel and next to him was a woman—blonde—about the same age.

Had to be Nelson's parents.

Mags looked over at him. "Stay here."

"Yes, ma'am."

"And be quiet. I'm serious. Don't make me arrest you."

Yeesh. Way to get dramatic on a guy. He held up his hands. "I'll stay here and be a good little boy."

"Ha!"

Half an hour later, Reid was still leaning on Maggie's cruiser when she exited the house with Nelson's parents. He straightened up, dropped his hands to his side, and nodded.

Mags stopped a couple of feet from him. "Mr. and Mrs. Marsh, this is Reid Steele. He's a friend of Brynne's. Not to mention Steele Ridge is named after his family. He's recently retired from the military and after the incident with Nelson, he stopped by the house to check it. He alerted me to the break-in."

She shot him a look. Hey, if that's what she was going with, he'd play along because she was basically saving his ass from a trespassing charge.

"Thank you," Mr. Marsh said in a voice tight with emotion. "You kept us from walking into that mess uninformed."

A little extra guilt took residence in Reid's chest because, well, his intentions hadn't been pure in this whole deal. He wanted a look around. A look that would hopefully give him intel on what, if anything, their son might be into.

But the Marshes didn't need to know that.

"Did you see anyone inside?" Mrs. Marsh asked.

"No, ma'am. I looked in the window, saw the mess, and called the sheriff immediately."

"I see." She let out a tired sigh. After the night they'd had, he wondered if she'd managed any sleep. She turned to her husband. "We'll have to stay at one of the bed-and-breakfasts in town."

Her husband nodded. "We can't stay here. It'll take days—weeks even—to clean that up."

"Mr. and Mrs. Marsh," Mags said. "Did you notice anything missing?"

Mr. Marsh huffed. "Who can tell with that disaster area?"

Reid jerked his chin toward the house. "Brynne might be able to tell. I think she spent some time here."

Brynne.

Once again, her name popped up.

Maggie angled her head, a small smile playing on her lips. What? Simple deduction. Big deal. Didn't mean he wanted to *interfere*.

Except, yeah, maybe he did. Little bit.

Mags reached for her radio. "I was just about to suggest that. I'll get her down here."

Brynne stood in the entryway to Nelson's house, her mouth partly open, at the sight of the normally neat and tidy living room.

So many memories in this home. From the time they were kids, middle-schoolers hanging out together, watching movies, eating popcorn, sulking about the cool kids who never paid attention to them, they'd been crashing here.

Together, they'd navigated adolescence.

Now, not one piece of furniture stood upright. The sofa, the chairs, the bookshelf with the CDs were all tipped and facedown on the recently resurfaced hardwood. The television sat in pieces, its various parts scattered.

That wasn't the worst of it. The worst came from the glass end tables that were now without glass. Tiny glistening ice picks formed a path across the floor.

"Oh, my God," Brynne said.

Mr. Marsh stood behind her, taking in what was left of his son's belongings. "It's a mess."

Understatement of the century. It would take days, at least, to clean this up. Nelson would be devastated.

Brynne spun back to Mr. Marsh, who was standing beside Maggie, his cheeks sagging and pale. Mrs. Marsh and Reid—whatever the heck he was doing here—had stayed outside.

"We can't tell Nelson," Brynne said. "Not until his condition improves. He loved this house. Knowing someone did this will devastate him."

Mr. Marsh nodded his agreement, but Maggie shook her head. What was that about?

"I'm sorry," she said. "We can't keep this from him. Not if it's somehow tied to his shooting. We were out here last night talking to the neighbors and nothing appeared disturbed. Whoever went in there, did it after we left."

Mr. Marsh did a double take. "I thought the shooting was random?"

"We haven't determined that yet. It could have been, but this break-in might indicate a connection."

Brynne angled back and once again inspected the carnage. "Someone who knew about the shooting could have broken in here, right? Don't thieves do that all the time when they know people aren't home?"

"It's possible."

Something in Maggie's tone, the patronizing flatness, hit Brynne the wrong way. What was happening here? And since when did she and Maggie ever have tense exchanges? "You don't think so?"

Maggie turned, set her hand on Mr. Marsh's arm. "Would you give me a second with Brynne?"

His gaze shifted to Brynne, then back to Maggie, but he kept any questions to himself.

The past twenty-four hours had been an epic nightmare. For Nelson's parents, she couldn't imagine the anger and heartbreak, but they'd always been strong and steady. Drama free. Right was right, wrong was wrong. Not a lot of gray areas. Which, Nelson had confided, sometimes made life with them rigorous.

Right was right.

Wrong was wrong.

Zero leeway.

Mr. Marsh left via the front door and Maggie waved a hand. "I wanted to speak with you alone. Parents, sometimes, are too close to the situation. Emotions take over and they don't see it clearly."

"Okay."

"Brynne, look, I'm concerned. None of this is making sense to me. Nelson was shot soon after coming out of your store, then your store is broken into, and now

Nelson's home. Someone is looking for something. If you know what that is, I need to know."

Brynne gawked. Now the sheriff thought *she* was involved? Outside of being the victim of a break-in, she didn't know anything. Absolutely nothing.

"Maggie, I promise you, I don't know. Believe me, yesterday terrified me. And then last night, coming back to find strange men in my store, it's crazy to me."

"Can you think of anything Nelson might have been doing that would prompt something like this?"

Brynne waved her arms around the room. "This? No way. He's an insurance salesman. Just a regular guy trying to make a living."

"Does he have money problems?"

"No more than any other twenty-five-year-old. He lives on a budget, but he'd gotten a raise recently so I think things had loosened up. He bought that television." She gestured to the carcass of the large-screen TV and shook her head. "He was so proud of that."

"All right. The Marshes have given us permission to look around. Would you know if anything was missing?"

"Oh, Maggie, I don't know. The big stuff, sure, but it's not like I know what's in his dresser. We're friends, not a couple. I don't know where he hides money or credit cards, but I've been here enough to know he keeps his iPod dock on the kitchen counter."

Throughout all the dinners and movie nights, she hadn't necessarily logged the details. Did it make her a rotten friend because she hadn't been that invested in what Nelson kept in his house?

She pressed three fingers into her forehead, closed her eyes, and concentrated on moving forward. Nothing in the past mattered. She opened her eyes again. "I'll go through the house. I don't know. Maybe something will click."

"Thank you. Anything you can tell me would help. Do you know if he has a computer?"

"Yes. Of course. A laptop."

"We haven't done a thorough sweep, but I didn't see it my first time through."

Which made sense because he always took his laptop with him. And since his car was still in front of the shop...

Brynne snapped her fingers. "It could be in his trunk. He carries it just about everywhere. He saved for it for months and doesn't like leaving it in plain sight."

"I'll have someone check that."

Maggie dug a tiny notepad and pen from her back pants pocket. Brynne had given her that notepad. She'd picked it up as a sample at a trade show, but found it too small to be of any use in the shop and thought Maggie could use it when she didn't feel like carrying the iPad she sometimes used.

"Walk me through here," Maggie said, "and we'll see if you notice anything missing."

Brynne nodded. "Sure, but Maggie?"

"Yes?"

"Why is Reid here?"

Maggie looked away, smiled a little. "Outside of him being nosy? Don't worry about it. Let's get started."

Avoidance. Not happening, lady. Brynne crossed her arms and tap-tap-tapped her fingers against her biceps. "After you tell me why Reid is here. It's a reasonable question. He doesn't really know Nelson. And he, of all people, knew Nelson wouldn't be home to accept visitors. What's going on?"

And then it hit her. *Ohmygod.* Reid must have come by to snoop and found this mess. He'd been the one to call the police.

Brynne opened her mouth and huffed out a breath.

Maggie put her hand up. "Just hang on. Don't let your imagination run wild. After last night you know enough about my cousin to realize he likes to insert himself into everyone's business. The big jerk can't help himself. He's an absolute dog with a bone. You'll probably find out anyway from the gossip pipeline, but Reid found the place like this."

"I don't understand."

"I say that a lot when it comes to Reid." Maggie gently smacked her notepad against her thigh. "He wants to help me figure out who shot Nelson. With his background, he's finding life as Mr. Average Citizen is dull. Comparatively speaking. He looked in the back window, saw the mess, and called me."

Outrage burned inside her. The absolute nerve of him. "Snooping. In someone else's house. Without permission. Isn't that illegal?"

"He didn't go inside."

"Why?"

"Mainly because he looked in the window first. I'm tempted to arrest him for trespassing."

"I think you should."

"If he doesn't stay out of my investigation, I may yet. First though, take me through the house."

After touring the disaster area known as Nelson's house and not finding anything substantial, Brynne walked outside, spotted Reid casually leaning against Maggie's car.

Dressed in long-legged jeans, biker boots, and that distracting black T-shirt that fit his muscular shoulders just right, the man screamed badass.

And he wasn't even trying.

That, for a girl who'd never been known for badassness, was just irritating.

As helpful as he'd been to her, he shouldn't be poking around another man's house. Despite being someone who liked keeping the peace, choosing her battles, and avoiding arguments, she couldn't deal with Reid invading Nelson's space. When it came down to it, people needed to keep their grimy mitts off of other people's things.

She'd learned that the hard way when the dippy blond intern had put her hands on Brynne's equally dippy husband.

Don't think about him now.

It had taken her months to put the end of her

marriage behind her. Months of self-reflection and hard work. After trying so hard to fit into the mold Kurt had expected, the nail and hair appointments, the makeup, the clothes, all that high-maintenance, time-consuming crap, still he'd dumped her.

Well, no more. The new Brynne wasn't caving to what men wanted.

Or expected.

Even if she did check her appearance in a mirror twelve times a day. Something she hated, but that nagging self-doubt always prompted her to fix her hair or her lipstick, maybe adjust her belt. Whatever.

Reid met her gaze and his eyes held enough challenge to intimidate. No surprise there. From the time she'd stepped into the Triple B yesterday, she'd recognized a certain assertiveness in him. That aggressiveness innate to alphas. Reid Steele, from what she knew of him, thrived on challenge.

Conflict.

Two things she despised.

But this? Snooping in Nelson's things? That was just flat-out wrong.

She hustled down the porch steps, teetering on her heels—damned shoes—but making quick strides toward him even if her pencil skirt slowed her down some.

Apparently he'd read something in her body language because he straightened up. Seeing the half a mountain that he was, she pushed her shoulders back, forced herself to stay strong.

Don't give in.

"Hi," he said.

She grabbed his elbow, walked him a few feet from Maggie's car and the Marshes. "I need to talk to you."

"Uh-oh. What's up?"

She faced him. "Why are you snooping around Nelson's house?"

Insolent jerk that he was, he shrugged. "Because he got shot yesterday and then two guys broke into your store looking for something. I know you're chummy with this guy, but"—he swooped a finger—"nothing about this sitch adds up. I don't think he's as squeaky clean as you think."

"You don't even know him!"

"I don't need to. Believe me, honey, all this stuff that's happened since yesterday? It's not random. I was gonna poke around. See if he had anything unusual hidden somewhere. Only, someone beat me to it. You can't think *that's* unrelated."

Maddening man. The arrogance. Unbelievable. *Stay strong.* She folded her arms, focused on not slouching. Not giving an inch. "How about not telling me what I think? I haven't given you that right."

Go, Brynne. Where was this girl when that rotten husband walked all over her?

Reid's head snapped back and he stared at her for a few seconds, his eyes moving over her face. *Stay strong.*

"You're right. I'm sorry."

Wow. *That* she hadn't expected. What she'd expected was a little alpha male tirade, a little condescension and lecturing about how naive she was. And maybe she was, but loyalty ran deep with her.

He touched her arm. "I am sorry. I get dialed in sometimes. I gotta tell you though, something is not right here. Did he say or do anything weird when he came to see you yesterday?"

Not only had he apologized, now he'd asked for her input?

This man. Full of revelations. If she wasn't so mad, she might let herself fall for him.

Oh, Reid, Reid, Reid, what are you doing to my five-year plan?

Sort of. She couldn't say that though. Too much of a betrayal when she wasn't even sure if she'd read the situation correctly. "No," she said. "I mean, he came to tell me he had to break our dinner plans for tonight, but that's it."

"Why didn't he call?"

"I have no idea. Maybe he was in town. It's not unusual for him to pop in on me when he runs to the post office or the bank. He said he wanted to see me before he left."

"Did he say where he was going?"

She thought back on his visit, ticking it back in her mind. "A conference. Someone got sick and he had to take his place."

"When was he leaving?"

"He said last night."

"Kinda quick, no?"

Yes. Exactly what she'd thought. "It is unusual for him. He tends to like planning."

"What else? Anything odd?"

The call. The one he'd received at the Triple B. She tilted her head back, stared up at a perfect blue sky, and squinted against the bright sun.

"Brynne?"

She couldn't admit that. Not to Reid. He was already suspicious and the call could have been nothing. Nelson could have been, as he'd said, stressed about the trip and acting goofy.

Didn't mean anything. Did it? Then again, if her choice of husband were any indication, her judgment wasn't exactly rock solid.

This was Nelson. She'd known him for years and he'd never disappointed her. Unlike Kurt.

Still, she wouldn't mind knowing who'd called him. Easy enough to find out, because for safekeeping she'd brought home an envelope with his belongings, including his phone. Apparently, since Nelson was a victim and hadn't shot back at his assailants, the police had no right or reason to confiscate his personal property. Chances were, after this latest development of Nelson's house getting trashed, Maggie would get a warrant to seize his phone.

Before that happened, Brynne would cruise the call log. No harm in that.

She looked back at Reid. "He was in a hurry. That's all."

"You're sure?"

"Yes," she said. "I'm sure."

At least for now.

After dealing with Mags and Brynne and their various issues with him, Reid did the only thing—tactically speaking—he could.

He retreated.

When it came to women being pissed at him, he was smart enough to know he should make himself scarce. So he headed back to the Hill to bug Jonah.

"Hey," Reid said, striding into the bedroom that Jonah had converted to a gaming room.

"Hang on, Meathead. I'm testing something."

His brother was deep-couch sitting, game controller in hand, his thumbs flying.

What else was new?

Half of Jonah's life was spent lounging around all day, making millions on gaming software he'd built.

Some freaking life.

But hey, the idea of making money by sitting on his ass all day worked for him. Reid? He'd shoot himself. One good shot to make the madness end. Anything to get him out of sitting inside all day.

The image on the giant wall-mounted screen froze and Jonah whipped his headset off. "Shit."

"What happened? Epic warfare wasn't so epic?"

"To you it's a joke. To me it's two hundred grand in development costs."

He ran his palms up his forehead and banged on his scalp. Since selling his company, his kid brother, from what Reid could tell, had been at loose ends. Maybe he'd secretly been working on the next big thing.

Only, the next big thing hadn't quite hit like the first big thing and baby brother was having some sort of billionaire crisis.

"Dude," Reid said, "chill. You're a stress monger. Take a break and get the hell out of this cave. Breathe some fresh air. Here's an idea. Maybe let the sun hit your skin."

"Oh, fuck you."

"I'll pass, thanks." He smacked Jonah on the head. "Off your ass. Let's get lunch in town. Unwind you some."

As much as Reid liked breaking Jonah's balls, he didn't want him having a stroke at the ripe old age of twenty-seven. His brother needed to decompress and if Reid had to carry his ass out of this aboveground dungeon, he'd do it.

Jonah didn't move from his seat and Reid smacked his head again. "Let's go. The software can wait. By the time you get back, you'll have a clear head. I promise you."

"Quit freaking hitting me. I hate that."

"Waah-waah."

Jonah pushed out of his chair, stretched his arms over his head, cracked his neck. Who the hell knew how long he'd been sitting messing with that game.

Reid's phone rang. Big brother number two. "Hang on. It's Grif." He picked up the call. "What's up? I just convinced Jonah to leave his cave for lunch. You up for it?"

"Can't. No time. Since Jonah's there, put me on speaker so I don't have to repeat this."

"Hang on." Reid tapped the screen again. "Go."

"The mayor just called. We got another shooting."

What in hell was going on in their little town? Two shootings in as many days.

"Come on!" Jonah hollered and Reid held up his hand.

"Who is it?"

"Some guy on the other side of town. Ed Wayne is his name."

Reid didn't know him, and the way Jonah was shaking his head, he didn't either. "Don't know him. Another drive-by?"

"No," Grif said. "The body was found inside the house by his cleaning lady. Two shots to the head."

Reid let out a whistle. A double-tap to the head meant the target not getting up. Total manstopper. "Someone wanted to make sure the job got done."

"I guess. The mayor says he's not a local. Moved here about a year ago. Kept to himself mostly."

Jonah stacked his hands on top of his head. "Two shootings. Unbelievable."

"I know," Grif said. "Our name goes on the town and people start dying."

"Yada, yada," Reid said. "We'll worry about that later. Guessing Mags is on this?"

"Yeah. She called in the State Police to assist."

"She's a smart girl. With two shootings, she doesn't want any screwups with the crime scene."

"Yeah. If you talk to her before I do, tell her whatever she needs, we'll get her. Hold up." Grif spoke to someone on the other end, then came back to them. "I gotta go. Just wanted to update you."

"We're out," Reid said. "Keep us informed."

He punched off, tucked his phone in the back pocket of his jeans, and let out a huff.

Jonah scrubbed his hands over his face, then blew out a long breath, and the tension rolled off him like a rogue wave.

"Listen, don't get crazy over this. We'll figure it out."

"I know. We just don't need any bad press when we're trying to revitalize the place."

"We'll be fine."

Reid wasn't sure he totally believed it himself, but the normally laid-back Jonah's stress level had been rising since he'd thrown a bazillion bucks into saving their hometown.

"Yeah. Let's go into town. Grab that lunch. Maybe

stop and see Mags." He gave Reid a backhanded slap on the shoulder. "Oh, hey, what did you need?"

"What?"

"What did you come in here for?"

Oh. Right. "Yeah. Wanted to see if you'd had a chance to look up any of that stuff we talked about this morning. Nelson. And Brynne."

Jonah moved to the desk in the corner. Handed Reid a folder. "I'm not done, but I got the basic history."

Reid flipped open the file, scanned the first document. Looked like something Jonah had cut and pasted together from different files. "No criminal record?"

"Nope. Squeaky-clean all around. Small mortgage on the house. He bought it off his parents. They must have given him a what-a-deal because he paid half the market value. He's got a car payment and some student loans and that's it. Zero credit-card debt."

"Huh."

How many twenty-five-year-olds had no credit-card debt? At least something. Even he, a guy who freaked over having any sort of debt, had a five-hundred-dollar balance on a credit card after buying clothes and a new pair of boots.

Reid flipped the folder on Nelson shut. "What about Brynne?"

"Now, she's kinda interesting." Jonah handed over another file. "I figured she banked in town, so I hacked into the bank's server."

Reid looked at him. "Holy shit. It's that easy? I gotta move my money."

"Nah. I've been working on it when I'm bored. I think your $3,187.59 is safe."

"You looked at my account?"

Jonah laughed. "Sure. Why not? And it's nice to see you're moving your extra money into a retirement fund."

"You shithead. Quit snooping in my stuff."

Mildly irritated, Reid tapped the transaction report

Jonah had printed. The columns were a little screwy. Another cut and paste job.

"Look here. Six months ago. Big transactions. Well, big for her. Three of them for eight thousand dollars."

Reid let out a low whistle. "When did she open the store?"

"Around that same time. So, yeah, it was probably to pay for her inventory, but where'd she get that money?"

"Loans?"

Jonah shook his head. "Nada. I pulled her credit report. No paper trail."

Well, shit.

He slapped the folder closed, headed for the door. "Let's go."

"Where?"

"We're killing two birds with one stone. We're going into town for lunch so I can get my baby brother the hell outside, and while we're there, I'm stopping to see Brynne. See if I can weasel out of her where she got close to twenty-five grand and why there's no paperwork on it."

Brynne returned to the shop, flipped the Closed sign to Open, and hoped she hadn't missed a mad rush in the hour she'd been gone. Not likely so early in the day, but the weekend crowd would start trickling in soon, so if the sheriff needed her again, she'd have to wait.

A girl had to make a living.

She set the envelope with Nelson's things on the counter, ripped it open, and dumped the contents. Later, she'd put it all in another envelope and return it to his parents. Or Maggie if she requested it.

Later.

Now *she* was snooping. And if she found anything unusual she'd march this phone right to Maggie.

Not feeling confident the phone had any battery life

left, she felt around the side for the power button. Like a lot of things they'd done together, they'd bought the same phone. Nelson had upgraded his to the newer version a few months back.

No juice. Dead battery.

She reached under the overhang of the desk where she kept her phone cord out of sight. If the phone company hadn't done one of their slick moves and changed the cord, she'd be in business.

And...no such luck.

"Bastards."

Nelson's car keys, along with his wallet, sat on the counter where she'd dumped the envelope. If she knew him at all, he had an emergency cord in his car. As with his laptop, he couldn't go five feet without his phone.

She dumped the phone, scooped up his keys, and headed for the door. While she was out there, she'd check the trunk for his laptop before Maggie's deputies got to it.

Outside, Mrs. Tilton flagged her down and Brynne stifled a sigh over the interruption. She had things to do and a store to run, and buying a raffle ticket wasn't on the task list. But, she did the obligatory hi-how-are-you-yes-I'd-love-to-buy-a-ticket. Mrs. Tilton was always selling something on behalf of her grandkids, and Brynne had grown to dread running into the woman. How many grandkids in sports could the woman have?

She held the ticket up and backed her way down the sidewalk in an attempt to not be rude, but...well...time was a precious thing. "Thank you, Mrs. Tilton. Glad to help."

"Tootle-loo. I hope you're a winner."

In seconds, Brynne had Nelson's car unlocked and rummaged through the center console. Nothing unusual in there. An old GPS unit Nelson never used since he had the newfangled phone, a box of mints, random receipts, a couple of old deposit slips and—huzzah—a phone cord.

Next up, the trunk. She hit the button on the key fob and—*ker-klunk*—the trunk lock disengaged. Exiting the car, she hit the lock button again, double-checked the door to ensure it had locked and moved to the trunk.

Aside from his roadside emergency kit and an empty box, the trunk was empty.

As in nothing. At all.

Was that weird? Even she had an umbrella in her trunk. Along with various samples and a few reusable shopping bags. Nelson's trunk? Nothing.

Why that struck her as odd, she couldn't know. He wasn't one for clutter, for sure, but didn't everyone have at least something in the trunk? Unless, of course, someone had beaten her to it.

"Hi."

Whoa. She spun back, found Reid behind her.

Her heart did a rapid *buhm-buhm-buhm* but at this point, it was hard to tell if that resulted from Reid surprising her or just Reid.

The way he looked? This one could do a girl in.

"Hi," she said. "Wow, you startled me."

He eyed the open trunk. "I see that. Looking for something?"

"Yes. His laptop. It's not here."

Wait. Slowly, as if her body hadn't quite caught up with her brain, she scanned the empty trunk again thinking maybe, perhaps, the laptop had shifted under the empty box.

She shoved the box aside. Nothing.

If the laptop wasn't in his trunk and it wasn't at the house, where the heck was it?

"This is so strange," she said.

"Why?"

"He never goes anywhere without his computer. Well…actually, that's not true. He'll run a quick errand without it, but then he just leaves it home."

"His office?"

"Maybe. But it's not typical. He usually brings it home."

Then again, what, in the last day had been typical? She lowered the trunk lid, gave it a good push, and checked it. All locked up.

"I'll have to let his parents know it wasn't in there."

"Or, maybe his folks gave Mags a spare set of keys and she grabbed it already."

"Right."

Maggie.

Reid pointed to the cord in her hand. "Phone?"

She didn't need to give him any more information. No, sir. He wasn't the police. He was just some hunk of a guy who flirted with her.

And helped her.

Sat with her while she waited at the hospital so she didn't have to be alone. Protected her while dealing with thieves inside her store.

Dammit.

"It's Nelson's. The hospital gave me his phone, but the battery is dead. Figured I'd charge it."

Reid's bottom lip jutted out. "So you could look at the activity?"

All these distractions were becoming a hassle. First Mrs. Tilton and now Reid. This little trip to the car was turning into quite an event. She pointed to the store. "Um...I need to get inside."

He stepped back, waved her through. "Sure. I'll walk you in."

Of course he would.

"Reid?"

"Yes?"

"Why are you here?"

He opened the shop door for her, setting his hand on her back as she breezed by him.

Call her silly, but having a man open doors for her would never get old. Her ex rarely did that. Unless, of course, they were around his coworkers. Then he was poised Mr. Attentive.

That should have been the first clue the marriage

wouldn't work. What she needed was a real man. One who didn't need to pretend. One comfortable in his own skin.

She glanced back at Reid's very fine skin.

Oh, honey. Not him. Too wild.

She marched to the desk, plugged the phone in, and the green battery light blinked. Success. Now all she had to do was get rid of Reid.

He wandered through the shop, casually taking it all in, his big hands gently moving over a silk blouse she'd just started selling, and Brynne's mind went all kinds of crazy imagining those big, gentle hands other places.

She cleared her throat, brought her mind back to the fact that Reid wasn't talking. At all. In her limited experience with him, Reid Steele's mouth was either going warp speed or it wasn't. And something told her to be wary when it wasn't.

She set the phone down, gave Reid her full attention. "Why do I think this isn't a social call?"

"Why do you say that?"

"Because when you flirted with me yesterday, I couldn't shut you up. Today you're quiet. If there's something you want to know, ask. I'm tired and I have work to do. So spit it out."

For months she'd been so closed off from the sting of her husband's rejection that her spine had completely disintegrated. Constantly being reminded to do better could do that. Tear a person down, make their self-esteem something that once existed, but no more.

Yet here she was, mouthing off to probably the most intimidating man in town.

She rubbed the heel of her hand over her forehead. "I'm sorry. That was rude."

He shrugged. "You think *that* was rude? Come to Sunday dinner and listen to how my brothers talk to me. You'll hear all kinds of rude."

Then he snorted.

Such a strange man. One she kinda, sorta liked.

And wanted to see with his shirt off.

Brynne, Brynne, Brynne, what happened to swearing off men?

He approached her, his huge body moving with that shoulders-back confidence that came with buff guys.

"I'm curious," he said.

"About?"

"This shop." He jerked his thumb behind him. "The shirt that's five hundred bucks."

She smiled. "Evie likes that blouse."

"I'm sure she does. But what I'm curious about is how a twenty-four-year-old woman affords a shop like this."

What the—? Half-stunned, she dipped her chin forward. "And that's your business how?"

"Aside from the fact that I brought you home last night and could have gotten my ass shot off by a couple of douchebags nosing around in here?"

"I didn't ask you to help me."

"No. You didn't. I was being neighborly. But if you've got something going on—"

Oh, now *she* had something to hide? "Like what?"

He cocked his head and her mind tripped back to last night. To Nelson's weird behavior, the shooting, and his house being trashed.

She should be insulted. Absolutely. Because she knew exactly what Reid Steele meant. Mr. Hunky Green Beret thought she and Nelson were involved in something that got him shot.

A wicked burn singed the inside of her stomach, just ate right through her, but she stepped forward, her spine securely in place.

After what she'd been through in the past year, she didn't deserve suspicion.

"Are you serious right now? You think, because my friend was shot right in front of me and I own a store with high-end items, that I'm doing something *illegal?*"

CHAPTER EIGHT

BRYNNE STEPPED CLOSER, THOSE DARK, heavy-lined eyes of hers sharp and accusing and—*sheeee-it*—that was hot.

I'm a twisted fucker.

He held his hands up and didn't bother to douse his grin. "You're not gonna hit me, are you? Because, gotta tell ya, I'd have a helluva good time pinning you to the ground."

Damn, this woman wound him up.

In all sorts of ways.

She gritted her teeth. "Oh my God. You're crazy. Get out of my shop."

She marched to the door, that curvy ass swinging, and all he could do was stand there. Like some love-struck dumbass.

His fingers twitched. He needed his hands on her ass. Pronto.

Given her current chilly mood, that probably wasn't going to happen.

"Hold up," he said, still not moving as she swung open the door. "Look at it from my perspective. My family's name is on this town, and one of your friends got caught in a mysterious drive-by shooting on his way from seeing you. Your shop was broken into, his house was tossed, and now we have a missing laptop and you trying to snoop in his phone. Tell me, Brynne, what's a guy supposed to think?"

She stood for a second, her eyes on him, slightly narrowed, and her eyebrows pinned together. She raised her fists and shook them. "How about that I'm a girl trying to figure out why one of my closest friends was shot! Could you have at least given me the benefit of the doubt?"

Crap. She had him there. All this having Jonah check up on her and basically invading her privacy when maybe he should have just freaking asked her what was up.

"You're right," he said. "I'm an idiot. I'm sorry."

Slowly, her face softened, her features returning to a relaxed state. Reasonable Brynne was back.

She closed the door. "I'm sorry, too."

"For what?"

"For calling you names."

"Again, come to my mother's. People call me names all day long." He stepped closer, got right into her space, itching to touch her, but no, he'd wait. Make sure they were square before he got handsy. "Look, there's a certain...chemistry...between us. I think I've made it obvious what I want, but I have questions. I want to help you, but nothing about the last day makes any sense. And it starts with you having large cash transactions right before this store opened."

"You checked my financials?"

"I did. And believe me, so will Maggie. You're in the middle of a shitstorm and if you want my help, start talking. What's with the money?"

For a few seconds she pinched her mouth closed and basically impaled him with a back-the-fuck-off look.

Wouldn't be the first time someone had done that to him. This time, though, he wouldn't make a comment. He'd wait. Why that was, he didn't know because generally, he'd hop all over making a smart-ass comment simply to rattle her. Knock her off balance. Something about Brynne Whitfield made him not want to knock her off balance.

Finally, she shook her head, stared down at her feet, and twisted her fingers together. "It was my settlement money. From my divorce."

Her divorce. Shit. No wonder she didn't want to tell him. The woman had a right to keep her failed marriage private.

She lifted her head, looked him in the eye. "I didn't want anything. At first. I was so angry. I walked out of there with my car and that was it. I wanted no reminders."

"Wow. He really worked you over, huh?"

"Oh, he sure did. I gave him everything I had. I tried so hard to be the perfect Wall Street wife. I lost weight, I kept up my appearance." She pointed to her face. "All the makeup and fancy hair? He loved it. Told me it made me beautiful. I gave up wearing my hair in a long braid. I loved that braid. He told me I looked silly. After that, for every damned function, I spent hours getting this look. Even when I was dead tired. And those people from his office? So mean. The small-town North Carolina girl just didn't fit."

"First of all, you're beautiful, I'm sure, even without all that crap on your face. What kind of idiot can't see that?"

"The kind that falls for his intern."

"No way."

"I heard about it over lunch with the wives. They were all talking about affairs their husbands had and the cheating that went on. Like it was no big deal. They'd gotten used to it. All they cared about was keeping their marriage intact. And the money and status. I didn't say anything, but inside? I was sick. And then that witch Marilyn, she was the boss's wife, turned to me and said, 'you know how it is.'"

Shit.

"That's how you found out he was cheating? Damn, that's harsh."

"I died. Right there. A little piece of me broke off. I didn't know who Marilyn was referring to. I just sat there. When he got home, I confronted him. Asked him flat out if he was screwing around."

"He denied it, I bet."

"Actually, no. He said it had been going on for a few months and he'd wanted to tell me. That the guilt was just"—she made air quotes—"'eating him alive.' That he was in love with her."

Holy crap. What a total dumbass that guy was. Who says that to someone?

Even he, bigmouth that he was, wouldn't do that to someone he supposedly loved.

"Jesus, Brynne. I'm sorry. Guys are fuckers."

She snorted. "Literally."

At that he smiled. "I can see why you've sworn off men."

"In less than one day, my life had blown apart. And I'd spent every waking hour since graduating from college learning how to be the perfect corporate wife, changing my appearance to fit his needs, and the only job experience I had was working retail part-time while in school. There I was, in New York, away from my family and friends, my real friends, trying to figure out what to do with my life."

"You came home."

"I did. The next morning, I packed my stuff, loaded my car, and came home. I didn't even tell him."

"Just like that? Good for you."

She nodded. "I was humiliated. And hurt. We'd only been married a year, but we'd been together since we were nineteen and he betrayed me. I didn't know what to do, but I couldn't stay there. And we didn't have years of marital assets to divide. All we had was a mortgage and a few credit card bills. He said if I gave him a divorce, he'd take care of all that. It seemed like a good deal for me. I walked away with a clean slate."

Interesting way to look at it. He imagined she could

have gotten a little money from the deal, but she'd chosen to start over. On her own.

With almost no work experience.

Brave girl.

But, hang on...

She met his gaze again. "You're wondering where the shop money came from if I walked away with nothing."

He sure was.

"The divorce was moving along and right before we signed the final papers, my lawyer called me. Kurt wanted to marry the intern."

"Come on!"

"Yep. Not only was he divorcing me for a twit, he was getting engaged. And, oh, guess what? His parents are devout Catholics."

Reid didn't know much about Catholics, but one thing he did know was that church weddings were big. And once you got married in church, that was it, no seconds. "Did you have a church wedding?"

"We had the biggest darned church wedding you can dream up."

"That's a problem."

"He wanted an annulment. Not only had he humiliated me, he wanted to erase me." She met his gaze, those big eyes turning hard. "Like I didn't exist. After all I'd given up for him. That's when I got mad. Really mad. I may not have been his skinny blond, but I had feelings. I'd done everything for him and he wanted to wipe me away."

Moisture filled her eyes and she paused a second, looked up at the ceiling. Reid curled his fingers. Fought to stay still and not wrap her up in his arms. Her husband was a douchebag. A douchebag who'd broken a sweet young woman.

And ruined her for the rest of the male population.

Ruined her for him.

For that alone, Reid should kill him. Just snap his neck.

"What'd you do?"

She shrugged. "I cried on Randi's shoulder. I'd been working at a boutique in Asheville, but money was tight. And living with my parents after all that time away wasn't working. I needed space. And a way to make a living. I was thinking about opening a shop in town and Randi encouraged me to do it. After attending all the charity fashion shows in New York, wearing the best clothes we could afford, and just generally trying to fit in with the elite crowd, I'd learned a few things. I thought maybe a boutique with beautiful, edgy things would bring people into town. So I went back to my lawyer and told him Kurt could have his annulment, but I needed to be set up."

Reid flashed a smile. "Oh, honey. I think I love you. You made him pay for the shop."

"I did. I walked away from our marriage without a dime and he wanted to erase me? No way. And you better believe I padded the numbers. I have a two-year cushion. Which means I have two years to build my little shop into something special. And I'll do it." She poked him on the chest. Hard. "That's where the money came from. Happy now?"

He'd been a shit for thinking the worst. "Happy? No. I want to kill this guy."

"You're not the only one. He shredded me."

Reid stepped closer. Barely an inch of space between them and the energy, that crazy crackling that filled his head every time he got near her, lit him up. She dipped her head, but he tucked one finger under her chin, forced her to look at him.

"You fought back," he said. "Guys like him, it's all about what they have and don't have. Things—possessions—are what matter to him. And you took his money. Damn, girl, I love that. You gave him one hell of a kick in the balls. If nothing else, be proud of that. This bullshit about him erasing you? Forget it. For years, he'll think about it. About how you wouldn't be erased."

"You know, I never thought about it that way."

"Well, then you should have." He brought his lips close to hers and her minty breath tickled his skin, making him instantly hard. Oh, man, he wanted this girl. "I'm sorry I invaded your privacy, but I'm glad I know. Because, seriously, I was attracted to you before, I think you got that, but now? I got me some serious hero worship."

She looked away. Just lifted her chin from his finger and stared out the shop window while Reid's chest got tight. *I want her.*

"Brynne, look at me."

"No."

He laughed. "Why?"

"Because I know what will happen."

"What'll happen?"

"I'll let you kiss me and I don't want that. I've sworn off men. Five years."

But then she did it. She looked up at him and all the air left his body.

He kissed her. Let her have it before she went on some tangent about sticking to celibacy.

Five years, his ass. Not if he had anything to say about it.

Reid Steele, hunk of the century, was kissing her.

Again.

And it was good.

Epic.

What am I doing?

Loving it. That's what. He wrapped his hand around the back of her head and she pressed against him, letting her body fold into his. His tongue eased into her mouth, just a gentle glide, and his breath was warm and he tasted like cinnamon and coffee and—ohmygod—so good.

Good enough that she might never stop. Ever. She was on fire. Every skin cell burning up, begging for more.

The bells on the door jangled and Brynne hopped back, out of Reid's arms and—wow—all that sexy, male heat disappeared. Instinctively, she inched forward again, her body wanting, needing, craving the closeness. If she could just take in the protectiveness and…safety.

Heaven help her, the woman who'd sworn off men, the woman who'd sworn to forever take care of herself, felt safe with him.

"Hello," Maggie said from the doorway, her gaze on Reid. "Sorry to…interrupt."

Gah.

Brynne straightened, pivoted toward Maggie and waved it away. "Not at all. We were just…"

What? About to strip each other naked? Jump each other? Hump like bunnies?

In the middle of her store.

What am I thinking?

Beside her, Reid snorted. "Quit while we're ahead, Brynnie."

She speared him with a look. But he had a point.

"What's up, Mags?"

Still eyeballing Reid, Maggie sighed. "I'd like to go through Nelson's car. I'm working on a warrant, but his parents gave me permission." She looked at Brynne. "I couldn't find a spare set of car keys. I think you have his."

Brynne headed to the desk. "I do."

Right next to his phone that was currently charging. She wouldn't mention that. Not yet. If Maggie wanted the phone, she'd ask for it.

As close as she and Nelson were, she wasn't family and if his parents gave permission, that was fine. But Brynne wouldn't be the one to turn over all his personal items without the sheriff requesting them.

Some lines shouldn't be crossed. Particularly when Nelson was unconscious.

She handed over the keys. "I checked the trunk when I got back. The laptop isn't there."

Maggie's jaw tightened. Probably from Brynne poking around in Nelson's car.

"I have no idea where else it could be," Brynne said. "He either had it on him or at the house. You could try his office. Maybe he left it. It would be unusual. Especially if he was going to a conference, I can't see him doing that."

Maggie held up the keys. "I'll check it out. Thank you."

"Of course."

The second Maggie was out the door, Reid turned to her.

"Okay," he said. "Let's get one thing straight. That kiss? That's my ticket to dinner. Forget all this swearing-off-men bullshit. If you're swearing off men, you shouldn't be invading my mouth with your tongue."

"You are insane. My God, you have no filter."

"Hell no. Why would I want one of those? I am what I am, babe."

And, oh, to have that confidence. Reid had a few years on her. Six or seven. Not all that much, but enough for him to be way ahead of her in the self-acceptance department. To know himself. Without question.

And be okay with it.

The way she felt now, she couldn't imagine it. The day she'd look in the mirror and be satisfied. No matter what.

Between her quest to be a size six—wishful thinking all around—and her constant questioning of what she'd done wrong in her marriage, that kind of confidence didn't exist.

"How do you know?"

"What?"

"You said you are what you are. How do you know what you are?"

His mouth dipped at the corners. "Is this one of those

men are from Mars things? Because I have no idea what you're talking about."

What an idiot. But she smiled up at him and patted his cheek. So darned handsome. "What I mean is, did you just wake up one day and not question who you were?"

"Oh." He grabbed the hand on his cheek and kissed her palm, flicking his tongue across it and making her body heat up again. Then he totally blew the moment by waggling his eyebrows. God help her, she might jump him yet.

"You know you're an idiot, right?"

At that, he laughed. "Pretty much." He threaded his fingers through hers. "I'm not sure I've ever questioned who I was. I'm just...Reid. The loudmouth guy who likes to get shit done and jump out of airplanes. It eats me alive."

"Why?"

"All I ever wanted was to be a Green Beret. I can't do it anymore." He pointed to his knee. "Can't pass the physical fitness test. And a desk job in the Army isn't my style."

Now this was interesting. "I'm trying to figure out how to be more and you have to learn how to be less. What a pair."

Another difference between them. All these differences. It'll never work.

"Man, you're tough on yourself. How is it your fault your husband was crappy? It would be your fault if you stayed with that dumbass. It's like that saying, the only bad hire is the one you keep. In your case, the only bad husband is the one you keep. Before you married that schmuck, did you question yourself?"

Had she? When it came to her weight, yes. Otherwise, not really. She'd known she wanted more than this little town. She'd done it. Went away to college, moved out from under her beautiful sister's shadow, and thrived.

On her own.

At least until her life blew up.

She shook her head. "Not like I do now. But you're right, maybe I'm looking at it backward."

"You are." He flashed a devastating smile. "Does it get me past that swearing-off-men rule?"

"Let's not get crazy," Brynne said, totally shooting him down again.

But hey, he'd gotten a helluva wicked kiss out of her. And if he knew anything at all about himself, he'd keep working her, slowly chipping away, and eventually, he'd win her over.

If that kiss was any indication, paradise loomed.

For now, he'd give her space. "I notice you didn't give Mags Nelson's phone."

"It's charging."

My ass. "Pretty sure she knows how to charge a cell phone."

"I wanted to look at it myself first. You showed up and distracted me."

"And it was mighty fun."

She spun away from him, headed to the desk. "You never stop."

Not if he could help it.

He followed her and lightly patted her ass. The one he wanted to take a bite out of.

"Yip!" Reaching back, she smacked at his hand. "Watch it, mister."

"Ooh, are you gonna get rough with me, Brynnie?"

Her eyes sparked, glistening under the glare of the overhead lights. "I just might. After I look at this phone."

She scooped up the phone. "I don't think you should look. You're already too involved."

Reid cornered the desk, peeked over her shoulder as

she fired the phone up. "I'm also the guy who also almost got my ass shot off last night. I'm looking."

She angled back and looked up at him. "I'm so sorry about that."

"Don't worry about it. I'm just guilting you into letting me look at the phone." He bent over, kissed the tip of her nose. "You're too damned irresistible. I hope you know that."

She held his gaze for a second, cast her eyes down, and ducked away from him.

If it killed him, he'd free that crushed spirit. This girl needed to look in a mirror and see how exceptional she was.

Twenty-four years old and making it on her own. How did she not see it?

She swiped at the phone's screen, pulled up the log. Only a handful of numbers. Interesting. Old Nelson was apparently diligent in clearing his phone's history. Not completely unusual, Reid supposed. When bored he tended to wipe out old texts and phone numbers.

Unless Nelson was decidedly unpopular, he ditched his history on a regular basis.

"Recognize the numbers?"

"Not the first one. And the second one came in an hour before he visited me at the shop." She tapped the screen again and pulled up the contact. RP. She angled back to Reid. "Initials?"

"Could be. Or a nickname."

He pointed at her laptop. "This on? We'll do a reverse lookup on the number. See what we find."

Five minutes and twenty bucks later, he had an Asheville address and a name for RP.

"Reginald Proman," Brynne said. "Who the heck is he?"

The bells on the shop's door jangled and they both glanced up.

Jonah.

Crap. All that time Reid had left Jonah sitting in the

Triple B. He'd forgotten his own brother. Who does that?

"Shit," he said.

"Damn straight, Meathead, are we eating lunch or not?"

"Oh, boy." Brynne held up her hands. "I'm sorry, Jonah. It's my fault."

"No, it isn't," Reid said. "You need to stop doing that. Taking the blame. I fucked up. Not you." He went back to Jonah. "I'm sorry. Yeah, we're eating. I need you to check something out first, though."

Jonah joined them at the computer. "What's up?"

"We pulled a number off Nelson's phone. Belongs to Reginald Proman. I need to know who this guy is."

Jonah pulled a face. "Then can we eat?"

Reid grinned. Had to love his brothers. "I'll even buy."

Jonah shoved them both aside so he could get to the laptop.

Again, the doorbells jangled. A woman came in, asked Brynne if she carried some kind of cotton underwear and Brynne sent her down to the general store.

She came back to them. "Sorry. It starts to get busy after lunch. I have my part-timer coming in at two."

"No prob," Jonah said. "This won't take long."

More bell jangling. Cripes. Brynne wasn't kidding. All of a sudden the place was Grand Central.

"Hi, guys."

Evie strolled into the store, her ponytail swinging, her big blue eyes lighting up. Reid's heart swelled. His baby sister. He'd missed so much of her growing and had a lot to make up for.

"Hey, Squirt."

She poked a finger at him. "I stopped being Squirt ten years ago."

"Not to me. Why're you home so early?"

"My afternoon class got canceled so I booked. Figured I'd stop and see Brynne on my way home. What are you guys doing?"

"I have no idea," Brynne said.

"Jonah is hacking."

Brynne gasped and her eyes bugged out. "He's hacking?"

Reid shrugged. "Sure. What'd you think he was doing?"

"Not hacking."

Evie swung around the desk, nudged in beside Jonah. "What are you trying to get into?"

"DMV."

"Ooh, can I do it?"

And holy shit. What the hell? Fucking Jonah. "You taught Evie how to hack?"

"Yeah. It's a useful skill."

"One that could get her arrested."

Christ his brother had a short memory.

Not too short, though, because he drilled Reid with a look. Yeah, Jonah knew what they were talking about.

"It's nothing big," Jonah said. "We play around."

"In the DMV."

Jonah sidestepped and let Evie take over.

Unfuckingbelievable.

But the kid's fingers sailed over the keyboard as she pounded out a bunch of code that was one of the languages Reid didn't speak.

"Brynne," Evie said, "wanna hang out tonight? Get a pizza or something?"

Brynne smiled and all the controlled emotion, the wariness, that simmered below the surface when around men—and Reid in particular—melted away. He wanted her to smile at him that way.

"I'd love that," she said to Evie.

"Not here you're not," Reid said.

Brynne and Evie both hit him with a who-the-fuck-left-you-in-charge scowl. As if that ever worked on him.

"No way," he said. "Not until we figure out what's going on with this Nelson thing. Brynne, you shouldn't even be in this shop alone. The place got robbed last night."

"Thanks for the reminder," she said, heavy on the sarcasm. "And I did ask Jules to come in early so I wouldn't be alone. I'm not an idiot, Reid."

"Never said you were. Making a point is all."

"Anyway," Evie said, "we can hang out at Mom's tonight."

Now his sister was thinking straight. Brynne would be safe at Mom's. With the security patrols and cameras they'd put in after Grif's daughter got kidnapped last month, no one unauthorized stepped onto that property without Reid knowing. "Yeah," he said. "Perfect."

Brynne went back to Evie. "I need to visit Nelson later, but after that, I could."

"Poor Nelson! I can't even believe it. It was all over the news last night." Evie lifted her hands from the keyboard. "Okay, Jonah, I'm in. Yay, me. What are we looking for?"

"Reginald Proman," Brynne said.

Reid held out his hand. "Really? You too, now?"

"Well, she's in. Why not?"

Again, Evie sent her fingers flying and despite himself, Reid was impressed. His kid sister. Go figure.

"Ooh," she said, "there he is. Reginald Proman. Suspended license."

"Okay." Jonah waved her off. "Get out of there, Evie. I'm up. Next one, I need to do."

Their baby sister made a pouty face. Too cute, she was. "Forget it," Reid said, "you shouldn't be doing this shit anyway."

He huddled up behind Jonah, looking over his shoulder as he punched in more mumbo-jumbo code. "Where you going now?"

"If our Reggie is on a suspended license, he might also have a criminal record. Doing a little snooping in Maggie's database."

"Well, shit. She'll kill you."

"Will you tell her?"

"Hell no."

Brynne and Evie started gabbing at warp speed about Nelson and his injuries. Why did women chatter like that?

Just bizarre.

On Brynne's computer screen, a report popped up.

"Bingo," Jonah said.

"Rap sheet?"

"Yep."

Reid leaned in, read the report. Brynne scooted next to him and he gave her room to squeeze in, their bodies wicked close as her hip connected with his crotch. Yeah, he liked that. Too bad they had clothes on. And, yowzer, the visions that brought to the front of his brain.

"What is it?" she asked.

"Well, sweet cheeks, Nelson has a friend who likes to dabble in gang-related activity."

"Well," Brynne said, "that's insane."

She nudged Reid from in front of her laptop and reread the rap sheet of Reginald "Reggie" Proman. Birthdate October 31, 1990. Two years older than she was. Same age as Nelson. Three arrests. One for selling an illegal firearm, one for auto theft, and one for painting gang graffiti on a city building. Idiot.

According to the report, he lived in Asheville. Could he have originally been from Steele Ridge? She didn't recognize the name, but that didn't mean anything. Reggie would have been two years ahead of her.

"Anyone recognize him?" Reid asked.

Brynne shook her head. "I'm wondering if he ever lived here. Maybe that's how Nelson knows him."

"I've never heard of him," Evie said.

They all turned to Jonah. He was closest in age to Reggie and, if Reggie had lived in Steele Ridge, Jonah probably would have known him.

But Jonah swung his head back and forth. "Nope. Never heard of him."

"Can we find a work history for him?" Brynne asked. "Maybe he and Nelson work—or worked—together at some point."

Evie looked up, her serenely beautiful eyes hopeful.

Jonah's mouth quirked. "What do you think, Squirt?"

"State income tax records. Let me do it. Please."

"Holy shit," Reid said. "I can't believe you're teaching our sister to break the law."

"I'm not teaching her to break the law. It's research."

But Reid was having none of it. He stepped in front of Evie, blocking her from the laptop. "No way. You wanna do this crap, do it when I'm not standing here. Really, you shouldn't be doing it all. Jonah knows better."

Reid's cheeks hollowed out. Carved rock. Hard and unyielding, and a muscle in his jaw throbbed.

Whatever was going on with him and Jonah and this hacking thing had the man ready to burst. Maybe it was simply wanting to protect his little sister, but somehow it seemed like more. Something festering.

And after all he'd done for her in the past day, the least she could do is help him get his way.

"Um, Evie," Brynne said, "could you let Jonah do it? I need to talk to you."

She latched on to Evie, dragged her to the stockroom. "We'll be right back! Girl talk."

What they'd talk about when they got there, she'd wing.

She opened the stockroom door, shoved Evie through. Her friend whirled back amid the shelves loaded with her inventory. "Are you okay?"

Was she? It had been a rough twelve hours and yes, she'd been pushing through. Painting on her get-it-done persona, but...

"I'm...I don't know."

"Is it Nelson? That had to be horrible."

Brynne flapped her arms. "I just...I don't know. Needed a second. This is cray-cray."

"Sure is. And believe me, with Reid in the middle of it, it'll only get crazier. Our mama says he's a magnet for chaos."

At that, Brynne smiled. "That's funny. He does love to get into everyone's business."

"Yeah, he goes all HAM on everything."

HAM—hard as a motherfucker. The first time Brynne had heard that, she'd cracked up. Being in New York, surrounded by older people, she'd lost touch with the slang of people her own age. Somehow, at twenty-four, she felt...old.

How had that happened? Most women her age were out at clubs, hooking up, searching for husbands. Her? She'd already had a husband and was in no hurry for a new one.

The life she had now? Hanging with Nelson and Evie and Randi? They were great friends. Reliable, kind, and loving. Always there to lend a hand. But something wasn't quite right. A void somewhere.

If Brynne went ahead with her plan to swear off men, that's all she'd have. No passion, no handholding or naked spooning at night. No intimacy that made her insides turn gooey.

The idea of that, years of loneliness, froze her lungs and she lunged forward, wrapped Evie in a crushing hug.

"Whoa." Evie squeezed back. "Girl, you're all right. I'm here."

Brynne squeezed her eyes closed, forced herself to breathe as visions of herself at sixty and alone filled her head. Can't do it. What kind of life would she have all alone like that? "I think I want to have sex with your brother."

"Jonah?"

Brynne laughed. Evie had multiple brothers. "No. The loudmouth."

A long snort flew from Evie. "Oh. Well, that's no big

deal. All the girls at school want to have sex with him, too. When he comes to visit, they line the hallway and watch him. He loves it."

Brynne backed up. "They really do that?"

"Oh, yeah. It has a major ick factor. He never does anything, though. He just says hello and keeps walking. I think he knows it embarrasses me. He's a jerk sometimes with getting on me all the time, but he's sweet, too. Like, taking-care-of-people sweet. You know?"

Yes. She did know. Since yesterday afternoon, Reid Steele had added Brynne to his list of folks to watch over.

"Thank you."

"For what?"

"Being a good friend. I love you."

"Hey!" Reid hollered from outside. "You two about finished? Got shit to do here."

Evie stretched her mouth open and scrunched her nose. "He's such a jerk."

"Coming!" Brynne gave her hair a flip over her shoulder, took a long pull of air—big girl panty time—and strode into the hallway.

The two men still stood behind her desk, Jonah banging away on her laptop while Reid stood to his side. When her heels clapped against the hardwood, he glanced up, his eyes steady on her, creating all kinds of flashing heat.

"Sorry," she said.

Still with that hungry gaze on her, Reid nodded. "No problem. You all right?"

"I'm great. Did you find anything?"

"No," Jonah said. "Reggie Proman can't hold a job. Mostly fast food or laborer stuff."

Again she squeezed next to Reid, let the heat from his extremely hard body work her hormones into an uproar. "If he has an arrest record, he might find it difficult to get work."

"True."

Reid poked a finger at the laptop. "You know what I think?"

Oh-boy.

"Here we go," Jonah said.

"I think your buddy Nelson might be awake by now. I say we go ask him."

CHAPTER NINE

BRYNNE CLOSED THE SHOP.

Her part-timer couldn't get there until two and the curiosity over this gang connection drove Brynne to make a decision she normally wouldn't. Closing the shop meant possible lost sales. But it had been slow all morning and the weekend traffic hadn't yet picked up. An hour wouldn't break her.

Jonah, bless his generous heart, had gone down to the Triple B for lunch and promised Brynne he'd go back to the shop at two and stay there with her employee until Brynne and Reid returned.

These Steele boys. Something else. The women of Steele Ridge needed to get to work and snatch them up.

Although the Steeles had a stake in this tragedy. With all they'd invested into the town—time, money, their family name—they couldn't have people gunned down in the street and businesses broken into.

What they all needed was answers. And if she could get those answers from Nelson, maybe it would help solve the shooting.

The main entrance doors to the hospital slid open, and Reid once again set his hand on Brynne's lower back, ushering her in.

And, wow, that felt good. A man touching her. A man

like Reid. One with big shoulders and a killer body and a never-quit attitude that made her feel...well...small.

In a good way. In a protected way.

Her husband never made her feel that. He wanted her to feel small in different ways. In helpless, controlled ways.

Not Reid. He didn't need to make women feel inferior to build his own power.

They reached the elevator that would ferry them up to the intensive care unit where, hopefully, if the morning had gone according to plan, Nelson had been taken off the vent. Even if he was still in ICU, off the vent, he'd be able to talk and she could ask him about Reggie Proman.

They stepped into the elevator and the doors whooshed closed. "Maggie won't be happy with us."

"Nope," Reid said. "I'll take care of it. Right now, we're on a fishing expedition. When we're done here, we'll take her the phone and any info we have on Proman." He looked down and grinned. "We'll leave out the part about hacking into her system."

Brynne snorted. "That might upset her."

"Ya think?"

The door slid open again. A sign hanging from the ceiling directed them to ICU and they made a right and strode through another set of double doors.

In the hallway stood Nelson's father. Next to him, seated on a rolling desk chair—what the heck?—was Nelson's mother, her head down, her hands twisting in her lap.

Something was wrong. The body language of these people she'd known almost her whole life indicated it.

Brynne picked up her pace, the hallway stretching out in front of her like something out of a horror flick. The faster she moved, the longer the corridor became. *Clip, clip, clip,* her heels smacked the cheap flooring and echoed against the walls. Blasted five-inch heels.

Get there.

Beside her, Reid's long legs kept perfect time, barely working to keep up. He'd sensed it, too. The negative vibe of the Marshes' body language.

"Whatever it is," he said, "you can handle it. I know you can."

Nelson's mom gave up on staring at her hands and lifted her head. She spoke to her husband, who stood beside her and patted her shoulder in response to whatever she'd said.

The sound of Brynne's heels drew her gaze left and her eyes, even from twenty-feet away, were...

Stricken.

Destroyed.

No. *No, no, no.* A weird cramp moved up Brynne's calf, but she kept moving, closing the space between her and Nelson's parents. *Clip-clip-clip.* Damned shoes.

She held her hands out, reaching for Mrs. Marsh. The older woman stayed seated but gripped Brynne's hands, squeezing so hard she hit bone and her eyes— God—her eyes were worse close up. Red and swollen and tortured.

Mrs. Marsh dropped her hands again. "Oh, Brynne."

Again, Mr. Marsh patted his wife's shoulder, but she went back to twisting her hands.

"Brynne," Mr. Marsh said. "I'm so sorry. Nelson is...He passed on."

Did he say...wait. Brynne craned her neck, moving closer, drawn in because what she thought she'd heard was that Nelson was...

No.

An enormous wave of cold radiated from her core. She shivered against the onslaught and her body rocked forward, then back. Forward and back, forward and back. Still standing behind her, Reid grabbed hold of her, his big hands wrapping around her biceps.

"I got you," he said.

But Brynne shook her head. "No. Nuh-uh. They said..."

Mrs. Marsh grabbed her hand again. "It was a…a blood clot."

Blood clot. The doctors had warned them about that. That the clot could break free and move to the lungs. A common occurrence, they'd said.

Common occurrence.

Brynne took it in. Tasted the nasty bile that came with it and swallowed.

Nelson was dead. Her childhood friend. Her *best* friend. The one who had gotten her through her divorce.

"He's…"

Her eyes went to Mr. Marsh, hoping, praying to whatever God would listen, that Nelson's father would tell her something else. Late April Fools'. Just kidding, hon. Ha, ha.

But no. He stood beside his wife, that damned hand patting away at her shoulder—pat, pat, pat—and she wanted to smack it away. Just make it stop. Because if she could make that patting stop, maybe, just maybe all of this would be her imagination. Some twisted tale spinning inside her mind.

"He made it through surgery, though. They said the vent would help."

Mr. Marsh shook his head. *None of that.* No way. Brynne went back to Mrs. Marsh and her twisting hands, but the woman wouldn't look at her. "I'm sorry, Brynne. I'm so sorry."

Get out.

She had to leave. Had to get out of this damned hospital with its disgusting closed-in air that reeked of illness and death and heartbreak.

She spun away, out of Reid's grasp, wobbling on the stupid heels. She headed for the door. Any door that would take her out of here. Away from it.

The loss.

Oh my God.

"Brynne," Reid said, "honey, hang on."

"I have to go."

The bright red exit sign at the end of the hallway flashed and she burst into the stairwell.

"Brynne, we're six flights up."

She bounded down the stairs, sucked in more stale, disgusting air, felt it close in around her as the cramped space—*worse in here*—wrapped its nasty, strangling grip around her throat and squeezed.

She kept going, Reid hot on her heels, his voice breaking through, but his words unclear. Jumbled.

"I have to go, Reid."

Another flight of stairs gone and a bead of sweat dripped down her back from the effort.

Or the heartbreak.

She wasn't sure. She hit the landing. Fourth floor. According to the giant blue number four on the door.

Three more flights of nasty, suffocating air. Oh my God. She'd die in here. Just like Nelson. Her lungs wouldn't survive this.

Midway to the next landing, she released a breath, a huge gasp, and—God—it was awful. That taste.

The death.

The pale orange walls shifted and curled in, and Brynne reached out, but the closer she got, the farther they were from her reach.

Can't do it. She stopped at the landing between floors and the wall was right there. She touched it—yes!—and rested her hands against it, let the cement surface cool her sweaty palms as she stared at the pukey paint. Smack! She slammed her open palm against it. Then did it again. A huge burst of energy firing through her arms. Smack, smack, smack.

Behind her, Reid latched on, grabbed her wrists. "Don't," he said. "You'll hurt yourself."

She tugged, tried to free her hands. "Let me go."

"No."

She struggled against his grip.

Too strong. She looked up at him, their gazes connecting and...

What was the point? Why spend all her energy fighting a man? Nelson would still be gone and the loss would still be devastating.

Slowly, she moved forward, her body propelling itself closer to Reid. Closer to all his massiveness that she could curl into. Taking his cue, he took a tiny step forward and she rested her forehead in the center of his chest, into safety, and breathed in the clean, fragrant scent of his laundry soap. Clean air. *Breathe.*

"Ah, Brynne, I'm sorry."

"He saved me," she said. "When my life fell apart, he saved me. I couldn't save him, Reid. How is that fair?"

"It's not fair."

With his military career, he knew all about the loss of friends.

"You're grieving," he said. "Give it a minute. There's no place we need to be."

We. *There's no place we need to be.*

She looked up again, into his eyes that had turned stormy. The color of the Atlantic during a hurricane and he held her, pulled her close, ran his hand over her hair, gently stroking while she held on. Held on to rock-solid Reid Steele.

And, oh no, that five-year plan just flew out the window.

The guys in Reid's unit would call this a clusterfuck.

A grand one.

After getting her out of that freaking stairwell, he hopped into his truck, snuck a peek at Brynne, sitting like a stone in the passenger's seat, staring straight ahead with that zoned-out, numb look he'd experienced a hundred times. Thousands if he counted the people he'd seen it on.

The poor girl had been through a helluva couple of

days. He itched to reach over and touch her, wrap her up, and tell her she'd get through it. That the pain would wear away eventually, burn down to an ache she could shove away somewhere.

"Here's what we'll do," he said. "I'm taking you back to my mom's. We'll get Mags out to the house, update her on what we found on the phone, and then you can sack out in the guest room. My mom will love it. You and Evie were gonna hang out tonight anyway. You'll get a good meal and my mother fussing over you and you won't be alone."

She glanced up at him with cloudy, unfocused eyes. Totally gone. Had she even heard what he'd said? And if she had, he doubted it registered.

"He's dead," she said.

And, ah, shit. He didn't need to respond to that. They both knew it, understood it on a primal level. Agreeing with her, reinforcing her pain, at this point, wouldn't do a damn bit of good.

Reid fired the truck's engine, shifted to drive, and swung out of the hospital lot.

"You're gonna be okay, Brynne. I swear to you. It sucks right now. Sucks the motherlode. But it gets better."

From the corner of his eye he saw her head move. A nod. At least she was tracking the conversation.

"When?"

He stopped at the traffic light and looked over at her. "When what?"

"When does it get better? Because the way this feels"—she curled her hands into tight balls and pushed them into her chest—"this ripping in my chest doesn't feel like it could ever get better. How do you suddenly lose people you love and get through it?"

If he knew the answer to that, grieving people everywhere would be a lot healthier. He shrugged. "Honest to God, I don't know. It's part of war, though, and I learned to find an outlet. Physical exercise was huge. I did whatever I could to work off the stress. When I got tired, I'd listen to music or fiddle with a guitar. More than anything, you need to let yourself feel it. Don't shove it away. It doesn't work. You'll eventually break down and all that shit'll come flying out. It's damned ugly when it does."

"The voice of experience?"

"Maybe. Or maybe I've just gotten smarter."

Behind them, a horn honked and Reid checked the stoplight. Green. The butthead behind him honked again. Where the hell was this guy going that he couldn't wait five seconds? Reid lowered his window, shoved his hand out and flipped the guy the bird.

It took a full two seconds for the guy to return the gesture and Reid looked back at Brynne. "He flipped me off. Should I kick his ass?"

Brynne let out a laugh. "No. Please. We don't need you in jail."

Reid hit the gas and the idiot behind them zoomed around. *Good riddance, dickweed.*

"I can pull over if you want to talk about this some."

She set her hand on his upper arm, let it rest there a second before she squeezed. That small gesture—the zero hesitation—sent his body into all kinds of activity—good activity—that made him think being home might not be such a bad thing.

"No," she said. "I'll be okay. Thank you, though."

"For what?"

"I'm not sure. Understanding maybe?"

Understand he did. "I won't lie and tell you grief is easy. It's not. It's a brutal bitch. One day you'll feel okay and the next you're a mess. Part of the battle is knowing that. But I promise you, in time, it'll get better."

"I believe you." She turned front again, dragged in a huge breath. "I don't know what to do now."

"Why do you have to do anything?"

A small smile tipped her mouth up. "Because it's what I do. I keep moving. But I've heard what you said about not shoving the pain away. I can do both. I can grieve and keep moving. I promise." She straightened her shoulders and stared out the windshield. "I should probably head back to the shop."

That was the last thing she needed. What she needed was quiet. "Jonah is there. He'll call if they need something."

"Your brother can't sit in my shop all day. I'm sure he has things to do."

"Yeah, he does. But he said he's good. And the thing about the Baby Billionaire? He'll let you know when that changes. Trust me."

"Doesn't he hate being called the Baby Billionaire?"

"Why would he hate it?"

"Well, it's a wee bit condescending."

The shock must really be screwing with her. Britt had laid that Baby Billionaire nickname on Jonah when he'd sold Steele Trap Entertainment, his software company. They'd been sitting around Mom's dining room table, had just finished dinner, and Mom set a giant cake in front of her youngest son. Even their dad had made the trip down from the cabin. All to celebrate Nerd Boy's accomplishment.

As much as Reid liked to get on Jonah, the kid had done it. He'd taken the thing he'd been passionate about for years and succeeded.

And Reid was proud of him. Not that he'd ever admit that shit, but yeah, baby brother had done good.

"I'm gonna disagree with you on that one. It might be condescending to people who don't know us, but he got that nickname when we were celebrating him. Mom was cutting cake and Britt said, 'Give the baby billionaire the first piece.' We all laughed, including Jonah. He's competitive enough to enjoy the fact that he's the youngest, geekiest of all the Steele boys and *he* was the one on the Fortune 500 list. *Believe* me."

"It really is amazing."

Sure was. "Yeah. He's a good guy. I want to kill him half the time, but he's got an open heart."

Silence followed. Reid wasn't good at silence. Silence meant too much thinking and heavy thoughts.

"My heart," Brynne said, "isn't open. Not anymore."

He hung a left to the mountain road that would avoid traffic and take him back to Steele Ridge.

Like he said, too much thinking. "Yeah, it is. You're just pissed at men."

"Which gives me a closed heart."

"Honey, after what I saw this last day, your heart is far from closed. Maybe you're cautious, but you're not locked down."

He took a quick glance at her, found her studying him, and if he weren't driving, he'd do things to her. Extremely fun things that would have them exploring various body parts and would most definitely take her mind off her troubles.

He went back to the road. This girl was grieving and his horndog self wanted action?

Total schmuck.

"So, Jonah's fine at the shop. We'll call him if you want. If he needs to bail, I'll run down there and keep watch until closing."

"You don't have to do that. You shouldn't do that. This isn't your problem."

"I know it's not. But I think you've figured out that I like you." He shot a smile her way. "For many reasons."

Brynne's lips quirked. Points for him on flipping that frown upside down, as his mama liked to say.

He punched up Jonah's number on his phone.

"Meathead, what's up?"

"We're heading back to town. I'll fill you in later, but I'm gonna run Brynne over to the house. You good there for a while?"

Jonah hesitated and Reid didn't bother filling the quiet phone line. If his little brother knew him at all, he took the unspoken hint that he shouldn't ask about

Nelson. If Reid wanted to update him, he would. Simple as that.

"I'm good," Jonah said. "Brynne's employee makes a nice view."

Reid laughed. "You're a dog."

"I learned everything from you."

Not everything, little brother.

"Whatever. I'll holler at ya. Later."

He punched off, tossed his phone into the console, and took the curve that looked out over Steele Ridge.

He checked the rearview and slowed the truck to a crawl. On days like this, with the sun throwing long rays over the trees and the church steeple, he figured Steele Ridge could be the model for some cheesy greeting card.

Small-town life. The thing he'd always run from.

Brynne shifted toward him. "Why are we stopping? Everything okay?"

Reid pointed out the window. "I've been all over the world and seen amazing places. I mean, there are places where the stars are so bright at night you'd swear they're fake."

"I can imagine."

"But there's something about this spot that's right up there with all those crazy cool places. I can't figure out why I feel that way, but I do."

"Oh," she said. "That's easy. This is home."

Home. Really? Could it be that simple?

"But it hasn't been my home for twelve years. Not really. Between school and the Army, I could count the times I've been here."

Something, in hindsight, he should be ashamed of. There'd been times, a few days' leave here and there, he could have come home, but chose to do other things. A weekend at the beach with the guys, a trip to Vegas.

"I don't think it matters how often. We all have a place that's home. We may live other places, but they're not home. Like me with New York. For a while, I loved it there. The culture, the excitement. It was all so different."

"But you came back."

"It wasn't home. Steele Ridge is. It's where I belong. The people who love me are here. That's what home is to me."

He glanced over at her, held her gaze for a few long seconds.

Home.

The people who loved him. And that he loved. All of them were here. Right in Steele Ridge. And after all the places he'd seen, the horrors he'd experienced, it took a twenty-four-year-old recovering from a bum marriage to enlighten him.

Dumbass.

"I'll think about that," he said. "Thank you."

"For what?"

Reid shrugged. "Making sense of it, I guess. Showing me how to change my thinking." He reached over, ran his fingertips down her cheek, and just touching her, the smooth, soft skin, lit something inside him. Maybe home wasn't such a bad place. He liked this girl. A lot. "You're a smart, beautiful girl, Brynnie. Don't ever let anyone tell you different."

Brynne sat in one of the Adirondack chairs on Mrs. Steele's porch watching the late afternoon sun dip while immersed in the quiet around her. A soft breeze blew and on any other day, she would love the peaceful calm.

Today? With Nelson gone, nothing would make her happy.

Evie pushed through the back door, two glasses in hand.

"Lemonade." She handed one off to Brynne. "Our mama makes it from scratch for Reid. She says he's a pain in the ass, but she loves him."

These people. So funny. "Your family is—"

"Crazy?"

"Spirited. But it's...nice. You know? Everyone helps."

One moment in their company brought a feeling of unity and love. Despite the smart comebacks and insults, the Steeles were a force.

"Yeah," Evie said, "but those boys *fight*. They're either arguing or laughing. Nothing in between."

"They're men. I think it's how they communicate."

"I guess."

Brynne took a sip of the lemonade and let the sweet tartness bring her taste buds alive. At least something brought her from her stupor.

The shock of Nelson's death hadn't quite worn off. That, combined with the emptiness left when Reid went off with Maggie half an hour ago, wasn't helping her mood. With Reid around, she was distracted. He had that way about him. All action and movement and, well, excitement.

Again he'd come to her rescue by relieving Jonah at the store and, Brynne guessed, took the opportunity to talk privately with Maggie after they'd turned Nelson's phone over.

Instinctively she knew Reid had theories and questions about Nelson he wouldn't say in front of her.

For that she'd always be thankful. As aggressive as he could be, his sensitivity to her situation, to her loss, could only come from someone who understood.

How had he done it, all those years in the military? Watched his friends get injured.

Or die.

Evie set her glass on the porch, twisted sideways and curled her jean-clad legs under her, her body nestling into the giant chair. Evie had that kind of body. Lean and flexible and...enviable. At least to Brynne, who'd never been blessed with a thin frame. One where she didn't have to try on thirty pairs of jeans to find one that fit her giant rear.

Evie propped her elbow on the chair arm and dropped her chin into her hand. "Is there anything I can do? I see how sad you are. I hate that for you."

Brynne took a second, stared out into the vast acreage beyond the porch. All that greenery enhanced by the orange glow of late sun. The place was stunning. Someday she'd have property like this.

And she'd buy it herself.

She looked back at Evie. "I don't know. I've never lost a friend before. It's…hard. Like it hasn't sunk in yet. When my grandmother died, we expected it. She'd been sick. But this?" Something in her stomach squeezed and she blew air through her lips, fought off the shaky feeling that came right before a bout of tears. "This, I don't know how to process."

Reid does.

"Reid does. You should talk to him."

Brynne finally smiled. "I was just thinking that! I swear you people are mind readers."

"I hope Maggie figures out who did this."

"The phone might help. And this gang guy—oh my God—that blows my mind. I had no idea Nelson even knew a gang member."

"Do you think—"

"What?"

"Nothing. It's dumb."

Brynne knew. How could she not? "You want to know if he was involved with a gang?"

"It's dumb. I mean, this is squeaky-clean Nelson. Did he even swear?"

"Not a lot. But something was weird yesterday. When he came to see me."

"Weird how?"

Exactly what Brynne had been trying to figure out. "I don't know, he was rushing. Distracted, I guess. And then he didn't have anything packed for this supposed trip he suddenly had to take. And where's his laptop? He always had that with him. And now Maggie can't find it."

"Did you look through his phone messages? The texts?"

"Yes. After we got back from the hospital. He'd cleared them all. All that was there were the numbers in his log."

Evie puckered. "Did you guys do an online search for them?"

"Not all."

"Do you still have them?"

"In my purse. Why?"

Evie flapped her hands. "Jonah and Reid are gone. We could do research without them yelling at us."

"Hacking?"

Evie hopped out of the chair, smacked her hands together. "Information gathering."

"Reid will kill you."

"And Jonah, too. He's always telling me not to do it on my own. But..."

Oh, this couldn't be good. "What?"

"I play. When I'm at school. I always make sure I don't leave a trail. He taught me how to do that. I'm getting good at it. I bet we could figure out who those numbers belong to and get a history. Just like we did with this Reggie guy."

As easy as all this sounded, a lot could go wrong and she didn't need the two of them getting arrested. Not when Evie shouldn't even be involved in this mess.

But the idea of getting answers and figuring out what Nelson was up to could be right at the end of Evie's fingertips. "You can do it safely? We won't get caught?"

"Yeah. This is the easy stuff. We just need to do it before Reid or Jonah gets back."

Minutes later, Brynne stood behind Evie, who'd settled into what she called Jonah's command center.

That *command center* thing might not have been far off the mark. Jonah had knocked out a dividing wall between two bedrooms and made it his own personal office/bedroom suite. On one side sat his bedroom and the other his office. In the office half sat a giant U-shaped desk with five oversized monitors, an ergonomic, reclining chair and a television that spanned half the length of the wall.

For gaming.

The setup must have cost a gazillion bucks.

Evie logged on to one of the three laptops—because, yes, apparently Jonah needed multiples.

"Evie, that might be the biggest television I've ever seen."

"I know. He doesn't even have cable in here. He's online all day. He works *a lot*."

"Does he play just to play? Or is it all work?"

"I don't know. Since he sold his company, I think the lines have blurred. He's bored."

One of the giant monitors on the desk flashed bright and Evie went to work, her fingers flying across the keyboard.

Brynne huddled behind her, watching over her shoulder as code streamed on the monitor.

"Is this the DMV again?"

"It worked last time. Give me two minutes."

"Sure."

Why not? It wasn't every day Brynne got to break the law. Was hacking into the local DMV a federal offense? Or just state?

She shook it off. Some things she didn't need to know. Unlike Nelson's activities. That, she definitely needed to know.

"I'm in," Evie said. "First number?"

Brynne read a number from the note she'd jotted back at the store. A few seconds later a report popped up on the monitor and Brynne scanned the name. Rebecca.

"Nope. That's his sister. She lives in Florida. No idea why her name didn't come up. I'd assume he'd have her in his contacts."

"Who knows? Moving on. Next number?"

Once again Brynne read off a number and another report popped up.

"Simon Barker," Evie said.

Simon, Simon, Simon. She knew that name. She tilted her head one way, then the other. Closed an eye.

When the silence dragged on, Evie angled back. And cracked up.

"What's funny?"

She waved her hands. "Your face. You're all twisty."

"I'm thinking."

"Do you know him?"

"He mentioned the name. I think it's someone from work. Sort of a friend. An acquaintance, I guess. Let's put that one aside and check a few more. Try this next number. It's a local one."

Brynne read off the number and the tippety-tap of Evie's fingers flying over the keyboard filled the quiet air. "There's nothing in the DMV on that one. Let me try one of those mobile trackers. I might get a hit."

More tippety-tapping before Evie's fingers went still.

"Got it," she said.

"What the hell are you two doing?"

Uh-oh.

Evie threw her hands up. "Whoopsie."

Brynne swiveled, found Reid standing in the doorway, arms folded and muscles bunching hard enough to crack concrete.

Whoopsie indeed. She set her hand on Evie's shoulder and squeezed. The I've-got-this signal. "You're back," Brynne said, her voice a little too high-pitched.

Evie faced her brother and held her still raised hands in front of her. "Don't freak."

"Don't freak? Really?"

He entered the room, his booted feet moving slowly. Stalking. Brynne wanted to spoon up all that prowling, contained energy dripping from him like gooey, luscious chocolate. God, the man knew how to make an impact.

Even mad.

He shifted his gaze to the monitor, then to Evie, and finally to Brynne and wowie, wow, wow the hardness in those eyes. Completely steamed. But, crazy as it was, so incredibly hot.

Obviously, it had been way too long since she'd been with a man.

"*What* are you two doing?"

Evie grunted, but Brynne held her hand out. When it came to her brothers, Evie tended to automatically go on the defensive and with Reid about to explode, Brynne wasn't chancing an argument. "We're checking the rest of the numbers from Nelson's phone."

He broke eye contact with Brynne, checked the monitor, then focused on Evie. "You're hacking again?"

"It's…"

"Hey."

Terrific. Now Jonah joined the party. He stood in the doorway, his lean frame casually propped against the wall.

"Well," Evie said, "the gang's all here."

Reid poked his finger at the monitor. "They're hacking again. You happy now?"

"Depends," Jonah said. "If she didn't get caught and didn't blow up any of my files, I'm happy."

"Unfuckingbelievable. You know our baby sister can go to jail, right? Just reminding you of that fact. *Again.*"

"She's fine. She's smart and knows how not to get caught."

"Thank you, Jonah," Evie said.

"You're welcome. But seriously, you can't be on my laptop without me. I gave you the password, but ask me next time."

"Sorry," Brynne said. "We should have thought it through."

"Ya think?"

This from Reid, who still stared at them like they'd bombed city hall.

Evie rolled her eyes, spun back to the monitor. "Oh,

relax. We're only on the third name. The first two were a bust. I'd just pulled this one up when you walked in. Ed Wayne. Brynne, do you know him?"

Didn't sound familiar. "I don't think so."

"Hey," Evie said, "he lives in Steele Ridge."

Before Reid even said a word, the energy in the room somehow shifted again and Brynne whipped around to where Reid stood, hands on his hips, fingers tapping, and the urgency firing off of him became a crackling buzz.

"Shit," he said. "Evie, get out of there."

"Why?"

"Because Ed Wayne was just murdered."

CHAPTER TEN

REID DIDN'T NEED TO BE a genius to figure out this wasn't some kind of fucked-up coincidence.

Ed Wayne.

Before Grif had called to tell them about the second shooting in Steele Ridge, Reid had never heard of freaking Ed Wayne. Now his number popped up in another guy's phone.

Right after they'd both been murdered.

He shook his head, squeezed his eyes closed, visualized the pieces coming together.

Mags. He needed to get this info to her.

"Evie, print me a screenshot of that report."

Brynne looked up at him, all big brown eyes. "What are you doing?"

"We're taking this to Mags. We have to."

"Dude," Jonah said, "be careful here."

Now he wanted to wax on about being careful? About not hacking into government databases? Seriously, he should kick his ass.

"*Now* you want me to think about it? You don't want me telling our police chief cousin you taught our baby sister how to hack into the DMV?"

"Oh, fuck you."

"Whatever, Jonah. You *know* it's fucked up. I can't believe you did it in the first place."

"Okay!" Evie held up the screenshot. "No fighting. Here it is."

Reid ripped the report from her hand, held his other hand out to Brynne. "Let's hit it, sweet cheeks."

He hustled her to the truck, opened the door, and she hopped in. The lack of sky-high heels and skintight skirt helped. Life at the Hill must agree with her because the minute they'd gotten there, she'd changed into jeans—nicely snug-in-the-ass jeans—and sneakers. The red V-neck T-shirt wasn't doing much for keeping his mind out of the gutter because Brynne had one hell of a rack on her. Something he'd known since he'd first spotted her at Mom's birthday party months earlier, but he'd never seen her dressed down like this. And T-shirts were her friend.

Her very good friend.

Depending on how a guy looked at it, that T-shirt might be *his* friend, too.

As pissed as he was that she and Evie had gone rogue on them, by the time he got to the driver's side, he needed to get his hands on her.

He slammed the door, looked over at her, still with the big, questioning eyes, and he was gone.

Gone, gone, gone.

I'm screwed.

He kissed her. A full-on assault that pulled a squeak from her throat. The squeak must have been a good sign, rather than fear or hesitation, because she wasted no time slapping her hand over the back of his head and angling her body into him as they damned near swallowed each other whole.

Oh, baby. For a girl trying to be celibate for the next five years, Brynne Whitfield sure knew how to kiss. She moved closer, pressing that amazing rack against him and he fought to keep his hands from wandering.

Groping her in front of his mother's house wouldn't win him any gentleman of the year awards.

They had to stop. Before he exploded. Except, he

gave as good as he got, deepening the kiss, letting her know whenever she gave him the go sign, he'd find them a nice spot to lose their clothes.

And then she was gone. Pulling away and taking all that hotness and lush skin with her. Still, he couldn't take his eyes off of her. Off of her face and her lips that had just been on him and he wanted…more.

A lot more.

She licked her bottom lip and Reid groaned. *Damn.* He glanced down at his crotch, where his jeans had gotten seriously uncomfortable.

He pointed to his engorged crotch. "That swearing-off-men thing? How's that working?"

"If we weren't sitting in your mother's driveway, I might do you in this truck."

Well, hello. Sweet little Brynne with the gutter mouth. He loved it.

"Look at you talking all trashy." He waggled his eyebrows. "I like it. But be careful, sweetheart, I might take you up on that."

He fired the truck and the headlights illuminated the darkening driveway. Losing daylight. Was it still the same damned day?

In the army, days like this, when bombs weren't going off and rat-a-tat-tat of automatic gunfire didn't litter the air, were a vacation. Barely eight months out and he couldn't deal with minor stress?

Assuming a couple of murders was minor stress. He didn't know these guys, right? *It's not about them, idiot.*

Nope. This was about Brynne and keeping her safe and figuring out what her involvement in this whole thing might be.

Once in town, Reid snagged a spot in front of the Triple B, midway between Brynne's shop and Maggie's office. After their visit to Mags, Brynne intended to pull any cash from the register at La Belle Style.

Smart move considering she'd already been robbed once.

Before hopping out of the truck, Reid grabbed his .45 and holstered it at his waist.

Maggie might not appreciate him walking into her office armed, but Steele Ridge didn't have an ordinance against open carry so hopefully she'd let it slide.

He opened Brynne's door, waved her out, and set his hand on her lower back, sliding his fingers just above the rise of her waistband, under her shirt to warm, soft skin and once again his mind drifted.

To Brynne.

Naked.

On the hood of his truck.

What the hell was that now? Twisted truck fantasies in the midst of all this bullshit. Excellent.

At this hour, the receptionist's desk was cleared, the chair empty, the lamp off. The rest of the place was lit up, though. The four bullpen desks were unoccupied, two of the chairs were tucked in and the other two pushed back as if the deputies had left in a hurry.

"Mags?"

"Back here," she called from her office.

He motioned Brynne ahead of him. "Let's see what's what."

They entered the office and Mags swiveled from her laptop. The collar button of her uniform was undone and her tie loosened. Call him a caveman, but Reid never could get used to seeing a woman in a necktie. But the uniform was the uniform and Mags having her tie loose indicated his cousin was running on fumes. She tended to keep everything tucked and buttoned.

She slid a questioning gaze to Brynne, then to Reid. "What's up, guys?"

On the corner of the desk sat a clear plastic evidence bag with what looked like Nelson's phone.

Maggie brought both hands up, ran them over her pinned back hair. The puffy, dark skin around her eyes screamed of a lack of sleep. Had she even had a catnap since yesterday?

He waited for Brynne to sit and took the chair beside her. "We, uh, have more information for you."

"About Nelson?"

Brynne's eyes got wide again and Reid nearly laughed. For a girl so easily convinced to hack a government database, she didn't look so cocky now.

"Yeah."

Mags picked up her pen—the cheap ones she used because she didn't want to spend taxpayer money on her favorite gel ones—and set her legal pad in front of her.

"I'm listening."

Reid grabbed the folded report from his back pocket, flattened it on the desk.

"We did research."

For a second, Mags didn't move. She just held his gaze, her eyes halfway to Panicville. "Reid, are you going to piss me off?"

"Probably."

"And here I thought we'd come to an understanding."

They had. As in Reid and Mags. No one counted on Brynne and Evie becoming cybercriminals.

Reid, the unsigher, let out the mother of all sighs. "We figured we'd help so we checked the Internet for the numbers in Nelson's phone."

"But you gave me the phone." She gestured to the evidence bag with the phone in it.

"Affirmative. We wrote the numbers down."

"I see."

Cuz, you're going to see a lot more in the next few minutes.

This thing could go one of two ways. Mags would either be thankful for the help or she'd tear into him for nosing around her investigation. And since she'd already told him to stay out of it, he wasn't feeling confident about her gratitude.

He sat a little taller, readying himself for his cousin's derision. "Turns out one of the numbers in the phone belongs to Ed Wayne."

Maggie flinched. A slight movement of her head, but

he'd surprised her enough that she opened a desk drawer for a pair of latex gloves and snapped them on. She dug the phone out of the bag and fired it up.

Brynne leaned forward. "It's the one that says EW. I got it from the log."

A whistle sounded and Mags set the phone down to let it finish powering up. When the screen flashed, she tapped it a couple of times. "I see that. And how do you know this is Ed Wayne's number?"

Reid pointed to the report he'd set in front of her. "It's from one of those reverse lookups. You might also want to check out a Reginald Proman."

Maggie skimmed the screenshot. "You got this on the Internet?"

Reid nodded. Mags didn't need any further information. Being family, she'd figure out how they obtained it.

"Do I want to ask if Jonah was involved?"

This one? Piece of cake. And when the hell had he ever uttered that obnoxious phrase? "Honest to God, he was not."

Not directly, since Evie was the one who'd discovered who the number belonged to.

"All right." Mags scooped up the report. "I'll take it from here. Thank you."

Wait. What? *"Thank you?"*

"Yes, Reid. Thank you."

"Mags, come on. Ed Wayne is dead. Nelson is dead. This is a connection."

She cocked her head, stared at him with that bland look she sometimes wore when trying to slow her mind down. "I'm aware of that. And as soon as you two leave, I will jump on it."

"Did you know Nelson knew him?"

"I can't comment on that."

Brynne stood. "Maggie is right. Let's leave her to get her work done."

"Reid." Mags folded her hands on top of the desk.

"You know I can't comment on an active investigation. A possible double murder no less."

"So you patronize me? Knowing I've had some involvement in this, you could have called me. Maybe let me know something was up with Ed Wayne and Nelson."

"Well, I guess I didn't feel I needed to say that since I've told you at least thirty times that you should butt out of my active investigation."

Which, somehow, made it worse. Hell on earth, he didn't know what he wanted, or expected, from his cousin. He knew the rules. Absolutely. Eight months ago, he'd have turned the phone over and moved on. Bigger fish to fry, nations to save, and all that.

Now? He had nothing. All of that hero crap gone. And he was trying to nose his way into a murder to make himself feel better.

Grif would call him the mother of all nonimpact players trying to be an impact player.

This is my life.

He pushed out of his chair. "Gotta go."

Maggie shook her head. "Oh, come on, Reid. Now you're going to walk out?"

Yep. *Sure am.* He kept moving. Didn't bother to look back.

"Perfect!" Mags said. "You always do this! You don't like something so you walk out. You know how this works!"

He stormed through the reception area, his feet pounding the tile hard enough to send smacks of pressure shooting up his ankles. Goddammit, this town. This was why he stayed away. When he came home, he felt...what? Useless? Trapped?

Ordinary. Decidedly not Special Forces material. *Shit.*

He pushed through the door, hung on with his fingertips for Brynne to follow him out.

They hit the street with his blood pressure on a steady climb and the heat under his skin burning him up.

He wanted his goddamn life back. Bum fucking knee. Who the hell loses a career by jumping off a truck bed?

Goddamned idiot.

Beside him, Brynne struggled to keep up, her much shorter legs double-timing. "Are you okay?"

"Ha!"

"All right. I suppose that means you are *not* okay."

Still, he kept walking, trying like hell to get rid of the harnessed rage tearing him up. "I'm good. Frustrated. I need a minute."

No talking. No goddamn talking.

"She's doing her job. That's all."

So much for no talking. Women. Always chattering.

"I got that. Loud and clear."

"So why are you mad?"

He stopped, set his hands on his hips and dug his fingers in until pain exploded. "I asked you to give me a minute. One minute of no talking. If I say please will that end this? *Please?*"

"I'm trying to understand."

She was trying? Really? How the hell could she understand when he didn't? "You're not the only one."

"What does *that* mean?"

The *un*sigher once again sighed. What the hell was happening to him?

"Great. Now you're sighing. I swear, men should be put in front of a firing squad with that sigh."

Him? All he'd asked for was a few measly seconds of silence. That's all. As if that were too much to ask. Done. Game over. He stopped, whipped toward her. "I told you I needed a goddamn second! I told you that. Why are you pressuring me?"

She stepped back. One giant move like he'd struck her and on top of all that boiling anger shredding him, shame piled on.

But Brynne rallied, pushed her shoulders back and poked him in the chest. "Because, you jerk, I want to help you!"

Fine. She wanted to do this on the street. Right in front of the goddamned Triple B where the busybodies were probably taking video. Fine. He'd go there.

No.

Fucking.

Problem.

But he'd lower his voice. Sure would. "I don't need help. I need my life back. I need this fucking bum knee to not hurt every morning. I need to be on a mountain somewhere other than North Carolina, staring up at a starlit sky with my unit. I need to *not* be in this fucking town, with the fucking small problems and the gossips and the ducks crossing the fucking street because I can't stand the idea of that being my life. *That's* what I need!"

She flinched again. A full-on lurch of her body. "Wow," she said. "That was..."

"I didn't mean—"

But, too late. He could see it on her. The cold look, the collapsing shoulders. All that closed-off body language a big neon sign assuring him he'd fucked up.

She looked up at him, those devastating brown eyes boring into him. "I think you made it clear what you meant. You've said you always wanted more than this. You told me that just a few hours ago. And now, here you are. *Stuck.* With all us small-town people who obviously aren't good enough for the big, bad Reid Steele. Well, you know what, Reid? Screw you!"

Talk about wow. Holy shit. Cute little Brynne who let her ex walk all over her had just told him off. In a grand way.

In front of the Triple B.

Oddly, it turned him on. *What an asshole I am.*

"Brynne, hang on."

She started toward her store, moving fast in a quasi run-walk that did amazing things to her ass. He reached for her and she whipped her arm free.

Faces appeared in the window of the Triple B, all of them watching the action.

Great. The whole goddamned town would be buzzing with this.

"No," Brynne said. "Now *I* need a minute." She stopped walking, flapped her arms. "No one is forcing you to stay here. If you want to leave, take that stupid job in Georgia and leave. Newsflash, Reid, this town didn't crumble without you and it won't crumble if you go. And we sure don't deserve to be treated like second-class citizens because you can't adjust to civilian life. Your family loves you, your friends love you. Why can't that be enough? Why can that *never* be enough for people?"

Oh, hang on here. What the hell was she talking about? Never enough?

He hadn't said that. Even if he felt it once in a while, he hadn't said it and definitely not to her.

But, oh, shit.

Her husband had dumped her. Left her for what she considered a skinnier, prettier, better-than-Brynne version of a wife.

Leading her to believe she wasn't good enough.

He'd hit a nerve. A big one. Probably the biggest one she had since her asshole husband didn't know a good woman when he had one.

And right now, the way Brynne was glaring at him, apparently, Reid didn't know that either.

She left him on the sidewalk. Had to. Otherwise, she'd scratch his eyes out. Make him bleed like she'd never imagined making anyone bleed.

What was it with the men in her life? They all wanted more. More, more, more. Boy, she knew how to pick 'em. No wonder she'd enacted the five-year plan. At this point, she should buy stock in a battery company because her vibrator would need all the juice it could get.

Five damned years.

Gah.

"Brynne, wait."

No. *Done waiting on men.* She kept walking. Marched right to her shop's door and unlocked it. "No, Reid. We don't have to talk about this. I understand." *All too well.* "Now, I need to deal with my banking."

Because that's what independent women did. They took care of themselves and didn't rely on men.

"Reid!"

Behind him, Maggie stormed the sidewalk, heading straight for him. Apparently, Brynne wasn't the only one who wanted a piece of him. He spun back, faced Maggie. Fabulous. Maggie could deal with the caveman while Brynne went inside and settled down.

To think she'd almost given up her plan for Reid Steele. *Puh-lease.* What had she been smoking? *He* was the heartbreaker the plan insured against.

Reid looked at a woman and her panties burned off. He didn't even have to touch. Just—whoops—panties gone.

Good thing they'd had this little exchange and she'd got her mind right.

Really good thing.

She swung into the store, considered locking the door, then opted against it. Why be a child about it and lock him out? No. She'd be an adult and not resort to those antics.

As much as she'd like to, she wouldn't.

Stay strong, girl.

Rather than leave her account number in the drawer, she kept the deposits slips and her checkbook upstairs. She trusted her part-timers, but people wandered in and out of the shop all day. Why leave her personal information lying around?

She glanced back at Reid and Maggie, in deep conversation on the sidewalk. With them right in front of the store, she could duck upstairs and grab what she needed.

She marched out the back door, up the outside steps to her apartment, and unlocked the crappy lock Reid complained about.

On that, he was probably right. She'd get a locksmith over on Monday to take care of it. She withdrew her key and a flake of cheap brass coating hung off the lock. She hadn't noticed *that* before, but she could have chipped it when inserting her key at some point. Who knew?

Once inside, she moved through the kitchen, down the tiny hallway, the worn carpet absorbing her steps as she made her way to the bedroom where she kept the banking info in the antique secretary that had been her grandmother's.

Damn that Reid Steele.

Just when she was starting to like him. Starting to? Ha. She liked him just fine. Had even fantasized about that big body on top of her.

What woman in this town didn't?

Gah!

She beelined into her bedroom and…froze.

A man in a black sweatshirt and jeans stood in front of her long dresser, his back to her, head tilted up to the ceiling.

And moaning.

What the hell?

Panic slammed her, knocking her back a step.

The man whipped around. His fly was open, his hand wrapped around his…*ohmygod.*

Masturbating.

In her underwear drawer.

For a second, she couldn't move, just stood there, paralyzed, her feet like blocks of cement. Inside her sneakers, she wiggled her toes and her brain fired. Shooting commands at her immobile body. *Move. Run.*

Go.

She shot off down the hall, a howling scream flying from her mouth, making her throat ache.

Behind her, something slammed and then a creak. The loose board under the carpet. *He's close.*

Run.

She ran harder, swerving into the kitchen. Door closed. Dammit. She'd lose time.

Ow. Something gripped her. Yanked on her hair. She bucked back as hot, lancing pain shot into her scalp and down her neck.

"Relax, bitch," he said. "Tell me where that phone is and I'll go easy on you."

Phone, phone, phone. Nelson's phone. Had to be.

God. What had her friend been into?

He yanked again and she bumped him, her lower back connecting with his body where the hardness of his erection stabbed into her.

Sickness tumbled in her stomach and another wave of panic took hold.

Get out.

She focused on the door, then slid her gaze over the sink to the kitchen drawer where she kept the sharp knives. *Weapon.*

"I don't...have the phone."

Another yank.

"Ow!" she screamed again, hoping someone would hear.

This time he held on, wrapping her hair in his fist and pulling her head back. He leaned in, his upper body connecting with the back of her, his breath hot and nasty, the smell of onions reaching her as his lips touched her ear. "Lying bitches don't get treated right. And since you interrupted me, I got something for you."

All those self-defense segments she'd seen on television paraded in her mind. That one guy, from a women's safety organization. Fight, he'd said. Hard.

And get a description.

Her mind ticked back and she pictured him in front of her dresser. Baggy jeans that hung low on his hips. Black sweatshirt with a hood. White guy. Maybe mid-twenties.

His hair. What color? Dark. She thought. How could she have missed that?

She needed another look. She lifted her foot, kicked back, connected with bone, but her shoe slid, lessening the impact.

"Ow," the creep said, his voice flat and even. "That was stupid."

He yanked again, tightening his fist around her hair and sending shocks of pain down her neck. Ow, ow, ow.

Scream, she thought, as he dragged her down the hallway. She started in again. Putting everything she had into the howls, praying Reid and Maggie were still out on the sidewalk just a floor below.

Right outside her bedroom window.

At the doorway, she grabbed on to the trim, wrapped both hands around it, and he yanked again. The pain, enormous and blinding, brought a bout of tears.

Hang on. Don't let go.

He stepped back, chopped at her wrist.

Hang on.

She gripped tighter. At least until she heard the distinctive click-click of a gun being racked.

Gun.

And then it was against her temple.

"Bitch, don't make me kill you."

Getting her attacker more wired wouldn't help her. She needed time. Time for Reid to get up those stairs and help her.

She let go.

For now.

"Now we're talking."

He shoved her to the bed, momentum making her stumble and she landed half on the mattress, half off.

"Good idea," he said. "On the bed. And pull your pants down. I'm gonna give it to you good."

CHAPTER ELEVEN

BRYNNE SCREAMED.

Reid heard.

In the middle of Mags stressing the need for them to come to an understanding about what had just happened in her office, she stopped talking. They both looked up at Brynne's window and a fierce blast of adrenaline pounded the inside of Reid's skull. He hauled ass, his body moving on instinct. *Help her.* Whatever it was, he'd get there.

He swung the shop door open—she hadn't locked it—and sprinted to the back with Mags on his heels.

"Let me go first," she said.

Fat chance.

Ignoring his cousin, he took the back steps two at a time, his longer legs leaving Mags in the dust. He burst through the door into the tiny kitchen and Brynne let out a wail from the end of the hallway.

Bedroom.

Shit.

Harsh stabs fired down his arms. *Ignore it.* He'd have to harness all the energy, channel it and make it work for him. Forcing his heart rate down, he ripped his sidearm from the holster.

"Shut up, bitch."

Man's voice. One man. Could he assume that? No. If

there were multiples, he'd have heard other voices. Maybe.

One target.

He'd work with that theory. For now.

"Back," Mags said quietly, drawing her Glock. "Don't be stupid. I'm the sheriff. Someone gets shot, I can explain it."

Point there.

Goddammit.

Using hand signals, she gestured left, down the hallway. Shadowing Mags, he crept along with juicy adrenaline charging his system and his mind zipping with possibilities. *Stay alert. Don't get shot.*

"No!" Brynne screamed again.

That's it. As much as Reid didn't want to irritate his already pissed cousin, this he couldn't do. Couldn't stand back and let whatever asshole was in Brynne's bedroom do who knew what. No way.

Almost to the bedroom, he focused on the door, sped around Mags and—whoosh—swung into the room, weapon trained.

A young guy in a sweatshirt stood over Brynne. And, *Jesus,* his pants were unzipped, his dick hanging out.

He swung back, .38 raised and angled sideways like the fucking gangsta amateurs did in music videos.

What an idiot. If he fired that thing the round would go straight through the wall.

Brynne locked eyes with Reid. Half her body sagged off the mattress and the panic, the full-blown, face stretched, I'm-going-to-die look he'd seen way too many times in his life stung him.

"Freeze!" Mags hollered.

But the idiot's finger slid to the trigger, a slow movement either meant to intimidate or this guy didn't know what the hell he was doing with that weapon. Either way, it wasn't good.

"Don't!" Mags said.

But, ah shit.

Boom, boom.

He fired two shots, both of them zinging between Reid and Mags. From her spot on the bed, Brynne rolled and kicked out, knocking the gun from the guy's hand.

"Freeze!" Mags said again.

But the guy leaped, straight at Reid who hopped left. No good. The guy plowed into him, the two of them going over. Reid landed hard, his right arm taking the hit, and the blow knocked his .45 from his grip, sent it skittering across the floor.

Shit.

Bad guy still on top of him, he pounded his elbow into the guy's cheek. Three quick thrusts that sent his head snapping back. Reid shoved him off, jumped to his feet, drove a hammer-fist to the man's lower back and connected with bone. The guy howled, brought both hands around to the injured area on his back. *Grab him.* Reid slid an arm around the target's throat and yanked.

"Get him on the floor!" Mags said.

Reid lowered to one knee, dragging the douchebag with him, tightening his hold on his neck. Douchebag clawed at him, digging his fingers into Reid's forearm as he gagged. A gurgling sound erupted, but Reid tightened his grip. *Come on, come on.*

Few more seconds and he'd be out.

"Reid!" Mags hissed. "Let him go. Right now."

Her weapon still drawn, she nudged him on the hip with the toe of her boot. "Stop it. Right now. You'll kill him."

The guy's body went slack and he stopped fighting. *There we go.* Reid loosened his grip. "You gonna behave?"

"Yeah," he croaked.

Reid let go, stepped back and held his hands wide while Mags moved in, weapon still on their target. Behind him, Brynne slumped to the floor. Child's pose, his yoga enthusiast buddy called it. Her shoulders hitched and she wrapped her hands around the back of her head, her body visibly shaking.

"On your stomach," Mags said. "Hands on your head. Don't do anything stupid while I cuff you."

Reid squatted next to Brynne. He made a move to touch her, to rub her back, but...no.

Careful here, buddy. With the trauma she'd just experienced, a man trying to rape her, to *control* her, she might not think too kindly of another man putting hands on her.

"Brynne?" he whispered. "It's me. Reid. Baby, you're safe now. Mags has him."

Brynne stayed hunched over, hands trembling and sheltering her head, and if Reid's temper hadn't already scraped a layer from his insides, well, seeing this sweet girl vulnerable and beaten down tore him up. Made his gut ache.

He glanced over at Mags cuffing the jagoff who'd wisely decided to comply.

Now, Reid wanted a piece of this guy again and angled toward him.

"Reid, don't be stupid. I'll arrest you. Swear to God, I'll arrest you."

And she would. To keep him safe from himself, she'd lock his ass up.

He jerked his head to the door. "Get him out of here."

One of Maggie's deputies, Glen, rushed into the room, his hat askew, his breaths coming hard. Old Glen needed to hit the gym if a flight of stairs put him in this condition.

"Sorry," he said. "Was on another call."

Mags motioned to their prisoner. "Take him to the jail. Put him in a holding cell."

"I get a phone call," Jagoff croaked.

"Yeah, you do. And as soon as I figure out what happened here, you'll get it."

While being escorted out, the jagoff looked back at Brynne still huddled on the floor, and the corner of his mouth lifted.

Smirking.

166 | ADRIENNE GIORDANO

And, shit on a shingle, something in Reid's brain snapped and handcuffed or not, this asshole was gonna get a beatdown.

Reid stood, headed right to the asshole, but—nope—Mags hopped in front of him. Just friggin' put herself in his line and shoved him back. "Don't give him what he wants." She kept her hands on his chest, gave him another light shove. "He'll get you arrested, too. You want that?"

Yes.

Only because it would mean he got to kick the son of a bitch's ass.

"Look at me," Mags said. Reid met her gaze. "Please, Reid. Just let it go. I'll deal with him. I promise you."

And she would. He knew it. Mags would talk to whomever she had to and make sure this asshole went to prison.

Reid looked over her shoulder at said asshole. "If you get out, you'd better hide. I'll find you. Come near this girl again and I'll bury you."

"Glen!" Mags snapped. "Get him out of here."

The deputy hustled their prisoner out and Mags dropped her hands. "Dammit, Reid. What are you *doing*? If something happens to that kid, we're screwed."

"Oh, something'll happen to him and you won't have to arrest me."

Because he sure as hell wouldn't get caught.

Reid dropped to his knees again, next to Brynne, set his hands on his thighs, still determined not to touch her unless she gave permission. But, Jesus, that was hard. To not hold her. To not offer some kind of comfort. It was an ache in his chest as she continued to crush her fingers over her head. Blue veins popped on the backs of her hands and the sick feeling in Reid's stomach railed at him. Trauma like this? It stayed. Squeezed so hard that it paralyzed. Mentally and physically.

That's it. He had to touch her, bring her back from whatever alternate state she'd put herself into. Survival sometimes meant compartmentalizing. Living in a parallel universe.

Avoidance? Sure. Why not?

He didn't have a problem with it. Hell, without avoidance, he'd be locked in a mental ward or self-medicating to kill the pain.

Mags unclipped her radio from her shoulder. "I'm calling an ambulance."

"Give her a second."

A couple of medics putting hands on her wouldn't help.

He lifted his hand, let it hover just above her back. "Brynne?"

No response. "Honey, I'm going to touch you. My hand on your back. Okay?"

A long few seconds passed while his hand hung in the air. He counted down from ten. At one, he'd touch her.

Eight, seven, six...

She nodded. Whoa. Under her hands, her head definitely moved. He'd take that as permission and lowered his hand. She flinched. He'd kill that fucker who put her in this condition.

"Honey," he said, "can you sit up? Mags is here. She wants to make sure you're okay. We both do."

Mags was female. And in this instance, as much as it made him nuts that he couldn't protect her from this, Brynne might need a woman's help.

And she'd get it.

For once, he didn't care that he was dispensable.

Reid got there in time.

He'd heard her scream and he'd...well...saved her.

"Honey," he said, his deep voice low and gentle and so unlike the cocky, sometimes commanding sometimes smart-ass one she'd heard from him.

"You're safe now," he said. "Please sit up. Just so we can get a look at you."

But she wasn't moving. Not until… "Is he gone? I don't want to look at him."

Because, like Reid, she might kill him. Or better yet, kick him in the balls. Hard. Hard enough to put him out of action for a good long time. She'd grab that knife she'd wanted to use as a weapon and chop his dick off. Chop it off and shove it down the disposal. No reattachment possible.

"He's gone," Reid said. "Probably already in lockup. You're safe. I promise you, you're safe."

She believed him. If she couldn't do it on her own, he'd keep her safe, she knew that about him already. If he could, he'd help her. No matter what.

He'd more than proved that. Even if he didn't want to be in Steele Ridge, he'd help her.

She released her aching hands. The pressure. Too much. She'd held too tight and made the muscles sore. Pushing to all fours, she stared down at her fingers where blood rushed back, turning them their normal color rather than the washed-out white from clenching too hard.

I'm safe.

"You're okay, Brynne," Maggie said. "It's just Reid and I in here."

Brynne nodded. "Thank you."

Reid squatted next to her. "Can I help you up?"

"No. I need to do it."

For herself. Just to prove she could.

"You got it." He made a move to stand, but she reached for him and gripped his arm. What was it she wanted from him? Did she even know?

She needed to rise on her own, without his help, but she wanted him close. Because heaven help her, something about Reid Steele made her not want to be alone. "Don't go."

"Staying right here. Whatever you need."

Squatting must have been killing his bad knee. Still, he stayed there, not moving simply because she'd asked.

"Let's stand up," she said.

With her hanging on to him, they both got to their feet and Reid motioned her backward, toward the bed.

Not there. She whipped her head back and forth, panic kicking in again. Her own bedroom and she couldn't be here. "Not here," she said. "I...can't."

Maggie pointed to the door. "Living room. Get her out of this room."

God. Her own bedroom, in her crappy little apartment that she was so proud of because it was hers. A place she'd rented on her own, way before the wicked in-laws had paid her to go away.

And now she couldn't be in it.

She left the room, walked right out and didn't bother to look back. At the end of the hallway she turned left, faced the living room. Something pinged in her chest and her breath caught. Ahead, the sheer curtain did little to veil the building across the street.

"Brynne?"

Reid's voice. She whipped back to him, her oxygen still caught.

Can't.

Breathe.

After three long seconds he hauled her toward the back door. "Outside," he said. "You need fresh air."

Yes.

"I...can't....Chest...hurts."

"It's a panic attack. Try to breathe. Slowly."

He opened the door, pushed her outside on the porch, and planted himself in front of her. "You're safe now. I promise you, nothing will hurt you again. Do you hear me?"

Nothing would hurt.

"Brynne? Did you hear me?"

She nodded. Opened her mouth. *Breathe.* Her chest

pinged again and a rush of oxygen—all that caged air breaking free—made her a little loopy.

"There you go," he said. "Not too fast or you'll pass out. Slow, even breaths."

He stayed focused on her, refusing to look away, and those darned eyes, the darkest blue she'd ever seen, undid her. Just steady and solid and...comforting.

Maggie stepped onto the landing. "Do we need that ambulance?"

Not an ambulance, but looking at Reid, knowing he was a wild card and not caring, made her think that she might require a shrink, because the five-year plan was cooked. "No," Brynne said. "I'm okay. Just needed air."

And the annoying alpha.

Maggie nodded. "Understandable. Can you tell me what happened?"

Reid ducked back into the kitchen, came out with one of her table chairs, and set it in the corner of the porch. Away from the steps.

"Sit," he said. "You need a blanket?"

"Blanket?"

"You're shivering."

She glanced down at her hands. Trembling. Huh. She hadn't realized. She squeezed her fingers closed, let her nails dig into the soft skin of her palms. *You're okay, girl.*

Considering what could have happened, yes, she was definitely okay.

She dropped into the chair and Reid disappeared again, returning a minute later with a blanket he set over her shoulders.

"Thank you," she said.

He jerked a thumb over his shoulder. "I'm...uh...gonna wait downstairs. Give you some privacy while you talk to Mags."

He took two steps and the flutter of panic started again. "Wait," she said. "Don't go."

"No?"

"No." She held out her hand, waited for him to grab hold. "Stay here. Please."

Maggie set her hand on the porch rail, gave it a testing shake, and leaned against it, obviously confident in its integrity.

"The insurance company yelled at him."

Maggie frowned. "I'm sorry?"

"Mr. Pippen. My landlord. The rails were loose. He had them repaired. I asked him what prompted that. He said the insurance company said they wouldn't insure him if he didn't fix them."

"Ha!" Reid said. "That cheap bastard. If the insurance company hadn't threatened him, he'd have let someone fall two stories."

Maggie slid the notepad Brynne had given her from her pocket. Who knew she'd be using it to take a victim's statement from Brynne?

"Tell me what happened."

"I came upstairs to get my deposit slips. I don't keep them in the shop. They're in my bedroom. I walked in and found him." She stopped, closed her eyes, pictured her assailant in front of her dresser, the drawer pulled open. "He was—" She waved a hand.

"Take your time."

"Masturbating."

That fucker.

The pressure in Reid's skull should have blown his eyeballs out, but this wasn't about him. He glanced down at Brynne and she immediately pulled her gaze away, staring straight ahead.

"He was just standing there," she said. "In front of my open underwear drawer."

Fucker.

Fucker.

Fucker.

Total dead man. He bit down, gritting his teeth so hard pain shot through his jaw.

Maggie shot him a look. In response he offered up a sarcastic don't-worry-I-won't-kill-him grin.

At least today he wouldn't kill him.

If the guy walked, all bets were off.

"I was so shocked, I ran. He caught me in the kitchen." She gripped a hunk of her hair. "Grabbed me and dragged me to the bedroom."

Fucker, fucker, fucker. And, yeah, this was just getting worse.

But she didn't need him getting all pissed off. Not now. She needed him to channel calm Reid. The warrior who contained his emotions and thought logically when surrounded by chaos. That's who she needed.

He squatted down next to her and clasped her hand. The corner of her mouth lifted into a pathetic smile. She pushed her free hand through his hair and patted his head.

Yeah, she'd figured out he didn't like hearing this. As hard as he'd tried to slap on his nothing-face, she'd tagged him.

Twenty-four years old, experiencing the worst days a person could, and she was giving him comfort?

"I think you're amazing," he said. "Just so you know."

At that, she really let loose on a smile. The full wide lips, eyes dancing one, and an enormous pressure built in his chest. *Stay.* Whoa. For years he'd wanted to be out of this place, now all of a sudden all he wanted was to stay and make this girl smile like that every damned day.

Throwing her shoulders back, she filled in the details of what she remembered while Reid squatted next to her. His knee barked like a mother, but he refused to move. If it took three hours, he wouldn't move, wouldn't break her momentum. Getting it all out was key. Then they'd deal with next steps.

When Brynne got to the part about the guy wanting a phone, Mags stopped jotting notes. "What phone? Nelson's?"

Brynne shrugged. "I don't know. I guess. He didn't say."

Mags shot Reid a WTF look. "All right. I'll send the phone to the state lab. See if they can find anything. Maybe there are hidden files or something. Can you think of anything else?"

"About the phone?"

"Regarding anything, but yeah, that phone. First Ed Wayne's number and now someone breaking into your shop and your apartment. It seems that phone is in the center of this."

"There's nothing. Nelson never, ever gave me reason to think he was doing anything dangerous. He was just...my friend."

Maggie touched her shoulder and squeezed. "I know. I'm sorry. If you think of anything, no matter how minor you think it is, call me. Whatever time."

"I will. Thank you, Maggie."

"You're welcome." She tucked her notepad away. "We'll go through the apartment and do the evidence collection."

"Okay."

Finally, Reid stood, stretched out his legs and—holy mother—that knee hurt. "Can she leave?"

Because there was no way she was staying here. Nuh-uh. Not until they figured out what the hell Nelson had roped her into.

"Yes," Mags said. "I'll call if I need anything else. Want me to lock up when the crime scene techs leave?"

Brynne stood. "Yes. Please. My keys are inside."

She swung toward the door, took one step, then stopped, stared at the door for a few seconds.

"Uh," Reid said, "how about I grab them for you?"

"Thank you. They're on the counter. I think."

He stuck his head in the door, spotted the keys next to a photo of her family. He swiped them up and handed them off.

"Not to add pressure, but you'd better call your folks. The Triple B is probably already command central for speculation on what's going on here."

"Great. Someone probably already called my mother."

"Brynne!"

Or her father.

Shit.

How was it that Brynne's luck could be this bad? First the cheating husband, then the humiliation of moving home. And just when she'd started to feel more secure—more settled being on her own—she'd watched her closest friend get gunned down. Like an animal, in the street.

She closed her eyes, tried not to think about the pain, the *fear*, Nelson must have experienced.

Now? He was gone.

Except for the questions he'd left her to grapple with.

And, oh, yes, her father.

She looked up at Reid. "This just gets better and better, doesn't it?"

He blessed her with one of those Reid Steele lightning-quick smiles that could create the dreaded panty drop and Maggie sighed. *Five-year plan. Five-year plan. Five-year plan.*

"Want me to run interference?"

With her father? He'd do that for her?

She waved at her father and mumbled. "I might. He's going to insist I go home with him. I don't want to. They'll bombard me with questions and I don't have answers."

"Got it."

Dad was halfway up the steps, his jaw set in that way that meant he was beyond listening.

To anything.

His eyes were on her. A fierce, protective connection she'd known all her life. A comfort to most, but there were reasons she'd left home and many of them circled around her father's unwillingness to let her make her own mistakes. To let her explore possibilities without his constant interference.

To let her breathe.

All of it done out of love, but sometimes love smothers. Controls.

A good dose of Reid Steele and his stubbornness might help here.

Dad reached the top step. "Are you all right? What happened?"

"I'm fine, Dad. There was an intruder."

"What happened? Did he hurt you?"

Yes. But she couldn't admit that. If she did, her parents would never leave her alone. "I'm fine, Dad. Reid and Maggie were right outside the store. They heard me yell and caught the guy."

Dad's eyes narrowed and he propped his hands on his hips. "Good. Good." He looked at Reid, then to Maggie. "Thank you. Both of you. You arrested him?"

"Yes, sir. I'm waiting on crime scene techs and I'll head over to deal with him."

Dad mopped a hand over his face, closed his eyes for a few short seconds, and Brynne noticed worry lines between his brows. "Dad, I'm okay."

He opened his eyes. "Your mother got the call from Ruth. I swear that woman has a police scanner. She didn't have any details and gave your mother a near heart attack. Then I tried to call you and you didn't pick up."

Her phone. She'd left it in the shop. "Oh, Dad, I'm so sorry. My phone is in the shop. I'd just run upstairs to grab a deposit slip and I…found him."

Finally, Dad stepped in, wrapped her in a giant bear hug, squeezing maybe a wee bit too hard. But, God, every daughter should feel this kind of love.

Even when it was sometimes too much.

"I'm okay. I promise. It was just scary."

"You're coming home. You can't stay here alone. I'm sorry, Brynne, I won't have it. We'll find you someplace safe to live."

She wouldn't bother with the argument that living half a block from the sheriff's office might be as safe as one could get.

Even with what had just happened, she believed that. But what if…

What if Maggie and Reid had not been nearby?

Don't.

Pondering those particular what-if thoughts wouldn't help.

Dad shifted his gaze from Brynne to Maggie and finally to Reid. The two men exchanged some sort of primal male posturing that, had Brynne been in any other situation, she'd find humorous.

Alphas. Simply extraordinary.

"Dad, I know I worried you. I'm sorry. But really, I'm fine. Besides, I had plans with Evie tonight."

A lie, but her father didn't know that.

"That's right," Reid said. "And you know my mother loves you. You can stay out at the house with them." He faced her father. "Mr. Snodder, we installed a security system that would blow your mind. Cameras everywhere and on-site guards. Between my mother sometimes being alone and Jonah with all his electronics, the place needed a serious security upgrade. No one gets near any of the buildings or houses without us knowing."

Go, Reid.

Dad held Reid's gaze a second. What argument could he make about her being safer at home with him and Mom versus at Mrs. Steele's with all her security and her big, extremely big, bad, extremely bad, Green Beret son?

"If I didn't think she'd be safe at my mother's, I wouldn't suggest it. Plus, I don't want to disappoint my sister. She likes spending time with Brynne."

"You know," Maggie said, "I'll let y'all work this out. Brynne, after we're done processing the apartment, how about I grab you some clothes and send them up to Aunt Joanie's? In the meantime, I'll call you if I have more questions."

These people. So kind. "Thank you, Maggie. For everything."

"Absolutely."

"All right," Dad said. "But if you need anything, you call me."

Reid held his hand out to Dad. "Sir, I promise you, I'll take care of her."

And, oh. My.

What five-year plan?

CHAPTER TWELVE

BY 10:30, BRYNNE HAD CURLED up on the couch
with Evie in the command center, watching Reid and
Jonah do battle in a new video game Jonah had bought.

Zombies aside, Brynne enjoyed watching them go at
it. All that competitive, male testosterone in full load was
something to be thankful for because, without a doubt,
the Steele brothers had managed to help her settle down
after what she'd experienced that afternoon. If nothing
else, they'd provided a sense of safety. For that, she'd
always be grateful.

In the morning she'd call Maggie for more
information on the man who'd attacked her and why he'd
even been in her place, but for tonight she'd pretend it
didn't happen.

For a little while.

"Dude," Jonah said, "you're dead. Give up already."

"My ass, I'm dead."

Reid flipped Jonah the bird and glanced back at
Brynne, a wicked grin on that all too handsome face.
They hadn't talked about their little spat on the street
earlier that day. Did they need to? Just to clear the air?
It wasn't as if they were a couple, right? So they'd shared
steamy hot kisses. So he'd slid his hand over her back a
time or two. Affectionate men did that. Didn't always
mean anything.

Beside her, Evie let out a soft snore. The poor girl had been up late all week finishing a paper and was zonked.

"Let her sleep," Reid said. "She's like me. She can sleep anywhere."

But with the way her head drooped forward, she'd wind up with a sore neck. "She doesn't look comfortable."

Reid kept his eyes on the giant screen, his fingers moving fast on the controller. "Jonah, you're fucked. Brynne, Evie is fine. She'll wake up if she's not comfortable."

"Son of a bitch," Jonah said.

"Yep. Sorry, bro. I just came back to life." He looked back at Brynne. "Stamina, babe."

Oh, he did not just do that in front of his brother. She laughed because, holy cow, the raw arrogance should have been annoying, but…nope.

"Well," she said, "at least one of us has it." Gently, attempting not to jostle Evie, she unfolded her legs and stood. "Thank you for everything, guys. I'm turning in."

Reid set the controller on the floor and grabbed hold of the ends of her fingers. "You okay?"

"I'm good. Just tired. Long couple of days."

"Shit, Reid." Jonah continued to stare at the screen where his video game character sat slumped in a chair. "I thought I had you there."

Reid hopped off his spot on the floor, wincing a bit as he stretched to his full height. The knee. Must be giving him trouble. But she wouldn't dare mention it. Some men didn't want the attention. They saw fussing as pointing out their weaknesses, and Reid definitely wouldn't want his weaknesses emphasized.

He smacked Jonah on the back of his shoulder. "Next time, pal. I'm gonna walk Brynne to her room."

No. Nuh-uh. With her luck, he'd weasel his way inside and they'd wind up in one of those crazy make-out sessions. This was his mother's house. What if the woman heard them?

She held up her hand. "I'm okay. Thanks. Really."

He gave her a nudge toward the door. "Whatever. I'm walking you."

"But—" Jonah looked over, studied her with squinty eyes. She ignored him, went on tiptoes so she could keep her voice down. "My plan. Remember?"

Reid laughed. "Honey, all I think about is that plan. Now, let's go. I'll say good night at your door. Besides, my mother is in this house and she still scares me. Just so you know, I called Mags earlier to check on your intruder. She hasn't called me back yet, but she will. Don't worry about it, though. He'll be dealt with."

He walked her two doors down to the guest bedroom where she'd dumped her overnight bag. The room had a set of French doors that led to an outside balcony. She'd never slept here before, but Evie had shown her the room when they'd first moved in and Brynne had helped decorate it. One thing her life in New York had taught her was a sense of style.

He propped his shoulder against the wall, flicked the knob on the door, and pushed it open. "Good night."

"Good night."

"And, about today. In front of the shop?"

Okay. Apparently they were going to talk about it. Good for him. "Yes?"

"What you said about this place not being enough."

"I overreacted. I'm sorry."

"Don't apologize. When I hit a hot button, I'd rather you tell me. So I know."

He tugged on the end of her hair and his knuckles skimmed the rise of her breast. A little zing shot right to her core.

"I want you to know," he said, "I'm gonna think about what you said. I don't know if I agree, but I'll think on it."

What could she say to that? Her ex wouldn't have given her that much. He'd have made up twelve reasons why all of it was her fault.

"Thank you."

"For what?"

"I don't know. Being you, I guess. Being comfortable enough, being *man* enough to at least consider you might be wrong."

"Ah, hell. I'm wrong ten times a day. That's no big deal." He leaned in a little, dipped his head close to her ear. "I want to kiss you."

His breath whisked across her skin and as close as he was, she wanted closer. To crawl right inside him and stay there where she'd be safe from Nelson dying and strange men attacking her. And why shouldn't she give herself the comfort of Reid Steele? This wasn't a marriage. Why couldn't it just be sex and comfort and fun? Why did it have to be an all-or-nothing thing?

She tilted her head, allowing him to nuzzle her ear. "Is there a 'but' coming?"

"After what happened today, I'm not sure it's appropriate." He backed away. "Besides, it's probably a five-year plan violation."

She reached up, slapped her hand over the back of his head, let her fingers play in the silky dark strands. "When have you ever been concerned about appropriate?"

She kissed him. Just let him have it by driving her tongue into his mouth and arching into him, pressing her body against his. His arms came around her, his hands, those long fingers cradling her butt where he pulled her into him, held her snug.

Down the hall, a noise came from Jonah's room and Brynne leaped back, bumped the doorframe, smacking her head against it. "Ow."

"Holy shit." Reid laughed and set his hand on her head, gently rubbing the spot. "You okay?"

"I'm fine. It was just…silly. You kind of unnerve me sometimes."

He hit her with one of his flashing Reid smiles. "I think I like that."

"I know I do."

I'm such a fool. A fool who'd be heartbroken when he got bored and took that job in Georgia.

"You know," he said, "I got a question."

"What?"

"Don't get mad."

"Oh, boy."

"No. I'm just curious and I don't mean anything by it."

"All right. Ask your question."

"Now that you're divorced, what's with the fancy hair and all the makeup?"

Her heart slammed a little and she fought the surging insecurity that came with constantly fretting over her looks. "You don't like it?"

"I didn't say that. I think you rock fancy hair and makeup. Total bombshell vixen. You just...You don't need it. I want to see you without it. A ponytail and no makeup. I'd bet you're even more beautiful that way."

She shrugged. "I guess after my ex told me not to be a 'country bumpkin,' it stuck in my head. If you hear it enough, you start to believe it and now I'm..."

"What?"

She couldn't admit it. Couldn't. A man like Reid wouldn't understand.

"Huh," he said. "I think I get it. You're afraid if you give up all the makeup and hair that you'll be exactly what he said. A country bumpkin."

There. He'd said it for her. She closed her eyes, let the relief wash over her because somehow, this god of a man understood.

She opened her eyes. "He sent me out shopping one day and I made a pit stop at a hair salon along the way. They had a makeup artist so I got my hair dyed and styled and my makeup done." She held her hand to her face. "I came home with this and he loved it. I guess that's what's locked in my brain. That I'm better this way."

"I'm sorry."

"For what?"

"That you married a douchebag."

Only Reid. Brynne snorted. "I should take offense at that."

"Why? It's not your fault he's a douche."

Huh. He might have a point there. Despite herself, she smiled. "Thank you. That means more to me than you could know."

"You're welcome." He leaned in, pecked her on the lips. "Do me a favor, don't let this guy ruin you. You're too special. Now go to bed before I risk my mother's wrath and invite myself into your room."

Mom shoveled a mound of grits onto Reid's plate and he nudged the bacon aside. No cross-contamination happening here.

"Thanks. I swear, I dreamed about your grits when I was overseas."

"You're welcome, baby."

After setting the pan in the sink, she turned back to him. Today's wardrobe choice included a pair of loose khaki pants and a short-sleeved pullover with a pair of— God help him—Chuck Taylors. His mother, the hipster.

"I made a plate for Jonah," she said. "Don't eat it."

"Yes, ma'am. I'll behave."

"That'll be the day. I heard one of the girls up and in the shower already. I know that's not Evie at seven o'clock on a Saturday."

"Yeah, probably Brynne. She doesn't strike me as one to laze around."

"You're probably right. I noticed the clothes she'd thrown in the dryer last night were gone."

Freaked after the intruder tried to jerk off in her underwear drawer, Brynne refused to use anything from there and had grabbed her dirty laundry before coming to the Hill so she could do a load of...uh...unmentionables.

But Reid couldn't think about Brynne's underwear while sitting in front of his mother. "I guess everything was quiet upstairs last night?"

"Of course. With the way you have this place wired, I'm afraid to touch anything."

Not wanting to tempt himself to sneak into Brynne's room, but concerned over leaving to sleep in the bunkhouse, Reid had slept on the sofa. As far from Brynne as he could get while still inside the house.

These past months of sleeping in a bed must have made him soft because suddenly everything hurt. His back, his neck, his hips, all of it.

So much for being able to sleep anywhere.

Jesus, he had to get used to this life. Whether he liked it or not.

His mother kissed him on top of the head. "I'm running into town for some shrimp. Thinking we'll do a family dinner tonight."

Reid perked up. "Shrimp boil?"

"You know it, baby."

Damn, he had a good mama.

"Hey, Meathead. Morning, Mom."

"Morning to my other baby. I'm going upstairs for a minute and then heading into town if you need anything."

Jonah grunted—sort of—and shuffled into the kitchen, his normal sleepy-eyed, hair-poking-up look firmly in place. For him, seven o'clock might as well be four.

"You're up early."

"I couldn't sleep. Just so you know, I'm meeting with an architect later."

"For the training center?"

"Yeah. He worked up some ideas. He's gonna be out of town for two weeks and wants us to look at it while he's gone."

No offense, but Reid hadn't even given Jonah a list of specs. Sure they'd talked general ideas, but what the hell did a nine-to-fiver know about building an elite training center? Plus, hello, Reid had already contacted a couple of architects. Barely into this and Jonah was stepping on his toes.

"Were you going to consult me on this?"

Jonah grabbed his plate from the counter, ripped the foil off, and flopped across from Reid.

"Didn't I just consult with you? He's giving us a jumping-off point. Don't get your shorts in a wad."

"Good morning, guys."

The two of them turned to see Brynne strolling into the kitchen. With her hair in a ponytail.

Nice.

He'd requested it and she'd done it, but—and not to be ungrateful—this girl, based on her own admission, had a tendency to do what the men in her life expected.

And that, he didn't want.

At least she'd still packed on the makeup, so maybe the ponytail was a compromise. Who the hell knew with women?

Jonah circled his fork at her. "Your hair is pretty in a ponytail."

"Thank you. I decided to take the day off. My part-timers are covering the store."

Excellent. And Reid didn't even have to suggest it. "There's breakfast, if you want."

"Just coffee for now. Thanks. Y'all are up early."

"I'm always up early. Jonah has an *appointment*."

"Whatever." Jonah shoved a load of grits in his mouth and swallowed. "All I'm doing is getting the guy's ideas. You look at them and give it a thumbs-up or down. We have to start somewhere."

"I could have given you a list to start with. You probably paid this guy a fortune for a concept that won't work. And, FYI, I already called a couple of architects. We're duplicating efforts."

Brynne cleared her throat. "What are y'all talking about?"

"Nothing," Jonah said.

"The training center," Reid said.

"Oh, fun."

Reid pouted over his coffee. Why he was pissed about this whole thing, he didn't know, but make no mistake, he was pissed.

"Screw off, Reid. You should have told me you were making calls. Believe me, I got enough to do. Do me a favor and decide where you are on this project. Two days ago you were bitching at me that you'd help get it built, but that was all. Now you're pissed because I'm not checking in with every move. I can't stop every three seconds to ask you if I'm doing this right."

Reid shot out of his chair, sent the damned thing flying. Across the table, Jonah did the same.

Mom stormed in carrying her purse and car keys. "You boys! Knock it off. Whatever this is, take it outside. Right now. You two will *not* ruin my kitchen. Or my furniture." She pointed at the back door. "You heard me. Out!"

More than ready to hand his brother an ass-kicking, Reid started for the door with Jonah on his heels and Brynne following behind.

"Guys, don't fight."

"Honey," Mom said, "save your breath. They're so stubborn they won't listen. They'll go outside and work this out the way they always do." She pointed at Jonah and Reid. "I'm going to the store, if y'all kill each other before my family dinner, I'll be upset. I swear you boys never grow up."

Jonah jogged down the porch steps behind him. "Great job, Meathead. Now she's pissed at us."

"Me? All you had to do was clue me in that you were talking to the architect and I'd have spit out a list of what we'd absolutely need."

"Yeah, but, again, on Thursday you were whining

about how I forced you into this. Decide what you want. Either help me or get the fuck out of the way."

Above their heads, Evie's bedroom window flew open. "Oh. My. *God!* You two are such jerks! The first morning I can sleep in and you're screaming at each other. Shut up!"

Oh, jeez. Poor kid. Waking Jonah up was one thing, but Evie was a sweet kid. She didn't deserve this. "Sorry, Eves. Go back to bed."

"Yeah, well, good luck with that!"

She slammed the window down, the smacking sound sending a flock of birds flapping and running for cover.

"Those fucking birds!" Jonah hollered. "Every damned morning outside my window chirping and waking me up. You think your life sucks? That I roped you into this? How the hell do you think *I* feel? You assholes crack jokes about the Baby Billionaire, but I put my ass on the line here. This whole thing could go bust and I'm out millions."

Whoa.

Reid knew it was a lot, but they'd never talked hard numbers. He tipped his head back, stared up at a glaring morning sun, let the rays warm his face. Selfish prick that he was, he'd never thought about Jonah's sacrifices. *Dumbass.*

"Look, Jonah—"

Jonah put his hands up. "No. I'm done talking. I'm going back to Seattle. Or anywhere away from here. You fuckwads can take care of all this shit. From now on, I'm just the money guy."

Hold on there, cowboy. What the hell was he saying now?

Beyond Jonah, Britt's truck roared up the drive. What did *he* want now?

Jonah slapped his hands on top of his head. "Great. Now we get to spend the next hour listening to him lecture us."

"Go inside. I'll deal with him."

Britt drove off the path, pulled the truck right into the yard before Jonah could make his getaway. Their older brother hopped out and whipped his sunglasses off.

Before he could start in, Reid got the jump on him. "Mom'll fry your ass if she sees this truck in the yard."

"Considering she just called me, I'm not concerned."

"Ah, shit!"

Jonah was totally melting down here.

"She called you?"

"Yeah. She said you idiots were screaming at each other and she wants a family dinner tonight. She told me to get over here and straighten it out."

Jeez with the melodrama. "Seems to me," Reid said, "there's only one way to settle this."

Britt waved them up the steps. "Let's go inside and talk it out."

"No," Reid said. "I got something better. Wait here. And someone call Grif. Get him over here. We're gonna get all this shit out in the open. Right now."

He climbed the steps, found Brynne in the kitchen, cleaning up the dishes.

"Honey, you don't have to do that. You're a guest here. We'll do it."

"It's all right. I like to earn my keep. And I didn't want to intrude so it's keeping me busy. You fight like that a lot?"

"With three brothers? All of us alphas in one way or another? Yeah, fairly common. We're gonna work it out."

"How?"

He jerked his chin to the door. "Go outside and you'll see."

Two minutes later, he swung through the back door carrying the four boxes he'd picked up at the post office the other day. He hadn't intended to use them so soon, but they'd hit DEFCON 2, the second highest state of alert used by the military.

DEFCON 1 meant nuclear war and nuclear war Steele style wouldn't just be ugly, it'd be *fugly*.

Outside, Jonah stood with his arms crossed, listening to Britt—nothing unusual there. Britt spent half his life taking care of everyone and the other half lecturing them on lessons he'd learned the hard way.

He was a pain in the ass, but when you needed a wingman, Britt was the guy.

Evie had made her way downstairs, dressed in flannel pajama pants and a pink sweatshirt. She stood at the base of the porch with Brynne, eyeballing the boxes.

She poked a finger at him. "What's that?"

"Nothing for you to worry about. Is Grif on his way?"

Britt scratched the back of his head. "Yeah. He said ten minutes. I think we…uh…interrupted something."

Grif. Fucking horndog. The lucky bastard.

"Were they—"

"Reid," Brynne said, "please. Just stop talking."

Brynne was shaking her head, but laughing at him. What? So he was curious. Big deal.

He set the boxes on the ground, checked the labels. "Jonah, this is you. Don't open it yet. We're waiting on Grif."

He shoved the box over to Jonah, checked the next one. *Mine.* Heh, heh, heh.

Always wanting to get in on the action, Evie wandered over. "Why are there only four? Don't I get one?"

"Sorry, kid. Boys only this time."

"This time? Try *every* time."

Well, that was probably true, but she could get hurt with this shit. Still, maybe he could order her one, teach her to use it.

Grif's car, that flashy Maserati he refused to give up, swung into the driveway. Finally.

Unlike Britt, he parked in front of the house and walked around the side with Carlie Beth bringing up the rear. At least Grif was in basketball shorts and a T-shirt rather than his normal GQ crap. His hair was wet, leading Reid to wonder if they'd interrupted something happening in the shower. He glanced back at Brynne, still happily yapping with Evie, and his mind went places. Places that involved a shower.

And the two of them doing naughty things.

Hokay. Back to business here.

Grif waved his arms. "You jackasses want to tell me why I got dragged here so early?"

"Shut up a second and you'll find out."

Reid put his foot on Grif's box and shoved it at him. "Open 'em up, boys. And, by the way, Jonah, this is coming out of the training center budget."

"What the hell, man?"

"You'll see why in a second."

This would be fun. He'd already cut the tape on each box so all he had to do was stand back and watch their faces light up.

Because one thing they all had in common? They loved their toys.

Grif got his box open first, stared down at it for a few seconds until a big-ass smile flashed. "Well, shit!"

"No way," Jonah said. "Paintball?" He squatted, scooped the weapon out of the box and snugged it to his shoulder, checking the fit.

"These babies are custom-made, boys. We're talking semi-burst and full auto capabilities. It's a 200-round magazine-tube-fed machine gun. Standard .68 caliber paintballs."

"It looks heavy," Evie said.

"Fifteen pounds, Eves."

"You know, I could carry fifteen pounds."

Sure she could. He just wasn't about to risk her getting hurt. Not with the way he and the boys went at it. Before this was done, not only would they be covered in paint, punches might be thrown.

"I know you could," he said.

He left it at that. Being a smart girl, she got the message.

"I can't believe you did this," Britt said.

Reid cracked up. "Our slingshot days are over. I ordered everything we need. Protective suits, goggles, masks, the works. This shit hurts when it hits you."

"Okay," Grif said. "What else? Yours is different, right? Better sights or something?"

"Nope." He held his hand up. "Swear. It's an even fight."

Jonah set the weapon back in the box. "Dude, these had to cost ten grand."

His brother was no dummy. "Don't worry about it. If it's a problem, take it out of the consulting fee you said I should let you pay me."

"The fee is your salary. For you to live on. Not to buy us paintball guns."

Reid shrugged. "What do I need money for? I got everything I need." He bent low, unwrapped his rifle. "Oh. I lied. Mine is different." He held it up, showed them the stock with the camouflage print. "Sorry. Couldn't resist. Now, let's get our gear on so I can kick your asses."

Chapter Thirteen

BRYNNE, EVIE, AND CARLIE BETH watched the men load into a battered pickup that, according to Evie, was Reid's. When he'd bought the new truck, Britt had insisted on keeping the old one as a work truck that they stored in the garage behind the house.

Not wanting to get their cars dirty, the guys decided the work truck would be used to transport them all to the heavily wooded north side of the property so they could attempt to maim each other with paintball pellets.

"They're such infants," Carlie Beth said, watching Reid and Grif hop into the truck bed. "This is how they work out their frustrations with each other. As if it would kill them to have a conversation."

Britt sat behind the wheel while Jonah handed up the weapons and boxes of protective suits and headgear.

Evie, now dressed in loose jeans and a long-sleeved black T-shirt, started toward the garage. "Girls, I'll be right back."

Where was she off to? "Where are you going?"

"To get the Gator. There's a bluff just above where my dopey brothers do their stupid war games. We can watch."

Brynne looked at Carlie Beth. The amazingly beautiful Carlie Beth with her slim figure and au naturel face. She obviously didn't have any hang-ups about leaving the house without her "face" on.

"They do this often?"

"Yep. They've tried slingshots, water pistols, sponge darts, and most recently Ping-Pong balls that shoot out of tubes. Grif came home from that fiasco with red circles all over his arms from the balls smacking him."

Men. "You're right," Brynne said. "They are infants."

"But, girl, watching all that male hotness in action? Talk about stimulating."

Evie zoomed up in a four-man ATV and skidded to a stop. "Get in and hang on."

Carlie Beth took the front while Brynne slid into the back. By herself. Something she didn't mind. After the horrendous past two days, she simply wanted to enjoy the ride, the wind hitting her face and the warm sun that battled the chill from the morning air.

All this land around them? The greenery, the random bursts of color from rhododendrons and birdfoot violets, all of it settled her mind. Let her breathe a little and relax.

A freak weather system storming the area was expected to drive temperatures into the eighties and she planned on soaking it up.

The ride took less than ten minutes and their maniac chauffeur skidded to a halting stop under a giant oak tree that offered plenty of shade. To their right was a sloping ridge that Evie pointed to.

"We're going up there." She shoved a bag at Carlie Beth. "Take this. I've got the other one."

Carlie Beth held the bag up. "What's this?"

"Ammo," Evie said. "I'm sick of these jerks telling me I can't play. I'm part of this family, too, and they never let me in on the fun. They're always on me about not drinking and not doing drugs and not having sex. Now I'm done."

And, wow. Evie had some pent-up frustration. Frustration that, oddly enough, Brynne understood.

She climbed out of her seat and Evie shoved a second bag at her. "Here's more for you. I've got the binoculars."

Brynne peeked in the bag and found what had to be a bucketful of acorns. "What's with the acorns."

"Slingshots."

Brynne laughed. "Slingshots?"

"Yep. They don't use them anymore so I hid them. I've been practicing and I'm pretty good. Girls, we're going to shoot my brothers."

Carlie Beth darted for the ridge. "They won't know what the heck is going on."

The three of them climbed the ridge and at the top dropped to their bellies. About twenty yards below was a worn path. If one of the brothers wandered through and looked up, the ladies would be busted. If they could stay quiet, though...

Brynne tested shooting an acorn and watched it hook left.

Evie, on the other hand, was a crack shot who'd hit the tree on the path below.

"I've been coming up here on weekends and practicing. I set up targets and ping them. This is the first time I'm doing live fire. Reid will pee his pants."

"I suck at shooting them," Brynne said. "I'll be the ammo girl for you two."

In the distance, the rat-a-tat-tat of gunfire destroyed the morning peace and a flock of birds flapped from a tree.

"We're rolling!" Evie said, bringing the binoculars to her eyes.

Brynne laughed. "This is too crazy."

"I'm teaching my obnoxious brothers a lesson. If they want to exclude me and make me feel unwanted, they're going to pay. Girl power!"

Twenty minutes in, after the initial high of an adrenaline rush faded, Brynne's lower back ached and boredom had set in. "Why are they so slow?"

"They're hiding from each other. Sooner or later,

they'll come through here." Evie scanned the area with her binoculars. "Shh, someone's coming. Right there, through the trees. Oh, that's definitely Reid. He's a sneaky one. He knows just how to duck into the trees and not be seen."

But he wasn't thinking about someone above him. For a solid three seconds, guilt leveled on Brynne. Reid was so darned competitive, having his baby sister pop him with acorns would drive him insane.

Good.

He deserved this. They all did. Brynne, having experienced life as a young woman constantly told what to do, where to be, how to dress, understood Evie's frustration. She might be their younger sister, but she deserved to experience life. On her own terms.

Baby sister or not, they should let her play with them. Period. These were paintball pellets, not actual bullets. As long as she was in safety gear, like them, they should make room for her.

And Brynne was all too happy to help prove the point.

Quickly, Evie handed over the binoculars. "Brynne, be my spotter." She pointed to an area just left of them. "He's in that clump of trees. It's hard to see him in that suit, but it's definitely Reid."

Brynne took up the binoculars, scanned right, then left. On her second pass, the leaves on a bush rustled and she zipped back to it.

There.

Protective gear covered him from head to toe, but that wicked body? His tall form, big shoulders, and lean hips? Nuh-huh. No mistaking it.

"Pssstt," Brynne whispered. "Here he comes. About to step out of those trees."

Evie giggled. *Giggled.* The girl was too cute sometimes. "Got him."

"I'd let him get a little closer. Just to make sure you can hit him from this distance. Wait for it...wait for it...now!"

Evie drew back and—fffttt—the acorn flew, just sailed through the air with amazing accuracy.

Ping!

She nailed him. Right in the back. With all the padding, it couldn't have hurt, but it darned sure startled him because he spun, dropped to a crouch and scanned behind him, his head pivoting while he checked the trees to his left.

The three of them ducked their heads, snorting quietly.

Evie scrambled for another acorn. "Load me up. He doesn't know where it came from."

Brynne checked her binoculars again. "Evie, that was perfect. It was so quiet, he didn't expect it. Hit him again."

Ping!

The second shot hit him in the helmet, the knock echoing. He spun again, this time looking straight up at them.

An explosion of gunfire—all that rat-a-tat-tatting— sounded from opposite directions, destroying the peace of nature, and the three of them gasped. Holy cow, that was loud.

Below them, Reid stood covered from front to back in red, yellow, and blue paint.

He dropped his weapon, flapped his arms. "*Evieeeeee!* Dammit! I'm dead!"

Their location now blown, the three of them scrambled to pick up their supplies and got to their feet, half running down the embankment and hopping into the Gator. Evie stomped on the gas pedal, but before they could clear the area, a paint-covered Reid tore over the ridge to intercept them. He looked like some kind of swamp monster in that getup.

Skidding to a stop, Evie released the wheel and held her hands straight up. "I'm unarmed."

Oh, the drama. Too funny.

Reid whipped his mask off and slammed it on the ground. "What the hell are you doing?"

"You wouldn't let me play. I'm making my own fun."

"Why would we let you play? You could get hurt."

"So could you."

Hoping to avoid a sibling smackdown, Brynne leaped from the backseat, grabbed hold of the only part of Reid's sleeve not covered in paint. "We need to talk."

"Now?"

She dragged him away from the ATV, well out of earshot, and spun on him. "Before you start screaming, you deserved that."

But, gosh, he looked so cute with his hair all poking up. Brynne's belly did a little squeeze and release and she bit her bottom lip because—yes—Reid Steele, in all his obnoxious glory, was stinking adorable.

"What? She just got me killed!"

"And rightly so. You should let her play. How do you think she feels, being the only one not included? That poor girl has to watch you guys go off and have fun, while she's left out. You're so busy telling her what she can and can't do all the time, you don't even see how much it hurts her to be left out."

Reid shook his head, let out a halfhearted grunt. *"What?"*

She might need a sledgehammer to get through that thick skull. "Stop being mad over losing that stupid game and listen to me."

"Stupid game? Are you *kidding* me? Whatever game we play, Jonah wins every fucking time. Well, not every time, but three out of four. I had this one in the bag!"

"Grow up," she said. "Evie is more important. You have no idea what you're doing to her emotionally. You're lucky she only hit you with acorns."

"Wait. *Evie?"*

"Yes. Evie. She's been coming out here practicing with that damned slingshot so she could prove to you that she can play. I'm telling you, it hurts her feelings. She just told me she feels unwanted."

That got his attention. His head snapped back and his

mouth hung open in disbelief. A few seconds later, he
held up a hand. "Hang on. She said that. *Unwanted.*"

"Yes. That was the exact word she used. She was
talking to Carlie Beth on the ride up here."

Disregarding the paint—it had to be washable,
right?—she stepped closer and tugged on the front of his
suit. "Let her play. You have no idea how something like
this can take root. She'll wind up resenting all of you for
it. Trust me on that."

Reid's face morphed into a tight mass of exasperation
and growing confusion.

"Seriously? She's that upset?"

"It's not just the war-gaming. She's complained about
you boys lecturing her all the time and popping in at her
dorm unannounced."

"Oh, hey now, that's not gonna stop. I've been a
horny twenty-year-old guy. I know what sleazebags they
are. No, sir."

"It doesn't matter to you that it embarrasses her?"

"Tough shit."

Oh, boy. She might need two sledgehammers for this
job. Paint be damned, she set her hand on his chest,
drummed her fingers. "Take a second here. Put yourself
in her place and think about what it was like in college.
Would you have wanted your parents showing up like
that?"

"I'm not her parent."

"You're sure as hell acting like it."

That shut him up.

"Crap," he said.

Progress. Excellent.

Still hanging on to his weapon, he brought one hand
up, dragged it across his face. "I just...worry about her."

"Which is great. But don't suffocate her. Please, let
her play these stupid war games. I know this is how you
guys work out your frustrations, but include her."

Behind them, another burst of gunfire sounded. This
one farther away. The guys moving away from them.

Reid sighed. "Okay."

"Okay, what?"

He started toward the Gator, his long legs moving at a clip. "I'm already out. If Jonah wins, again, I'll put a bullet in my head. And our war games are *not* stupid." He stopped, turned back to her, and their eyes connected for a long few seconds. "Thank you for helping me with Evie. I never realized. In fact, to show my appreciation, as soon as I get you alone, I'm gonna try to do you. Just a warning."

Brynne burst out laughing. What an animal. Total caveman.

Yet, she could get used to this. Reid listened to her, heard her opinions, and didn't roll his eyes when he didn't agree.

Even when the idea might be silly.

Like a five-year swearing-off-men plan.

At the Gator, he set his weapon on the small flatbed, kicked out of his boots and unzipped his suit.

Her eyes wary, Evie watched him. "What are you doing?"

"You wanna play, don't you?"

She hopped up. "Yes!"

"Fine. The suit'll be big, but you've got that sweatshirt on. It'll protect you."

Brynne unzipped her hoodie, handed it over. "Take mine too. It'll fill out the suit. And it has a hood."

Evie shoved her hands into the hoodie while Reid stripped his suit off. "We'll cuff the sleeves. And the pants so you don't trip." He handed her the suit. "Whatever you do, Squirt, do *not* let Jonah win this thing."

Evie lost.

But since she'd ambushed Jonah and killed him, Reid

was a happy guy. Plus, Britt had a decent smile on his face from the win. All good.

Given that they were all there already, their mom moved her family dinner to lunch and Britt, Grif, Carlie Beth, Aubrey, who'd just returned from a sleepover, and Reid stood in the yard waiting for the water to boil in the giant electric turkey pot.

The back screen door smacked open and Jonah stepped out carrying another giant pot. Probably the shrimp.

"I'm not taking this as a loss," Jonah said as he walked toward them. "You can't send Evie in as a ringer."

"You're just pissed because she killed you."

"Damn straight I'm pissed. We're doing a rematch."

"I need to order her a gun. Or we have to do it when she's at school. She doesn't like being left out."

Britt shrugged. "We knew that. Didn't we? She hasn't exactly been quiet about it."

Reid took the shrimp from Jonah and dumped them into the boiling water. "We ignored her. If she did that to one of us, we'd be pissed."

"The meathead is right," Jonah said. "Order her some gear. Get her all set up. I'll even let her win one."

"Hell, no," Reid said. "If she wants to play, it has to be level. She'd hate it if we let her win."

Jonah turned toward the house. "Mom's got another couple pots in there."

"I'll help you," Reid said.

He had a few things to say to Jonah anyway.

They reached the porch and Reid held his arm out, blocking Jonah from going in. "Hang on."

"What's up?"

"About before."

"When?"

"This morning. When I was giving you shit about not including me in the meeting with the architect."

His baby brother's shoulders sagged in that here-we-go-again way he'd become an expert at. "Dude, I wasn't boxing you out. I figured you didn't want to be involved in the details."

"I didn't. But I *suppose*, if I'm going to be involved, I need to be in it all the way. I just can't picture me doing that."

"When you were Army, you helped train foreign military. What's the difference if you're doing it here or overseas? The concepts will be the same."

Huh. Point there. Behind him, female laughter drew him from the conversation and he angled back, spotted Evie and Brynne sitting in Mom's Adirondacks that they dragged off the porch. Brynne laughed at something Evie had said and threw her head back. Her ponytail swung and the bright sun hit it just right and something inside Reid collapsed. A total cave-in. He wanted this girl.

And it wasn't just for sex.

Crap.

He couldn't do this anymore. This grieving for the life he'd left behind. It took too much energy, and worrying about being a washed-up Green Beret wasn't helping. He needed to leave it in the past and not be so freaking negative. He should just take that job in Georgia. Get back to action and try to recapture a miniscule piece of what he'd lost. Even if private security wouldn't put him back at the tip of the spear, he'd be able to travel. To get out of Steele Ridge.

Except, the knee.

And Brynne.

He turned back to Jonah. "Can I think about it?"

"Yeah. Don't leave my ass in the wind, though. If you don't want it, give me enough time before the build-out is done so I can find someone to run the place."

"I will. And if I decide it's not for me. I'll find someone. I've got all the contacts."

Evie's laugh—that adorable frickin' belly laugh— streamed back to him, followed by Brynne's laugh. On the other side of the screen door, his mom and Carlie Beth were teasing Grif about something. He couldn't think too hard about the women in his life. If he did that, he'd wind up stuck in the Ridge. *Not happening.*

After lunch outside, the entire brood sat around the table, patting stuffed bellies and moaning about too much food.

Did someone say dessert?

Brynne sat next to Reid, something he didn't much give her a choice with, and while his mama told a story about Daddy running his car into a ditch when they were kids, Brynne quietly excused herself. Bathroom break.

Finally. All afternoon he'd been trying to get a minute alone with her, but with his family? Forget it. Someone always had to butt in.

He stood and held his hand out. "I'll…uh…show you where it is."

She looked over at him, a small smile playing on her decidedly unpainted lips. Au naturel, here we come.

He couldn't wait to see her without all that crap on her face.

For now, she had his number. Everyone at this table did, considering she'd spent the night in this house and knew exactly where the john was.

Yes, he was a dog.

No shock to anyone.

They made their way into the house, down the hallway toward the powder room, but Reid grabbed her arm.

"The upstairs one is bigger."

She halted, tugged her arm free, still grinning up at him. "I'm aware of that. I don't need a lot of room to pee. Here is fine."

He shrugged, opened the door and gave her a light shove, huddling in behind her.

"What are you doing?"

"I promised I was going to try to do you. It'll be tight in here, but I'm always up for a challenge."

She burst out laughing and that weird collapse inside him happened again. "Damn, I love when you laugh."

And he was on her. Moving closer, dipping his head, expecting some kind of smart-ass comment. Nope. She pulled him closer.

Well, hello, Brynnie. "You're not gonna lecture me about your crimes-against-men plan?"

"No. I like kissing you. A lot."

Yes. *Advantage, Steele.* "Then I'd say we should do more of it. Don't you?"

Someone banged on the door. "Hey!" Evie said from the other side. "The walls are not soundproof and I need to tinkle."

Reid swung the door open, smiled at his baby sister. "Well, come on in then."

Evie huffed out a breath. "You're an idiot, Reid. I'll go upstairs."

"What are y'all fighting about?"

Reid poked his head out, spotted Mom entering the kitchen. "Nothing. Evie said I'm an idiot."

No answer.

"Mom!"

"You're not an idiot," his mother said.

With that response, he sure hoped she never had to convince a jury of it.

Brynne swatted him on the butt. "Get out. I really need to pee."

"We'll finish this later."

"Absolutely."

He walked back to the kitchen where Mom was scraping plates. "I'll rinse and load 'em," he said.

"Thank you, baby."

Being on his own for so long, he never minded helping with chores. He'd gotten used to washing his own dishes. Plus, the military had taught him a certain sense of order, gave him a hint of OCD about things being stored in proper places.

In combat, there were only so many things he could

control. Keeping his personal space tidy was one of them. He'd enjoyed the discipline of it, the knowing where he and his things needed to be at all times. The sudden punch of loss, the not-so-subtle reminder that the life he'd loved was gone, blasted him square in the solar plexus.

Dang.

Leave it behind.

He rinsed the first plate and set it in the dishwasher.

"I like her," Mom said. "Brynne."

Phew. In a lot of ways, Reid was a self-admitted mama's boy and the idea of his mother not liking a woman he brought to her didn't sit well. It had happened before and the sick feeling, the lack of approval from the first woman he'd ever loved, never went away,

"I like her, too."

"She's a little young."

"Is that a problem?"

"Not for me. She's been through enough that there's wisdom there."

"She's smart. Really smart. And easy to talk to."

Mom leaned against the counter and puckered her lips in that way that meant she was about to hit him with something. "Does spending time with Brynne impact the job in Georgia?"

His mother. Always cutting to the quick. "Not sure yet. The job is there if I want it."

"You're not sure?"

The clunk of the ancient doorknob on the powder room door sounded and a second later, Brynne entered the kitchen and eyed the small mountain of dirty dishes.

"What can I do?"

"We got it," Reid said. "Have a seat."

"Absolutely not. I ate, I'll help clean."

"You know," Mom said, "the potpourri you sent is in that cabinet right behind you. Dig it out for me and we'll test it in the kitchen. See if it'll get rid of the shrimp smell. If it works, I'll buy it by the truckload and use it in Jonah's running shoes."

"Ha!" Reid said. "Good one."

"I swear that boy's shoes could take out an entire nation."

Brynne froze. Just stood there staring at his mother like she'd stolen her prized pony, and the tension in the room built to a thick wall of unease.

Holding a plate, Reid paused. "Everything okay?"

She shook it off, opened the cabinet, gazing at the quart-sized bag of potpourri.

Reid stuck the plate in the dishwasher, slapped off the faucet, quickly dried his hands, and touched her arm. "What's wrong? You sick?"

"No. I just…"

"What?"

She looked up at him and tears bubbled up in her eyes. "The potpourri."

"What about it?"

"I can't get any more of it." She reached for the bag, held it in both hands for a second, her fingers tight around it as if afraid to let go.

What the hell was up with this stuff?

"Oh," Mom said. "I thought you were testing it in the shop?"

"I am. Was." Again she shook her head. "I was testing it. For Nelson."

Nelson. *Shit.*

Mom set the bowl she'd just scraped in the sink and spun to Brynne. "My dear girl, I'm so sorry."

"From the time we were kids, he loved chemistry. Wherever we went, he'd mix flavors. Ice cream, soda, whatever. He got into mixing scents, too. I told him he should start a side business. The aromatherapy market is huge and he had a gift for creating pleasant scents. And I own a store where he could test samples. We wrote a business plan. Not for us, for him. I just helped. He'd even invested in a label machine and packaging. Logos were his latest obsession. So many logos."

For a few seconds, she held the bag in front of her,

her eyes cast downward, her lips dipping at the corners.

"You should take that with you," Mom said. "He'd want you to have it."

She let out a hard breath, handed Mom the bag. "Actually, he'd want you to have it. His intention was for people to experience it. So you should enjoy it. That would make him happy."

Reid couldn't stand it. The crackling in her voice, the tears. He hugged her, wrapped her up and squeezed while he kissed the top of her head. What the hell else could he do?

"Baby, I'm sorry."

She pressed her forehead into his chest and let out a massive breath. "It's just...sad."

He wouldn't bother with the normal it'll-be-okay platitudes. Tragedy like this would never be okay. She'd learn to deal with it, to shut the pain away, but it would always be there, scratching, needling, tunneling its way to the surface.

After a minute, Brynne stepped back. "Thank you for that. You're a great hugger."

"He is!" Mom said.

There could be worse things to be known for.

Brynne held the bag up. "Let's put this in a bowl. Nelson would want that."

CHAPTER FOURTEEN

AN HOUR LATER, JONAH HAD gone off to his meeting with the architect, and Grif, Carlie Beth, and Aubrey headed home. That left Brynne to enjoy a sunny afternoon with the rest of the Steele bunch.

Her phone rang and she left the table to take the call. "Hi, Maggie."

"Hey, Brynne. I just stopped by the store. Your employee said you were off today."

Not wanting Jules, her part-timer to be alone, Brynne had called her backup, a college student only available on weekends.

Someone wanted a phone they apparently thought Brynne had, and until they figured out what the obsession with this phone was, Brynne would stay clear. It would cost her a bundle to have two employees on, but she seemed to be the target and if she weren't at the store, her employees would be safe.

"I decided to take the day off," Brynne said. "What's up?"

Somehow, she knew it wouldn't be good and steadied herself, staring up at a blazing blue sky that reminded her life could still be beautiful. Even during challenging times.

"I wanted you to hear this from me," Maggie said. "The man who attacked you was just released on bail."

Oh, no. "I see."

"I tried to hold him. I really did. The prosecutor didn't think we could make a case for no bail so we fought for a higher bond, hoping it would be too much for him to raise."

"He raised the money, huh?"

"I'm sorry. We'll keep an eye on him. Make sure he stays away from you."

She swung back, found Reid still sitting at the table, but his eyes were on her. With him around, she'd be okay. Unless he decided to run off to Georgia. *Don't be a fool and fall for this guy.*

"All right. Thank you. Maggie?"

"Yes?"

"Can I ask what his name is?"

Maggie hesitated, then let out a long sigh. "Well, if I know my cousins, as soon as you hang up, they're going to hack into the county database and find out anyway so I'll just save them the unlawful access charge and tell you. His name is Dexter Sweet. They call him Dex."

"Does he have a criminal history?"

"Mostly gang-related activity. Assault and theft."

"That's all you know about anyway."

"Correct."

"Okay, Maggie. Thanks for calling. I know you didn't have to."

"No prob. Call me if you need me."

"I will. Thank you."

She tapped off, stowed her phone in her jacket pocket, and walked back to the table, where Reid reached a hand to her.

She grabbed hold, took the quiet, steady comfort he offered, and reminded herself to be thankful. Outside of Evie, before this week she'd barely known these people, and now they'd welcomed her into their tight circle and helped her through the worst days she'd ever experienced. Even if Reid left town, she'd always be grateful for his family's support.

"So," she said, taking her seat again. "That was Maggie. The guy who…" what? Attacked her? Just the thought made her stomach flip. "The intruder was released on bail."

Reid made a noise in his throat. "Shit. But I'm not surprised."

"His name is Dexter Sweet. She figured one of you would hack into something to find it, so she told me."

Evie leaned forward, propped her chin in her hand. "Did she tell you anything else?"

"He's been arrested before. Assault and theft. She didn't go into details."

"We need Jonah," Reid said.

Evie popped out of her chair. "I can do it."

"Eves," Reid said. "No."

Already at the porch, Evie waved a hand over her head. "I won't even have to hack. We can just do an Internet search. For twenty-five bucks we can get whatever we need."

Britt cocked his head. "She's got a point there."

But Brynne didn't like it. Reid being involved was one thing. And Evie and Jonah had already done enough. "I don't want to drag you all into this."

Britt waved that away. "We live in this town. Our *name* is on this town. We're already in it."

Evie came back with her laptop, went to work, and in less than five minutes she provided them with Dexter Sweet's address and very spotty work history. And it hadn't even cost anything.

Reid sat forward and stacked the plate and plastic cup still in front of him. "E-mail me that address."

"Why?" Britt asked.

Ignoring him, Reid stood, grabbed the plate and cup, and made his way to the house.

Evie held up her hands. "What should I do? Send him the address? He's scary when he's not yelling."

"He's all right," Britt said. "Send me the address. Not him."

"Wait," Brynne said. "You're not going after this guy, are you?"

Britt pushed up from the table. "Not if I can help it. Reid might have other ideas."

Reid dumped the plate in the sink and cup in the garbage and walked through the kitchen, down the long hallway to the basement door.

Downstairs, he flipped on the light for the back corner where he kept his gun safe. Above him, boots—Britt, no doubt—clomped against the floorboards.

Whatever. Reid entered the safe code, pulled open the door, and scanned his toys. For years, he'd been buying and selling weapons, upgrading his rifles, legally modifying here and there to make them suit his needs.

He grabbed some extra ammo for his .45 and set it on top of the safe. The smaller and more concealable Sig Sauer 9mm might be a good backup gun. A knife also never hurt. He chose one with an assisted opening and, what the hell, added a flash bang to his arsenal.

"What's up?"

Britt. Mr. Responsible. Mr. Don't Get Hurt. Mr. I will lecture you until you shrivel and die.

Terrific.

Reid glanced back at him, at the set shoulders ready for battle. "Nothing. Grabbing some stuff."

"From the gun safe?"

Uh, yeah. "Yes. From the gun safe. I like to play with my toys. Now leave."

"Why? So you can sneak out of here? Hunt down the guy who attacked Brynne? Good luck, little brother."

Acting from habit, Reid started with his knife and strapped it to his ankle, yanking his jeans over it. Maybe he'd grab the .22 for the other ankle. Couldn't hurt.

"I'm talking to you," Britt said.

Reid did a quarter turn and propped his wrist over the safe door. "Yeah, I heard you. Don't worry about me. You do that too much. I'm a big boy."

"Who's about to go off—alone—and probably do something stupid."

"I need answers."

"Clearly."

Here we go. When big brother got this way, Reid had learned it was best to confront it straightaway. Let him say his piece and move on. "Okay. Have at it."

"What?"

"You know what. Give me the ten-minute lecture on getting my head on straight and not taking unnecessary risks. Go ahead. Unload on me and let me get on with what I need to."

Britt snorted, shook his head a little. Another one of his older-brother tricks to get Reid talking.

"Reid, what's going on with you?"

Aside from his life going down the toilet? Not a lot.

"In regard to?"

"Everything. Life. Brynne. You two got a thing going all of a sudden? Because she's barely divorced and…"

Now the lecture about what a pig he was. Excellent. "Yeah, I know. Grif already told me. I'm an animal and she doesn't need a guy like me."

"Actually, if you'd shut the hell up and listen, I'd tell you the opposite. You're in a bad place. You're not done—emotionally speaking—with leaving the Army and now I see you getting involved with a woman whose divorce is baby fresh. Between the two of you, it's a train wreck."

Well, jim-dandy. Now Mr. Responsible was adding shrink to his list of talents.

"Britt?"

"Yeah."

"I'm not talking to you about this."

"Why? Because you don't want to admit it?"

Yes. Reid banged his forehead against the safe door.

He could turn around, load one of his nine-millimeters and put a bullet in his head. It'd be a lot easier than this conversation.

But Britt wouldn't go away. Not a chance. The guy was a total pain in the ass when it came to stuff like this. Reid supposed he should be grateful someone cared enough—loved him enough—to get into his business.

"I like her," Reid said.

"I see that."

"Maybe I more than like her. And, yeah, I know she's coming off a bad deal with her ex, but she—" He waved his free hand. "I don't know. She gets me. Doesn't take everything I say too seriously. It's like she knows I'm a dumbass and doesn't mind."

"You're not a dumbass. Mostly."

"You know what I mean. She's...forgiving. I usually need a lot of forgiving."

"And what? Because of that, you're taking off, loaded down with weapons to do God knows what?"

"I'm gonna find the guy. Talk to him."

"With a knife, a .22, and most likely your .45."

Reid flashed a grin. "I like to be prepared."

Never one to appreciate sarcasm during his lectures, Britt pressed his lips into a tight frown. "You think this is funny?"

"No. I don't. I swear to you, my intention is to talk to him. If things go sideways, I'll improvise. She needs help. And Mags can't do it. I'm not a cop. I can bend the rules."

"Not alone."

"What?"

Britt stepped forward, shoved him out of the way. "I'll go with you. Now, let me see what you've got in here that I might like."

CHAPTER FIFTEEN

REID RODE SHOTGUN WHILE BRITT parked the work truck four doors down from Dexter Sweet's residence.

The house sat in a sketchy area on the southern slope of Asheville that hosted sagging porches, roofs ten years overdue for replacement, and weeds choking out the landscaping. Having run around the Asheville area during high school, he knew these neighborhoods and the minute they'd entered the address into the GPS, he and Britt realized they'd be entering one of the worst areas the city had to offer.

For two hours they sat with the engine off and the windows open, waiting for some sign of Dexter, but nada. So much for getting an idea of his comings and goings. A cop hooked a right onto the block and they ducked low, out of sight, so they didn't have to answer any questions. *Well, gee, officer, that guy tried to rape my girlfriend—girlfriend?—and I'd like to bust him up good.*

Yeah. Probably not a good thing to say.

"Two damned hours," Reid said.

"Yep. And don't say it."

"What?"

"You know what. I know you, little brother. You're antsy and bored and ready to do something."

Freaking Britt.

"Well," Reid said, "sitting here isn't doing jack."

"*Well,*" Britt shot back, "getting shot by the guy you nearly strangled won't do jack either."

"I'm not gonna ring his doorbell, for Christ's sake."

"What'll you do, then?"

Hell if he knew.

Reid grunted.

The front door of the house next door to Dexter's swung open, and a middle-aged guy wearing a blue work shirt, pants, and black rubber-soled boots exited. He hopped off the porch and headed down the sidewalk toward them.

"Neighbor," Reid said. "Let's talk to him."

"Why not?"

"Sir?"

The guy stopped, eyeballed them and the truck, but didn't come near it. Living in this neighborhood he knew better.

"Yeah," the guy said. "Help you?"

"We're looking for Dexter Sweet." Reid pointed to Dexter's house. "He still live there?"

"You cops?"

"Uh, no. Not even close."

"He lives there. I don't think he's home. If you want trouble, take it out of here. Mostly, you can find him hanging out by the projects, wasting his goddamn life. What did he do now?"

No love lost here. Reid propped an elbow on the doorframe, looked him in the eye. "He's bugging my girl. I want to know why."

"He's not the brightest bulb. You and your girl should stay away from him. He's running with the wrong crowd. Sooner or later, he'll wind up in the joint. Can't say I'd be sorry."

"Sounds like you're not a fan."

The guy shrugged. "Used to be. Not anymore."

"Why's that?"

"Caught him selling weed to my son."

Well, *that* would strain the bonds of friendship. "No shit?"

"Yeah. Cops arrested him. First offense so he got off easy. Now he's back and I'm trying to keep my kid away from him. It's a shame, too. His folks are good people." The guy glanced down the block. "I need to run or I'll be late for work."

Reid dug through the glove box, found an old pencil and an envelope with an insurance card in it. He tore off a piece of the envelope and wrote his number down.

"Do me a favor. If you see him, give me a call. I'll keep you out of it."

The guy shrugged. "Sure. But, take my advice, stay away from Dex. Nothing good can be found there."

The guy hustled off down the block.

"Okay, Ace," Britt said, "what now?"

"Dexter is a bust."

This field trip netted them a big zilch. Zero.

But apparently, Dexter sold weed. That could be something. Maybe not. Who the hell knew?

Reid ran a hand over his mouth. "I don't know. Nelson gets shot and right after that, Brynne's store and apartment are broken into. Now"—he waved a hand— "Dexter is looking for a phone he thinks she has. And, in Nelson's phone, we found the phone number of Ed Wayne, another murder victim. Coincidence?"

Britt shrugged. "If it is, it's convenient."

"Right. We need to figure out the connection between these three guys."

"I'm guessing you have an idea."

"Bet your ass." Reid circled his finger. "Let's roll."

"Where to?"

"Ed Wayne's house. I want to see what that fucker was up to."

After carrying Mrs. Steele's Adirondack chairs back to the porch, Brynne sat scrolling through her Facebook page while Evie lounged on the porch swing, using her foot to sway while she released her competitive juices on a live trivia game via her phone.

"What color did Oscar the Grouch used to be? I have eight seconds."

"Orange."

"Orange? Seriously?"

Brynne sneered at her.

"Okay, okay." Evie thumbed in the response. "No need to get huffy. Just…orange? *That's* surprising."

"He turned green overnight. Something about getting caught in a swamp."

"Aren't you the useless book of knowledge."

"Just saved your butt."

Evie set her phone down. "I won. Thank you *very* much"

"You're welcome."

"We should do something."

Yes. They should. Because in the past six months, Brynne had had three modes. Working, sleeping, or hanging with Nelson.

And right now, two of the three weren't options and despite brain-ravaging fatigue, without the help of a medication, sleep wouldn't come, so a nap was out.

Evie gestured to the laptop. "What are you working on?"

"Nothing. Facebook. But it's horrible. Everyone is posting about Nelson and funeral arrangements and…I don't know. I want to pretend it doesn't exist."

"Yeah. Totally get that. Maybe Maggie—or Reid—will figure something out."

Brynne set her laptop aside. "I've been thinking and thinking and I'm telling you, I can't come up with anything. Other than when he stopped to see me and him acting a little rushed, nothing strange had occurred. He was just Nelson. Same as always."

"Was he hanging around any new people or anything?"

"Not that he said. There was a new woman at work that he'd mentioned, but it was just a passing comment. He was helping train her and ran late for one of our dinners."

Wait. Facebook. All those people commenting. Some names Brynne recognized. The others? Who were those people?

She went back to her laptop, clicked in the search bar and typed in Nelson's name. His profile came up and she scrolled down, scanning the latest posts.

Evie rose from the swing and peeked over Brynne's shoulder. "What are you doing?"

"Checking his Facebook page."

"Maggie probably did it already, but you'd know some of the people."

"That's what I'm thinking."

She scrolled down the page, scanning the condolences, the poems, the photos of Nelson, all posted by friends and family who'd shared his life. Halfway down, one of their childhood friends added a photo of a group of kids at a high-school football game. Brynne clicked on it, found Nelson in the bunch, and there she was, twenty pounds heavier, right next to him.

Back then he'd been her lifeline. The one boy who wanted to spend time with the chubby little sister of the prom queen.

Adolescence spent in her sister's shadow meant misery, but Nelson always made her laugh. Always accepted her for what she was.

An angry longing sparked and she shook her head, fought the brutal rush of sadness. No. Not sadness. This was more. This was a gutting she'd never recover from. It might, as Reid said, get better with time, but the loss would stay with her.

She continued through the posts, scanning as she went, searching for anything that might appear odd.

Nothing.

Worse, reading all the tributes wasn't helping. She

clicked over to Nelson's photo albums. Maybe there she'd find something.

Evie pointed to one album with a photo of some intricate scrollwork. "What's that?"

Brynne clicked the album. "Logos for the business he wanted to start. He'd bought logo-creating software and was testing out different designs on Facebook. He'd toss a design out and ask everyone to vote."

"Kinda cool."

"Yeah." Brynne clicked on a variation of the Canterbury cross with rounded edges. "I think this is the one he decided on."

"It's nice."

It was indeed. And for all the time he'd spent on it, he wouldn't even be able to see it on any packaging. Such a waste.

Jonah appeared at the screen door. "Reid just called. He wants me to bring you into town. Grif's place."

"Is something wrong?"

"No. He said there's some stuff he wants you to look at. See if you recognize it."

After a death-defying ride down the mountain, insane-driver Evie swung her compact into the driveway of Carlie Beth and Grif's place and hit the brakes. Brynne's head snapped forward from the sudden stop and she let out a laugh.

Like Reid, Evie had two speeds.

Fast and faster.

All of them, in one way or another, shared distinctive traits. Jonah and Reid and the constant sense of competition. Jonah and Evie with their love of hacking, the challenge of cracking the code, so to speak, and Britt and Reid with their protective instincts.

Grif? She wasn't sure. She hadn't spent enough time with him to see what his family trait might be. Somehow she had a feeling that was about to change.

Jonah slid out of the car and pushed the seat up for Brynne, who'd insisted on sitting in the back to save him from folding his legs into that tiny bit of space.

Glancing up at the small-framed house with the cute porch, Brynne shielded her eyes from the sun. The house looked recently painted, its exterior gleaming in the sunlight.

Carlie Beth opened the wooden front door just as Reid came around the side of the house and—*there he is*—Brynne held her breath, let that little jolt of excitement subside.

After months of dedication to her plan, of refusing to even consider dating, it felt...good...freeing even, to look at a man and allow herself the instant heat of attraction.

"Hey," he said, "you okay? You look weird."

How romantic.

But that was Reid. Master of the inappropriate comment. And yet, buried in that inappropriateness, he'd already gone into protector mode, sensing something was off.

Jonah and Evie disappeared through the front door, leaving Brynne and Reid alone in the driveway. She looked up at him, at his eyes that screamed of mischief. Maybe she needed a little mischief for her battle-weary heart.

"I'm good," she said. "I'm..."

"What?"

Should she do it? Take the risk?

On Reid Steele?

"I'm...happy to see you."

He bent to snuggle her neck and the feel of his lips on her skin and that ultra-manly scent he liked sent another jolt of blazing heat straight to her boobs.

And lower.

He nibbled behind her ear, then kissed the spot. "How happy?"

She laughed, but pushed him away. If he kept that up, they'd go at it right on Grif's driveway. "Relax, player. Why are we here?"

He slung an arm over her shoulder, jerked his head toward the back. "We're in the yard."

"Why?"

"Uh, I didn't want to pour garbage all over my brother's house."

"Huh?"

"We drove by Ed Wayne's house."

"You stole his garbage?"

"Bet that sweet little ass of yours."

"Can you get in trouble for that?"

He set one hand on her lower back and led her to the side of the house. "In the law enforcement world, garbage sitting on a curb in plain view of the public is considered abandoned property. Lucky us, it falls outside the confines of the Fourth Amendment." He gave her a winning smile. "The one that protects citizens from unreasonable searches."

So, yes, Reid had a constitutional right to pick that bag up off the street and search it. "Yes, but Maggie will skin you for butting into her investigation."

"I'm risking it."

He steered her into the yard. To the left was a metal building. Carlie Beth's blacksmithing forge. How cool was that? Carlie Beth had a talent and she'd put that talent to work, supporting herself and a child for years before Grif moved back to town.

Sitting on a giant blue tarp were two torn-open construction-sized garbage bags, their contents spread across the length of the tarp. A light wind blew and the stench of rotting food drifted toward her.

"Ew. That's pleasant. I'm sure your brother appreciates the mess."

"Bringing it back to the Hill would put my mama on a questioning binge. Grif's was closer anyway. Plus, I'm not afraid of him like I am my mother."

He led her to the patio table where they'd spread some papers and weighted them down with rocks.

Poor Carlie Beth. The Steele brothers had invaded her yard and quite literally trashed it.

Reid lifted his arm away, taking all the weight and

heat and comfort with him and slipped on a pair of latex gloves from a pack on the table. He slapped a pair into Brynne's hand, swatted a rock aside, and picked up a document.

"Put those gloves on. If we find something that could be evidence, we don't want our prints cross-contaminating."

Once she had the gloves on, he handed her the document.

"We found copies of paperwork. Car insurance renewals, bills, that sort of stuff. Didn't you say Nelson worked for an insurance company?"

"Yes. NC Allied."

"This is a receipt showing an automatic bank draft from Wayne's account to NC Allied."

Brynne skimmed the document. "You think that's the connection to Nelson? He was his insurance guy?"

"Not sure."

"It could be why his number was in Nelson's phone. He gave his cell number to certain clients."

"Were they friends outside of work?"

Brynne shrugged. "I don't remember him mentioning an Ed Wayne, but it's possible." She dug her cell phone from her purse. "Let's check his Facebook page and see if they were friends."

Brynne signed on to Facebook, went to Nelson's page and scrolled his friends list. No Ed Wayne.

"Nothing," she said.

"Can I take a look?"

"Sure." She handed over the phone. "I looked through his posts earlier to see if anyone had left any threatening or nasty posts."

"And?"

"I didn't find anything."

While Reid scrolled, Brynne wandered to the tarp, scanning the discards of Ed Wayne's life. In the far left corner, a smaller white garbage bag had been torn open and the papers inside shoved into a pile and weighted down with more landscaping rocks.

She squatted next to the pile, removed the rock and sifted through the pages. More receipts, copies of spreadsheets, scrawled notes on sticky pads.

"This pile looks like it came from an office. The pages aren't dirty or wet."

"That's what we figured. Maybe he has an office in his house."

The wind blew a few pages from the pile and she slapped her hand over them, caught them before they blew away. She assembled the pile again and held it while reaching for a rock. *Hold on.*

Second page. The edge of a circle peeped out. She slid the page free.

"Wow."

Reid looked over. "What?"

She held up the page, hopped to her feet. "Give me that phone."

"You find something?"

She shoved the page at him. "This. It's a Canterbury Cross. And I saw one on Nelson's Facebook page."

"Now we're cooking," Reid said. "What's the deal with the cross?"

Whatever it was, it got his little Brynnie all fired up because the energy in the yard went berserk. An immediate surge that made the air nearly crackle.

Brynne swiped at her phone like a junkie in search of her fix. "Nelson was playing with logo designs for his potpourri business. He posted examples on Facebook. There it is!" She cupped her free hand over the screen to block the sun so Reid could see it. "This is the one most people liked. It's similar to the one in your hand."

Yep. Sure was. "Why would Ed Wayne have it?"

"I don't know. We need to find out what he did for a

living. Maybe Nelson hired him to do packaging or something."

Reid peeled off, hustled over to the white garbage bag and dropped to his knees. "Let's dig through here. Look for a work order or something."

The back door opened. Britt, Jonah, and Evie filed out just as Reid handed Brynne half the stack.

"I think we got something," Reid said.

Britt squatted next to him. "Seriously?"

"See that cross? We found it in this pile of crap. Nelson had the same picture on his Facebook page."

"What is it?"

Brynne answered that one. "It's the logo for Nelson's potpourri business. We're wondering if Ed Wayne was somehow involved. Like, a packaging manufacturer or something."

Reid pointed at a second stack. "Put gloves on and go through that. See if you find anything."

"Like what?"

Was he an investigative encyclopedia? "No clue. I mean, what the fuck do I know about potpourri?"

Jonah laughed and dropped to his knees. "I'll take a stack."

After gloving up, Britt paused, held up a copy of a receipt. "Mint leaves."

"What about them?"

"Think about it. Potpourri is made from dried plant material." He held up the page again. "Mint leaves."

"Well, excuse me, Mr. Granola, for not tracking that thought." Reid snatched the page from him and scanned it. "And hello, who needs the ten-pound bulk bag if they're not making potpourri."

His bad knee barked at him and he stood, took a few steps back to stretch his legs. "Brynne, did Nelson have a partner?"

"No. At least, not that I knew of. And when I helped him with all the paperwork for incorporating, he never mentioned anyone else."

Carlie Beth wandered into the yard, carrying a box of green garbage bags. "Y'all better pick all that up before Grif gets home. He will go crazy if he sees this mess."

His brother, the high-class one, always worried about appearances.

"Where is he now?"

"At a meeting with the chamber. He said he'd be home by five."

Reid checked his phone. "Thirty minutes." He shoved his phone into the back pocket of his jeans and circled a finger. "Let's clean this shit up. I'll start with the nasty stuff. Shove all the papers in a separate bag so we can go through them." He turned to Jonah and Britt. "Take Evie and Brynne back to the house. I need the truck."

"Where are you going?"

"Got a few errands to run."

Brynne eyeballed him. "What kind of errands? What are you up to?"

Nothing she needed to know about.

"It's personal."

"Reid," Britt said, "don't be stupid here. Maggie is already pissed at you."

"Don't you worry about Mags. I got all that under control."

Reid sat in the truck outside the sheriff's office, fighting the urge to turn tail and handle this latest discovery his way.

His way being a quick sneak and peek on Wayne's house. The inside. Which would mean breaking in. If they'd found the logo in the guy's garbage, imagine what he'd find behind closed doors?

He tapped his fingers on the bottom of the steering wheel, adrenaline plowing through him, urging him into action and eating away at reason.

Reason. Who needed that shit?

In front of him, the door to the sheriff's office opened and the receptionist strode out, spotted him sitting in the visitor's space, and waved.

If ever there was a sign he should do something, this might be it.

That something being he should quit stalling and go inside to show Mags what they'd found in Ed Wayne's garbage.

The sneak and peek would be so much more fun, though. Why the hell would he choose to get his ass chewed out by Mags when he could be breaking into a dead guy's house?

But he loved his cousin and he didn't want to screw her up on this investigation.

And that, kids, was the deal breaker on the sneak and peek.

"Ah, shit."

He smacked his hand over the manila envelope he'd stolen from Grif's home office and pushed the door open on the ancient F-150, taking comfort in the squeaking door hinges. Some things just felt like home. He made his way to Maggie's office before the urge to fall back on his old ways took hold.

Inside, the bullpen desks were all empty, the receptionist's space neat and tidy. She must have been knocking off for the day.

"Mags?"

"Enter!" she hollered, making Reid laugh.

He found her behind her desk, furiously typing on her computer. When he entered, she stopped typing and swiveled front to face him.

"Hey, you."

"Hey."

He stood there, staring at her, her staring back and....*shit*. Now that he was here, having to admit he'd ignored her order to stay out of her case, that sneak and peek was looking like the better option.

"Oh, no," she said. "What'd you do?"

Now, that was harsh. Automatically she assumed the worst? That he'd done something wrong?

Maybe because you did, dumbass.

"It's not bad," he said.

"Every time something starts with 'it's not bad,' it's bad. And coming from you? I can only imagine."

Considering what he was about to tell her, he'd give her that.

Reid tore the envelope open lengthwise and flipped it so the logo fell onto Mags's desk. Being the ace cop she was, she'd obviously noted his attempt not to touch the document and remained still. Not even a twitch of her hands.

She held his gaze for a few long and supremely agonizing seconds and then looked down. "What's this?"

"It's a logo."

"Whose?"

Sticky part. Right here. If it were anyone but Mags, he'd employ the ultra-schmooze and talk his way out of it. The military had taught him more than combat training. Being part of Special Forces meant dealing with people, talking his way into buildings or bartering for necessities when a mission went sideways.

So, yeah, he could talk his way out of Mags being pissed at him.

He just wasn't sure he wanted to.

Mags was his go-to girl. His closest confidante, the one he brought his most important life decisions to.

And he couldn't lie to her.

"Straightaway," he said, "you're not gonna be happy, but I promise you, this has a good ending. Let me finish before you yell."

His cousin huffed out a breath, sat back in her super-duper sheriff's chair, and folded her hands in her lap. "Will I have to arrest you?"

"No. I can honestly say I haven't broken any laws."

"All right. That's good news."

Reid pointed at the logo. "I got that from Ed Wayne's garbage. And before you scream at me, the bag was on the curb."

Mags locked her jaw, drew a breath through her nose, and closed her eyes for a few seconds. Yeah, definitely testing the bonds of familial love here.

She opened her eyes and scooted her chair closer to the desk, all the while keeping her sorta-pissed stare on him. "You did a trash pull on Ed Wayne's place?"

"Yeah. I was driving by."

"Nope. Stop talking. You were not just driving by. You have no reason to be in that area. Other than you were nosing around in my case again."

"I—"

She poked two fingers at him, her face flooding with color. "Don't you dare lie to me."

He dropped his head, focused on the toe of his boot. *Careful here, buddy.* Whatever he said next could change their relationship, annihilate any trust she had in him.

He raked his hands through his hair, prepared himself to beg for mercy. "Yes. You're right. I was snooping. I didn't go near the house, though. I saw the garbage on the curb and grabbed it. Didn't go past the sidewalk. I swear to you."

Her shoulders relaxed a millimeter. "At least you have some good sense. Dammit, Reid, I asked you, begged you to stay out of it."

"I know. But after that asshole went after Brynne, my brain fried. You know how I get. Sometimes I lose my shit. And now the guy is out. I had to do something. If it scores me any points, my first thought was to run back to Ed Wayne's and have a look through his house. I didn't do that. I came here instead."

"Ha! You're not a total loss then."

Gee, thanks for that.

Sighing, she leaned forward on her elbows and stared down at the document. "Tell me what the hell this is about."

Phew. First hurdle cleared. "Nelson was starting his own business. Potpourri."

"Brynne said something about that."

"Yeah, she helped him incorporate and was testing samples of his stuff in her shop."

"What does that have to do with Ed Wayne?"

Reid held up his finger. "Slow down, Sheriff. Getting there. First off, we found a copy of an automatic bank draft showing a payment to NC Allied, Nelson's employer. Then Brynne was looking at Nelson's Facebook page and found a post with different logos he'd asked his people to weigh in on. *Then*, I do a trash pull on Ed Wayne's place and find this." He gestured to the page. "The same logo Nelson chose for his business. Is that a coincidence?"

Mags picked up her pen, jotted a note. "We're already checking ballistics on both cases."

"What did Ed Wayne do for a living? We're thinking maybe he and Nelson were working together on the potpourri business."

"He worked for an ad agency. One of those smaller boutique setups. A lot of online stuff."

Huh. Their theory on them being partners might not be such a stretch. "Maybe he was the marketing guy for Nelson? Helping him come up with slogans or whatever?"

"Could be. We're going through all his finances and outside of the phone link, this is the only other connection we've found between the two." She pointed at the logo again. "I'm keeping this. Did you touch it? At all?"

"No. I wore gloves."

No sense letting her know he'd dragged his whole family in on the action.

She jerked her head. "Good. And thank you for coming to me. I know it's killing you."

"A little bit, yeah."

"For the most part, you did good. I wish you'd have

left the garbage for us to handle. Wait until the crime scene guys realize they missed that, go back and the garbage is gone. At least you were sensible about not touching it."

He grinned. "I'm not a total loss, right?"

Clearly not amused, her nostrils flared. "Just, please, I don't know how many times I have to say this, but let me handle it. Anything else comes up, you call me first. Got it?"

"Yes, ma'am. I promise I'll call you."

Chapter Sixteen

BRYNNE WOKE TO A DARK room and an owl hooting.

She blinked twice, then a third time, her gaze fixed on the bamboo ceiling fan swirling above her.

Tupelo Hill.

It took a second for her mind to adjust, to realize, for only the third time in six months, she wasn't in her own bed.

The first night, at Randi's, she'd hated it. The bed had been perfectly comfortable, the room warm and settling, but Brynne hadn't slept well. Too many images—of Nelson, his wounds, the blood—plagued her thoughts, jolting her awake every thirty minutes. Then the night before, Dexter Sweet and what he'd tried to do to her filled her dreams. Nightmares really.

She glanced at the clock. *Merciful God, thank you.*

Tonight? At the Steeles', with Reid somewhere under this roof, she'd slept a solid four hours.

The owl hooted again, the sound seeping through the French doors leading to the balcony.

In a blatant abuse of power, Mother Nature had created a freak warming trend and by the time Brynne had gone to bed at eleven, the temperature hit 73 degrees and the stars, well, a thousand angels must have been winking from that black canvas of a sky.

She pushed the covers away, rolled to her feet, padded to the door, and peeked through the blinds. Yep. Still a bazillion stars.

And she wanted to be out there. To breathe fresh air and forget about the past few days, to forget about Nelson leaving her and the giant hole that would never be filled.

Her stomach clenched, the pressure shooting up into her throat, cutting off her airway.

Air.

Fresh air.

Just outside this door.

But Reid had warned her about the alarm. Was the second floor wired? Knowing what she did about Reid, probably.

On the nightstand, she reached for her phone. Yes, it was three in the morning, but he said he slept like the dead. If he was asleep, a text probably wouldn't wake him. Still, how badly did she want to get outside?

She peeped out the window again. He had said to call him if she needed anything. Anything at all. Calling, though, would wake him up.

Text. Definitely a text.

Are you up?

Seconds later, his response came.

U okay?

Yes. Need some air. Can I open the balcony door?

Come downstairs. We'll walk.

A walk. In the middle of the night, under a sky full of stars.

With Mr. Sex on a Stick.

She stared down at the phone. At Reid's text, at his name on her screen.

She liked it. Seeing his name there.

"I'm in trouble."

Shaking her head, she tapped out another message.

Be right down.

Rather than flip the lamp on and blind herself, she hit

the spotlight button on her phone, illuminating the room enough to dig through her duffle bag for a pair of yoga pants and a lightweight, long-sleeved fitted T-shirt that—yes, she knew what she was doing—accentuated her small waist and big boobs.

But after six months of celibacy, of being alone and without affection?

Why should she deny herself the attention of a fine piece of man candy like Reid?

She whipped off her nightshirt, slipped into her bra, the sheer, lacy beige one she'd gotten as a sample from the lingerie vendor trying to convince her that Steele Ridge and La Belle Style needed a little naughtiness.

With the way her nipples poked through the cups of this bra, she definitely saw the naughtiness. And if she got really lucky, so would Reid.

From what she could see, the T-shirt had a few wrinkles. A spritz of wrinkle releaser took care of that minor detail.

Her phone buzzed. Reid.

Any time now.

Mr. Impatient. Well, he could wait a few seconds longer. She moved into the adjoining bath lit only by the motion-detecting nightlight. She brushed her teeth and glanced in the mirror.

No makeup.

Not even foundation.

Still, her eyes were bright—for three in the morning—and her skin was clear, cheeks a little flushed.

If things with Reid progressed, sooner or later he'd see her without makeup.

And something told her he wouldn't be scared off by it.

Her phone buzzed again. *Oh, my God, that man.*

Ignoring him, she shoved a brush through her hair, considered slipping it into a ponytail. He liked it that way. Had said it himself. But she liked it down and she'd already compromised enough by forgoing the makeup.

Compromise.

Something she'd never experienced in her marriage.

That's over.

She fluffed her hair one last time, liked the way it swooped over her shoulder, and for once didn't pick herself apart.

Quietly, she opened the bedroom door and made her way downstairs, the steps creaking a bit and making her wince.

Light from the first floor splashed halfway up the stairs and Reid appeared at the landing, his gaze locking on hers, taking in her face and the obvious lack of makeup, and she stopped moving. Just froze right there as panic flicked at her skin, that old insecurity crawling around inside her, bringing her back to the woman who'd never been good enough, pretty enough, thin enough.

Could she do this?

No.

Ready to head back to her room for her armor of makeup, she turned.

"Don't," he said. "I'm staring because you're amazing. Flat-out slaying me."

Well, all right then. She stood for a second as all that zapping on her skin settled and the panic slid away.

She turned back, met Reid's gaze, and the approval she saw there...Well, Reid Steele might just get lucky tonight.

Moving down the stairs, she broke the intense eye contact because—God—what was she doing?

Her and Reid? The most unlikely couple ever. What with his oozing cockiness and her supremely lacking self-confidence, they might as well be on different continents.

But he made her feel...pretty.

No.

Sexy.

At the second step, she halted, stood eye to eye with him, and he smiled.

"I like your T-shirt," he said.

Smart-ass. "Somehow, I knew you would."

"I'm a guy. Most of us like breasts."

And, oh, boy. Reid talking. Heaven help her.

He held out his hand. "You ready?"

She nodded. "I am."

This was it.

Finally.

Alone with Brynne. Who'd left her makeup off. She'd trusted him enough to know he wouldn't turn tail just because she didn't have her face all painted up.

The truth was, he liked her better this way. Dressed down, her hair loose and not sprayed to cement. Just a sweet country girl with curves to spare and the ability to knock him to his knees.

He disarmed the security system, waited for the beep, led her through the front door, then relocked it.

Just in case.

Way out here, he didn't expect any unwanted visitors. Not tonight. A night so perfect he might be the luckiest bastard alive.

A May night with temperatures twenty degrees above normal and a cloudless night sky surrounded him. He focused on breathing. On taking it all in. On enjoying the moment. Not letting his memories of all the different night skies he'd seen make him pissy.

"Where are we going?"

"Just down the path here."

The path—a dirt road, really—wound around to the bunkhouse he'd commandeered for himself when things at Mom's house began to get cramped. As in, his mother, as much as he loved her, started to make him nuts.

In the bunkhouse, he had quiet. And could walk around butt naked.

As they moved away from the lights of Mom's house,

Brynne nudged closer, squeezed his hand a little tighter.

"Wow," she said. "It's...dark."

He lifted their joined hands and kissed the back of hers. "There's nothing to be afraid of here. And look at that sky. Amazing."

They trudged on, into the blackness where only the outline of his cabin served as a guide and all around them crickets and birds chirped.

"What is this?"

"It's the cabin where I sleep. My mom was driving me nuts. Throw in Jonah and I needed some quiet."

"*You* needed quiet?"

Okay. So maybe he deserved that. Just because he was a loudmouth didn't mean he didn't like peace every now and again. "Does that surprise you?"

"A little bit, yes. You're always so...alive. Ready for action."

"Even us hyper guys need downtime."

He led her around to the back, where the cabin sat on an angle with the wooded tree line on one side and open land on the other. The structure itself blocked the view from the road, leaving a secluded, private area.

"Wait here."

"Where are you going?"

"Just up on the porch. Got a surprise for you."

He hopped up on the covered porch, pulled the tarp off the metal-framed futon he'd found in the basement and relocated to the bunkhouse.

"Heads up, sweetness. Coming through."

Grabbing on to the top and bottom rail, he scooped the futon up, carried it from the porch to the grass and set it down.

"What is this for?"

"Stargazing."

"Really?"

"Yep."

"How cool is that?"

"Very cool actually." After popping the frame open,

he extended it into his own personal chaise lounge and brushed his hands over the cushion. "Stretch out. You'll love this."

She settled in and he dropped next to her, extending his legs as he tilted his head to the sky.

Perfection.

"You do this a lot?"

"Not every night. When it's clear."

"Isn't it cold?"

He shrugged. "Sometimes."

"What about the security people you told my dad about? And the cameras? Doesn't that freak you out?"

He smiled over the girl who didn't like people looking at her. She'd have to get over that. "Not an issue. I futzed with the cameras. The area we're in? Cameras can't get to it. Total blind spot from that corner"—he jerked his thumb to the far end of the cabin—"to this one."

"Oh, that's brilliant."

"Thank you."

Obviously satisfied with his answer, she inched closer, rested her head in the crook of his shoulder and stared up at the explosion of stars. She let out a little sigh and...well...if she didn't knock that off. *Whoops.* Too late, Reid's mind wandered and, yep, the start of a woody.

That bad boy hadn't seen a lot of action lately, so he was all kinds of fired up.

"I can see why you like this."

Oh, honey. He laughed a little and she turned her head, looking up at him in the dark. "Sorry," he said. "My mind wandered. *Anyway,* being out here reminds me of overseas."

She nestled into his side and propped one elbow on the back of the cushion. *Brynnie, Brynnie, Brynnie.* She felt so damned good his body might combust.

"You miss the military, huh?"

"I do indeed. I trained hard. Not just the physical stuff. College, too. Straight As. I learned to speak Spanish, then Portuguese. All to make sure I qualified for Special Forces."

"You reached your goal."

"Yeah. And I was happy, you know? A lot of people strive for a goal and get there and it's not what they think, right? Not me. It was everything I expected. And more."

"You're lucky. And correct about goals sometimes being disappointing. I sold myself short. All I wanted was a husband and a family. I got there and..." She shook it off, waved her hand. "Doesn't matter."

"It wasn't what you thought."

"Definitely not. But I learned from it and I'll never regret it. I know now what I don't want and that's the important part."

"And, hey, it brought you back to the Ridge and here we are under an amazing sky."

She leaned in a little, totally taking the lead—which he kind of loved—because a few days ago, she'd been too closed-off to even flirt with him.

But this time she met him halfway and he dipped his head low enough to kiss her. He brought his free hand up, cupped her cheek, and ran his thumb along her jawline, taking it slow. They had time.

He backed up half an inch. "I like kissing you," he said. "I'd like to do a lot more to you. Assuming it fits in the five-year plan."

She sighed. "Well, I think it's safe to say you've obliterated my plan."

"When I'm good, I'm good."

"And so humble, too."

He burst out laughing. Damn, she was cute. And, yeah, a little young, but wise. Wise enough to set him straight when he needed it.

He slid his hand over her waist, under the hem of her shirt to the warm skin underneath.

"So, Ms. Whitfield, if I tried to get your clothes off, would you smack me?"

She gawked. "You want me to take my clothes off here? In your yard. Just down from your mother's house?"

He shrugged. "It's kinda a fantasy of mine. You, out here,

naked. And it is the middle of the night in the pitch black."

"A fantasy? Really?"

"There's the truck one, too, but that'll take some maneuvering."

"Holy cow."

"What?"

"You're just...a lot."

Uh-oh. That didn't sound positive. "A lot how?"

"You say things and I can't figure out if it's enviable honesty or totally inappropriate."

"If I get an opinion on this, which by now you realize I always have an opinion, I'd say honesty. I mean, why not put my intentions out there. I'm attracted to you. I want what I want. Why play bullshit games?"

"You scare me a little."

"I *scare* you?"

What the hell did that mean? He'd done his damnedest to stay levelheaded with this girl, not push too hard, and he scared her?

Shit.

"Not like physically scare me. I'm...you're...different."

Marginally better, he supposed. "Different is good sometimes. You're different for me, too."

"I'm not a Victoria's Secret model."

"Never said I wanted one." He inched his hand up higher under her shirt, dragged his thumb over the underside of her bra.

Lace.

Nice.

She whipped off a smile and angled closer. "Oh, good answer. I love when you touch me. Crazy things happen when you touch me."

"Say the word and it gets a whole lot crazier."

Say the word.

She could. Right here, right now. Wanted to even. Six long months of...of...nothing. Now the superhero wanted to shag her.

In his yard.

How incredibly wicked for a girl whose most daring sexual escapade was doing it on the living room floor. Woo-hoo! The floor.

I'm so not ready for him.

Reid Steele, conqueror of women. Something else to feel inferior about. Great. He'd be bored with her lack of sexual experience.

How pathetic was that for a divorced woman?

She snuggled closer. "I want to."

"What?"

"Say the word."

"Okay. Is there a 'but' coming?"

"No."

He laughed, ran a hand over his face. "You're funny."

"There's something I should tell you."

"Oh, man. That's never good."

This time she laughed. One thing about them, they shared a twisted humor.

"Actually, it *is* good. I'm just nervous about admitting it."

Again, he rubbed his thumb over her boob and—wow—his hands were nice. Big, rough hands that made her feel delicate. Small. Being the chubby girl for so long, even after losing weight, she still carried that extra ten pounds and the cellulite that went with it.

Reid leaned in, nibbled the side of her neck.

That would do it. She lifted her chin, giving him fuller access, and the long dormant and neglected parts of her stirred.

Hello, girls.

When Reid's hand moved fully over her boob, she sucked in a breath. "I'm not...experienced."

There. Said it.

His hand stopped. Just halted right on her boob and oh, God, this was bad. Bad, bad, bad.

He'd run. Why wouldn't he? A man like him could find any number of willing—and talented—women to sleep with.

He backed away and even in the dark, she saw it, the analyzing gaze. The choosing of his words.

"What do you mean?"

It was out there now. Might as well spill it. "Please don't laugh at me."

He kept his hand on her. Good sign that. If he'd pulled away, she'd have cried. The rejection, for a girl like her, before she'd even told him, would carve her to pieces.

"I will *never* laugh at you."

Then he kissed her. Gently. Just a light peck on the lips.

Tell him. "I'm afraid I'll"—she stopped, squeezed her eyes closed—"disappoint you."

She held her breath a second, waited for the humiliation to wash over her. But…nothing. She exhaled, dropped her forehead to his shoulder, let her body sag from the relief.

Free. That's what she was now. Free of her bad marriage. Once and for all.

"Sweetheart, you've got to be the sweetest thing. You're not going to *disappoint* me. Pretty much, I've never had a disappointing experience when it comes to"—he waved his hand—"this. And with you, with what I've got in mind? Definitely not disappointing."

"But that's the problem."

"What?"

"What you have in mind. I may not know how."

"Jeez, Brynne, I'm a smart guy, smarter than Jonah smart. Seriously. My IQ is off the charts. But God help me, I don't know what the hell you're talking about. So please. Just trust me to do the right thing here and talk to me."

Up to now, he'd been nothing but kind to her. Kind was an understatement. He'd been exceptional. Taking care of her, seeing to her safety, letting her help him with Evie. Why should that have to change? And really, she couldn't live like this anymore. The scared little mouse.

She lifted her head, met his gaze. "I've only ever done it one way. With my ex. He's it."

"You were a virgin when you met him? *Really?*"

She nodded. "Yes, *really*. I was the chubby girl in high school. No one noticed me. I lost weight between my freshman and sophomore year in college, went back to school, and met Kurt. He was the first. And he…well…let's say he wasn't adventurous."

"Okay, seriously. The more I know about this guy, the more I hate him. I mean, what the hell is wrong with him? And what the hell was wrong with you for marrying a guy who could look at you and not want to do you on every possible surface in every possible position? I mean, honey, you are spectacular. Sexy, cute, sweet, nice, all of it wrapped in one curvy little package. It's like hitting the fucking Lotto and this douchebag didn't see that?" He banged his palms against his head. "In my mind, the things I've done to you are borderline ridiculous. I imagine you screaming from orgasms constantly. And you manage to marry the one guy who's dumb enough not to enjoy it." He ran his hand over his face. "Lucky for you I came along."

Had this idiot just said all that to her? "I'm *lucky?*"

"Well, actually, I think I'm the lucky one." He sat back, wrapped both arms around her and hauled her on top of him. "I get to play out my fantasies and show you what you've been missing all at the same time. Jackpot!"

Without bothering to ask, he grabbed the hem of her shirt and lifted. She raised her arms, let him draw the shirt over her head and toss it over his shoulder.

"I need to see this bra."

With her straddling him, he lifted his hips and—wowie—that was quite the healthy erection. He slipped his phone from his back pocket, the little blinking blue light shattering the darkness.

"You're not..."

"Yep." He swiped at the screen and light washed over her, lighting up the sheer lace bra like Times Square.

"Shit," he said, gawking at her. "I wasn't prepared for that wickedness."

She looked down at her protruding nipples and her shoulders caved in.

"Hey." He dragged his fingers under her chin. "Don't shrink away. You're beautiful. You need to own that. Don't ever let anyone tell you otherwise."

Coming from him, she believed it. As much of a player as Reid probably was, he didn't lie. The man, as she'd just semi-painfully experienced, spoke his mind. Always.

"Thank you," she said.

"Sugar, don't thank me yet. You're gonna have a long night. What say we start with you on top?"

"Me? On top?"

In her mind, her hips would spread wider than the Grand Canyon and she'd rather spare herself that humiliation.

Plus, she wouldn't know what to do. Theoretically, she knew, but had never tried it because—oh, right—her ex always had to be in control of the sex. And he wanted plain old missionary style.

Every time.

She dropped her chin to her chest, her cheeks heating up under his stare. Twenty-four years old and divorced and she still didn't have the confidence to handle a man like Reid Steele.

But letting him control this? Could she do that? Let the man dictate what he wanted?

Yes. She could. But this time, she'd have a say. They'd both get what they wanted.

She set her hands on his chest. Tapped her fingers.

"You're thinking," he said.

"I feel fat up here. Like my hips are everywhere."

"They're not. Your hips are perfect. Well, they would be if you'd get your pants off."

At that, she laughed. Leave it to Reid.

"Brynne?"

"I want to. With you. I just…" She shook her head.

Be honest. As outspoken as Reid tended to be, he'd expect it.

"What?"

"I don't know what I'm doing. Up here. Me on top."

"Plan B."

"Plan B?"

He rolled. Just whoop! And she faced the stars blanketing an amazing night sky. So bad. All of this. Sex in the middle of a field? Seriously?

Smiling down at her, he kissed her, long and slow, and she pulled him on top of her, loving the feel of his massive body, so much bigger than hers, pressing her into the crappy futon.

He broke the kiss, wormed his hands down to her waistband. "Lift up."

She raised her hips, let him slide her yoga pants down, and the friction of his calloused fingertips against her bare skin ignited her.

"Oh, wow, oh, wow," she said.

"What?"

How to explain it. What she felt. Because that crazy intense heat burning her alive? Never before. Making love had never been an issue for her. She'd never minded.

But that was it. Overall, she didn't get the allure.

And she'd never experienced hot flashes.

"I want to love this. With you."

"Well, hell, no pressure there. Way to kill a moment, Brynnie."

She smacked herself on the head, laughing a little. "No. That's not what I meant. It's…sex."

He scooted down her body, dragged her pants off and hooked his fingers under the strings of her underwear.

"Lookie here. I may have to see these in the light, too."

She gripped his wrists. Hard.

"I swear, if you shine that flashlight on me again, I will murder you right here."

He grinned at her, ran his fingertips over the lace just above her crotch and...*wow, wow, wow.*

"I guess we'll wait on that," he said, sliding her panties down, those rough fingertips making her insane.

Insane.

She gripped two handfuls of his hair, all that thick dark hair, and pulled gently because—yes—she wanted to experience everything with him. All the things she'd imagined, but had always been laughed at for suggesting.

"I want to try it. Me on top. Now. Before I lose my nerve."

Whoosh. She was on top again, straddling him just above his hips. Before her good sense reined her in, she scooted down, went to work on unfastening his jeans. Fast, fast, fast.

He let her do it, let her fingers hurry through the process, and then he helped her get his pants off by lifting his hips.

"You in a hurry, Brynnie?"

"You have no idea. Problem?"

"Nope. We've got all night."

She wiggled down his legs, taking his jeans and boxer briefs with her, and his erection sprang free and—yippee. Big boy. Brynne gulped because...because...*this* would be a new experience.

Who knew her ex-husband had such a pencil dick?

Scooting off him, she whipped his pants over his ankles, grinning like a girl about to have a very good night.

"What's the shit-eating grin about?"

She straddled him again, just below his hips and grabbed hold of him. Her reward came by way of a guttural groan and somehow, his erection grew harder.

"I'm smiling about you," she said. "Thank you."

"For what?"

"For making me feel pretty. And making me want sex again."

He let out another groan, arched against her hand still wrapped around him.

"Condom," he said. "Back pocket of my jeans."

With her free hand, she reached back, grabbed his jeans, and dumped them on him.

A second later, the crinkle of foil sounded. "Let me," he said.

She let go of him, kept her gaze on his while he dealt with the condom.

"You ready?" he asked, his voice thick and low and raspy.

She hovered over him, letting her instincts help her along. His erection rubbed against her, the heat of him pouring into her, and she lowered herself the rest of the way and...

"Oh," she gasped as he lifted his hips and entered her.

She tipped her head back and he brought his hands up, over her chest, the roughness of his palms bringing her nipples to full attention through the sheer lace of her bra. Regretfully, he moved his hands back to her hips where he nudged her along, guiding her.

"Not too fast," he said. "Yeah. Perfect. Right there."

With one hand, he banged on the mattress and groaned—ooh, he liked that, whatever it was. She repeated the movement and his smile flashed.

"You are a wicked girl, Brynnie."

He bucked his hips, squeezed his hands over hers, coaxing her along, faster, slower, faster again, teaching her without saying a word.

Reid had that way about him. The ability to show her what he wanted, without making it a thing. Without demoralizing her.

Still inside her, he sat up, kissed her hard, his tongue ravaging her mouth, running along her lips, and she clung to him, wrapped her arms and legs around him, loving the feel of him, this perfect circle that was the two of them. He rolled, pushed her to her back and held himself up, staring down at her, those dark blue eyes somehow so clear, connecting with her in the pitch black.

He tucked one hand under her thigh, pushed it up, and was so deep inside her she thought she'd come apart. Just split in two.

"That hurt?"

Hurt? Was he kidding? Experimenting, she lifted her other leg.

"Oh, man," he said, pumping his hips. "Damn, girl."

"That feels amazing."

He pumped harder and she clamped her hands on his rear, holding him, refusing to let go because, yes, yes, yes, the storm inside her started. That swirling euphoria, building, building, building, one layer, then another.

Perfection.

The night. The man. The sex.

She dragged her hands up over his hips to his chest, explored the bulging muscles. A man's man.

Finally.

Pressure expanded inside her, an enormous squeeze that stole her breath, and the corner of Reid's mouth lifted. So damned smug.

She didn't care. For what he was doing, she'd let him be smug. She brought her hands to his cheeks, ran them up into his hair, let them get lost in all that silky softness, and he pumped harder.

The hand holding her leg disappeared and he propped himself on his elbows, his gaze still on hers, holding her stare, and she worked her hips in time with his.

A soft growl came from his throat and he smiled at her.

"Wicked woman."

Her body stiffened and she strained against the building orgasm. "Reid?"

"Yeah?"

"I loved being on top."

He kissed her, drove his tongue into her mouth and—

now, now, now—she exploded. Her body fracturing into a million different pieces, the release so perfect.

So good.

Reid reared up, threw his head back, working his hips faster and harder, and she touched his chest and ran her fingers over his nipples. He cried out, a fierce, guttural moan.

He collapsed, all that massive muscle falling on top of her, smothering her under him, but she wrapped him up, hugged him to her.

"You're a beautiful man, Reid Steele. Don't let anyone ever tell you otherwise."

"So," Reid said, feeling way happier than a man had a right to be. "You liked being on top, huh?"

Curled next to him, huddling against his chest, Brynne dipped her head, nipped at his skin. "Don't tease me."

He shifted to his side, slid his other hand over her hip to her back, drew her closer, skin to skin from chest to thigh. Just how he liked it.

And he'd never again curse Mother Nature, because she'd given him a gift tonight. Hot as hell in the middle of May, enabling them to lie out here naked as a couple of jays.

Brynne's hair fell in a tangled mess that said she'd just been supremely shagged and his body started to stir again.

This woman. She might screw him to death. And he might like it.

"I'm not teasing you," he said. He kissed her lightly, lingered for a second, let her feel his growing hard-on. "It makes me happy. That you liked it."

"Oh, I liked it. Believe me."

"As you can tell, so did I."

She laughed, dipped her head in that sweet, cute-as-hell move that meant he'd embarrassed her. If it were light out, he'd probably see her cheeks turning red.

Killer combo, this one. Sweetness and vixen all in one.

And she's mine.

For now anyway.

But what the hell did that mean? All he'd wanted was to get out of this place. Away from small-town life. To travel and see places.

Coming back here? Permanently? That hadn't been in the cards. And Brynne, she had a business here. Family. From what he could tell, she wouldn't be leaving any time soon.

Hell, this shouldn't even be on his radar. Not after one night. Even if it truly was extraordinary.

She snuggled against him, ran one leg up his. "I think it's funny that you rigged the security cameras so there's a blind spot."

That blind spot might have been his subconscious at work, because yeah, right now? Freaking genius move.

"I didn't want the security guys watching me when I lie out here. I come here to be alone and think. They don't even know. I hear them drive by when they're patrolling."

She gasped. "Seriously? What if…"

He pulled her in close. "They won't. Not unless they hear screaming."

She levered up. "I feel so naughty. We just had sex in your yard! Where someone could have just walked up."

"I mean, if you want to get dramatic about it, yeah. But, honestly, chances of someone walking up were slim. Besides, they'd go to the front first and we'd hear them." He waved a hand. "But if the risk factor gets you hot, have at it. As you may have noticed, I wouldn't mind."

"What time is it?"

"Plenty of darkness still left, sweetness. And I have a bunch of new positions for you to try."

CHAPTER SEVENTEEN

AFTER SNEAKING BRYNNE BACK INTO the house, Reid sacked out for a few hours before the glory of his mama's brewing pecan coffee got his ass moving again.

He shuffled into the kitchen, found his mother at the giant farm table paying bills. Yes, she still wrote checks rather than paying online. He liked that. Reminded him of childhood and the sense of routine he'd experienced back then. Before Dad had decided to spend ninety percent of his life at the cabin. His parents' relationship would always be an enigma, but certain things were constant. Like his mother paying bills twice a month. In the morning. At the kitchen table.

"Morning, Mom."

"Hey, baby. Your mug is there and coffee is hot."

He popped a kiss on her head. "Thank you."

"Give me ten minutes to finish up here and I'll get some breakfast going."

He poured his coffee, topped off Mom's, and slid into the chair across from her, setting his phone in front of him in case Brynne texted.

Mom eyeballed the phone and he nudged it to the side. She hated phones at the table. "I know," he said. "But I'm waiting on a couple of important calls."

Really, he was just hoping Brynne might call begging him to do her again. Yeah, he was a menace. *Sue me.*

Mom went back to her bills and Reid checked out her white top with a screen-printed photo of a dark-haired woman, her large hazel eyes staring straight out. The image was in shadow, but the woman's eyes? Totally intense.

The shirt seemed kinda edgy for his mom, but lately she'd been dressing more hip and when Reid looked close enough, the woman's eyes were the exact color of Jonah's.

And wasn't that interesting? A woman with Jonah's eyes. Micki's eyes.

Reid put thoughts of his absentee sister out of his mind. Nothing about Micki made any sense and if he spent too much time thinking on it, he'd get aggravated. About a lot of things.

His phone rang. At barely 7:00 a.m. it had to be one of the guys from overseas.

The number was local, though. An Asheville exchange. "Sorry, Mom. I gotta take this."

He scooped up the phone and headed to the living room. "Hello?"

"Is this Reid?"

"You got me. Who's this?"

"It's Blake Boden. I talked to you yesterday in front of Dexter Sweet's place?"

"You're the neighbor?"

"Yeah. You said to call if I saw him. He just got home."

"He's at his house? Now?"

"Yeah. I had the early shift today and saw him getting home. He's all banged up. Probably stoned."

Reid thanked the guy, disconnected, and called Britt.

Of all his brothers, Britt would actually be awake now. Probably communing with nature or some shit.

"Hey," Britt said. "What's up?"

Yep. Big brother. Wide awake. "I got a call from Dexter's neighbor. He's home. You up for riding shotgun?"

"If it means you not going alone, yeah."

"I'll pick you up in twenty. I'm out."

He punched off and strode to the kitchen where his mother was just closing her checkbook.

"Mom, I need to go."

"But I'm starting breakfast. You have to eat."

"I'll grab something. I'm gonna hit the shower and head out. I shouldn't be long. I'll tell Brynne to stay put until I get back."

With the hours she kept last night, she'd probably sleep all morning.

His mother let out a sigh, the one perfected by mothers worldwide. "Well, all right. Just be careful."

"Don't you worry. I will."

Time to pay a visit to Dexter Sweet.

By 8:15, Reid and Britt were clomping up the battered porch steps of Dexter Sweet's home.

As he'd done yesterday, Reid had loaded himself down with weapons and had passed a couple on to Britt. If anything went sideways, they were at least both armed.

"Let's stay cool," Britt said. "Don't get crazy."

"I got it."

Reid rapped on the peeling front door and waited. A minute later, the door swung open and a woman in her forties—maybe early fifties—stood there. She wore what looked like a housekeeper's uniform from one of the chain hotels, and her feet were bare. She studied them both with hard, accusing eyes.

"Help you?"

"Is Dexter home?"

"What do you want with him?"

"All due respect, ma'am. That's personal."

The woman smirked. "Well, I'm his mama and it don't get more personal than that."

Tough cookie. Beside Reid, Britt cleared his throat. "Morning, ma'am," he said in his aw-shucks voice. "We just need to ask Dexter a few questions."

"You cops? He's not talking to any cops without a lawyer."

Reid took that one. "No, ma'am. Not cops. I'm Reid Steele. This is my brother."

"Steele?"

There we go. "Yes."

"The Steele Ridge Steeles?"

Now mama bear was getting it. Two guys bearing the name of the town where her son was arrested had showed up at her door. "Yes, ma'am. That's us. We're here to talk to Dexter about his arrest. If he's straight with us, maybe we can help him."

Not likely, but if they were gonna get past mama bear, Reid wasn't holding back on much of anything.

Her gaze shifted from Reid to Britt and back. *Come on, lady.*

She stepped back, held the door open.

Bingo.

"You can come in. Have a seat. I need to wake him up."

Reid glanced at Britt, jerked his chin, and stepped into the house.

Just behind the door was a staircase and mama bear headed up, so Reid and Britt moved to the tiny living room. The inside, although spotless, had more of the same rundown feeling as the outside. Tattered furniture, mismatched curtains, and wood floors in need of refinishing. Still, he sensed the occupants cared, had even tried to make the place welcoming with throw pillows and a few plants.

All of that, he saw. What he didn't see was a junkie's house. Maybe mama bear was a single mother trying to make ends meet and her son went wayward. Who the hell knew? But the smell of lemons in the air, the tidiness of the place, the *effort*, sure didn't give Reid the impression the woman was a checked-out parent.

Rather than sit, the Steele boys remained standing. With any luck, this wouldn't take too long.

A round of yelling from the second floor ensued and Britt pulled a face. Apparently, Dexter wasn't happy. Oh. Well.

Mama bear's feet, now covered with sneakers, appeared through the spindles on the steps and then the rest of her came into view. She hit the bottom, grabbed her purse off the hook and slipped it to her shoulder.

"He'll be down in a second. I need to go to work. But I'm calling Dexter's uncle. He lives around the block. He'll make sure nothing gets crazy. He'll call the cops if he needs to. And I know who you boys are. If anything happens to my son, I *will* find you."

"Ma'am," Reid said. "I promise you. If things get crazy, it won't be our doing."

At that, she harrumphed. Above them, a floorboard creaked. "He's up," she said.

"Thank you."

She left via the back door and Reid checked his watch. If the uncle lived around the corner, they had maybe ten minutes to get whatever they could out of old Dexter.

Reid glanced up at the steps, tapped his foot and smacked his hands together. "I'm tired of waiting." He headed for the steps. "I'm gonna catch him off guard. You can stay here if you want."

"My ass."

"Atta boy."

At the second floor, Reid noted four doors. Two on one side, one on the other and at the end of the hallway a bathroom. Music drifted from one of the doors on the right and he stopped at the first door. Listened a second. Nothing. Next door.

He turned to Britt, jerked his thumb and they moved to the second door. Reid set his hand on the knob, gave it a quick turn and shoved the door open.

Dexter Sweet stood in the middle of the room.

In his underwear.

Damn, could this get any better? Now he had to talk to two apes in only his briefs.

And it wasn't lost on Reid that he got to give this guy a serious mind fuck by trapping him in his bedroom like he'd done to Brynne.

"Well, this'll work out just fine."

"What the fuck?" Dexter hollered. "Hey! You're the dude from that bitch's place."

Steeer-rike! Reid cocked his head, fought to control his rising blood pressure over this dumbass calling Brynne a bitch. He could work this, though.

"How does this feel, Dexter? To be trapped in your own room?"

"Fuck you."

"No, thanks." Reid pointed to the bed. "Have a seat."

"Touch me and I'll sue you."

Reid waved that off. In truth, he'd love to pummel this asshole. Beat him to an unrecognizable pulp.

But he wouldn't.

First, he had no doubt the kid would indeed press charges. Second, this piece of shit had information he needed and pulverizing him would only slow this investigation down.

Reid stepped farther into the room and the smell of cheap cologne, that crap all the high school kids wore, made his eyes water. He nodded to Britt to block the door. "Listen up, Dexter, you're gonna help yourself out here."

"I am?"

"Bet your ass." Reid waved a hand. "Might as well sit down."

"Can I put my pants on?"

"Nope."

The kid hit him with a hard stare and Reid glanced at Britt, who rolled his eyes.

Reid went back to Dexter. "Dude, you're pissing me off. And believe me, I'd have no problem finding a place to dump your body. You may have noticed, you're not my favorite person."

Keeping an eye on Britt, Dexter eased his way to the bed.

"Britt, watch him." Reid checked out the dresser, scanning the top. Nothing but some crappy looking jewelry, a couple of condoms, and three bottles of high-school cologne.

"Okay, Dexter, we'll make this quick. You tell us what you were looking for in my girl's place yesterday, and we'll walk out of here without tearing your arms off. How does that sound?"

"Fuck you."

Reid opened the top drawer of the dresser.

"Hey! That's my shit."

"Yep. Sure is. And I'm about to go through it." Out of the corner of his eye, Reid spotted Britt straightening up. "Don't move, Dexter, or the big guy by the door will take you apart. Trust me, he's a dirty fighter."

Good old Britt. Nicest guy to walk the earth, but he could fuck a dude up.

Not finding anything of interest, Reid slid the top drawer closed, opened the second. The underwear drawer. People usually kept all kinds of interesting crap in the underwear drawer.

He riffled through some boxers and a yellow pair of tighty-whities. "Dude, yellow? Tsk, tsk, tsk. We'll make those your second strike. While I finish raiding your dresser, why don't you start talking? What phone were you looking for the other night?"

"I don't know anything."

Sigh. "Sure you do."

Reid opened the third drawer. Socks. All neatly folded inside of each other so they wouldn't separate and get lost in the drawer. Also a terrific place to hide things. Starting on the left, he began squeezing each set of socks, running his fingers up and down, feeling for anything foreign.

The bed squeaked and Reid looked up, found Dexter standing. "Sit down, Dexter."

"Get out of my shit, man."

"This is how stupid you are. The first two drawers, you didn't move. I get to the third and all of a sudden you're on your feet. What's in this drawer you don't want me to see?"

"Nothing."

Dexter took two steps—idiot—and Reid had enough. He pivoted and slipped the punch Dexter tried to throw. Boom, he clocked him with a right hook. Dexter's head snapped sideways, as he fell back on the bed.

"Shit," Britt said.

If the fucker passed out, that'd be a problem. Reid watched for a few seconds as Dexter, flat on his back, arms sprawled, blinked. Slowly at first, then more rapidly.

"He's fine." Reid went back to the drawer. "Watch him while I dig through this stuff."

Now he yanked the socks apart, waved them around in case anything was hidden inside. Four pair in, something crackled. Now that was interesting.

"What have we got here, Dexter?"

Inside one of the socks, Reid found a roughly three-by-three inch foil package marked potpourri.

Potpourri.

He flipped the package and—whoa—there was the logo they'd found on Nelson's Facebook page. Reid studied it for a long second, the pieces suddenly coming together. *And, oh shit.* The logo on the back, the packaging, Ed Wayne and Nelson.

He rummaged through the rest of the socks, found five more packs of potpourri. And if this was potpourri, Reid was Betty White in disguise.

Using the edge of a sock, he lifted the packets and walked back to Dexter, still sprawled on the bed.

"Sit up. Right now."

"Fuck you."

Oh, his patience was about cooked. "Okay," he said. "I'm gonna make this easy." He held his phone where Dexter could see it. "See this? I'm calling the cops."

He dialed random numbers. Four, two, three.

"Wait!" Dexter said.

Good boy.

Reid tucked his phone away, flapped the package in front of Dexter. "What is this? And if I think you're lying, I'm calling the cops and telling them you're out on bail and then I'm pointing them to that sock drawer. That, douchebag, is enough for a warrant to search this whole goddamn place. Then you're fucked. Start talking."

The kid's head dropped forward, his shoulders slumping with the movement.

Come on, come on.

Behind Reid, he sensed Britt moving and held his hand up. If instincts served, old Dexter was about to make a smart move for probably the first time in his life.

"It's weed," he said.

"Weed?"

"Yeah. I sell it."

Which meant what in regard to Nelson? Middleman? "Where do you get the stuff?"

"I don't know. I get it from my buddy. He's a gang member. I sell what I can and he gives me a cut."

"You in the gang?"

"Not yet. I was supposed to get that phone. They think your girl has it."

"What's on the phone?"

"I don't know."

"But they think it has something to do with this weed?"

The kid shrugged. "Yeah. They sell the weed to shops. Convenience stores and shit. They say it's potpourri, but the shop owners all know what it is. They keep it behind the counter and wait for customers to ask for it. I figured your girl was selling the stuff. All I know is my buddy told me to go to her place and find a phone. Told me to grab any I found."

What the fuck?

Reid whirled back to Britt and their gazes locked. Brynne had given him some of that goddamned potpourri to give to his mother. His *mother*. Based on the quantity she'd given him, it couldn't have been pot.

But this other stuff in the packets with Nelson's logo made him wonder what Brynne knew. Despite her denials, did she know, or at least suspect, Nelson was somehow involved with selling weed?

No.

Couldn't have.

Could she?

Britt snagged the truck keys from Reid. "I'm driving."

"Whatever."

Right now, he didn't care. He needed to call Mags and clue her in on Dexter's little stash.

Ten minutes later, being the good soldier he was, he'd alerted Mags to the Dexter situation, got a ration of shit for their efforts, and in the end, a thank-you from their more-than-slightly pissed-off cousin, who called the local PD and had Dexter hauled in again.

They'd gone rogue, again, but at least they'd provided usable intel.

"So," Britt said, pulling away from Dexter's house. "What are we thinking about all this? What's with the weed?"

As they passed an older man—probably Dexter's uncle—hoofing it down the sidewalk, Reid slipped one of the foil packs out of his front pocket and held it up.

"Shit, Reid. You took one?"

He sure did. "Time to see if our little Brynnie has seen them before. The crap she gave me was in a bigger, clear bag. Way more than this. No one gives away that much weed."

Britt shook his head. "This is nuts."

"Yep. It appears Nelson was growing weed, or was at least involved in the packaging of it. Then they sold it as potpourri."

"You think Brynne knows?"

"Big brother, we're about to find out."

CHAPTER EIGHTEEN

WHEN JULES CALLED ABOUT A missing payment for a vendor, Brynne decided to hitch a ride into town with Jonah and Evie. One thing she didn't need now was an accounting mix-up that might send her into collections.

She pushed through the front door and found Jules and Val, her other part-timer, straightening some T-shirts on the front display table. "Hi, Jules."

"Hi," Jules said. "Wow, look at you all casual."

Brynne held her arms wide and did a little spin to show off her jeans and V-neck graphic T-shirt with the hammered metal around the sleeves. "Yep, decided days off entitled me to dress down."

"I like it. And I love your hair back like that. It really shows off your eyes."

The other big change. A ponytail and only a half-ton of makeup versus the full ton.

"Anyway," Jules said. "Sorry to bug you on your day off, but the sales rep called and said accounting is bugging him about the payment for our last order."

"No. It's fine. You know I'm a freak about this stuff. I appreciate you calling. I'll see if I can get a copy of the canceled check and send it to them."

"Also, Reid called a few minutes ago. He said his mom told him you were here."

Reid? She checked her cell phone. Three missed calls. Damned mountain screwing with the cell signal. "Shoot. I missed his calls."

An incoming text buzzed her phone. Reid again. *Where the eff r u?*

Alrighty then. Was he being funny or rude? Hard to tell via text.

Just got to shop. Where the eff r u?

Let him respond to that, because good old nice Brynne wasn't about to put up with any nonsense from a pushy male. Been there done that.

Jules picked up another T-shirt and refolded it. "He said he'd be down at the Triple B. He seemed kinda mad."

"Mad? About what?"

"Don't know. I told him if I saw you, I'd send you down there. But if you don't want to see him, we can pretend I didn't see you." Jules held up her fist. "Girl code."

At that, Brynne smiled.

Her posse.

The shop door swung open and Reid pushed through, his jaw set, his big shoulders back, muscles bulging and—bam—he stole her breath. Just left her with no air.

My man.

He stopped moving, slowly turned, and his laser-sharp focus landed on Jules.

She threw her hands up. "Hey, she just walked in."

He strode toward them, grabbed Brynne by the elbow, and ushered her back to her storage room. Fierce energy flew off of him, charging the air, and something inside of Brynne went haywire. A weird mix of tension gripped her shoulders. *Please don't let him do anything stupid.*

"I need to talk to you," he said.

For a second, all that charged energy Reid brought with him went still. Just...nothing, and Brynne's pulse hammered.

Clearly, he was upset—with her—and her newfound confidence began to crumble.

No way. She couldn't let that happen. Not again. Whatever Reid's problem was, he wouldn't make it her issue.

She shook him off and followed him into the storage room where he stood sandwiched between two shelves.

"Time to be straight with me. Do you have any of that nasty-ass weed in here?"

Screw this. Brynne stood in front of him, her face stretched in an almost comical look of horror. He'd asked her a simple question. If she didn't have any weed in here, the answer would be a simple no. Anything beyond that was a stall tactic.

"Excuse me? You say 'time to be straight' with you like I haven't been. What the heck are you talking about?"

Yep. Not good.

He'd get the answer for himself. He swung right, pulled one of the boxes from the shelf and rifled through it.

An invasion of her privacy? Totally.

Did he care?

Not a lick.

He needed answers. And even if she didn't know Nelson was selling weed, if he'd left her a stash of it, Reid would find it in one of these boxes.

Damn. After a stupendous start—pure perfection—of doing wicked things to Brynne, this day had gone to shit. First the weed and now her stalling when he'd asked her a question. Goddammit, he needed answers.

And his knee was fucking killing him. He'd had a good couple of days without major trouble and now? Throbbing. Go figure.

"Reid!" she said. "That's my inventory. What the hell are you doing?"

He shoved the box of socks back onto the shelf and turned to face an owl-eyed Brynne.

Reid dug out the weed he'd swiped from Dexter and held it up. "Looking for these."

He handed her the package, let her study the logo on the front.

"Potpourri," she said. "Did Nelson make this?"

"Since that's the logo we found, I'm assuming he did." He turned back to the shelf, started in on another box. More socks. How many fucking socks could the woman sell? "It's not potpourri."

"Then what is it?"

He slammed the box back to the shelf. "Weed, Brynne. It's weed. Pot. That your good friend was packaging and selling."

Now she looked up at him again, her mouth plummeting open as her face flooded with color. "What are you *talking* about?"

"I found Dexter this morning. Britt was with me. He told us the whole thing. The phone your intruders are looking for has something they want on it."

"But we gave the phone to Maggie."

"Well, sweet cheeks, I don't know what to tell you. Maybe there's a second phone, but right now I'm making sure you don't have any of this crap in your storage room."

"Sweet cheeks? Who do you think you are, talking to me like that? Have you lost your damned mind? And *really*? You think *I* knew about that? That I'd sell it through my shop?"

No.

Not entirely.

But the questions ricocheting around his brain blew a hole in his filter. Just tore that sucker up. "You two were pretty damned close. Maybe you didn't want to see what was right in front of your face?"

He went to the next shelf up, grabbed one of the clear plastic storage bins. Hair clips or some such shit.

"Reid, you can't be serious. After what we've been through these past few days, you think I'm lying about Nelson?"

"How do I know?"

"Because, idiot, I've been telling you I didn't know anything odd about Nelson. Are you even listening to me? Probably not. Why should you? Not when you can just take charge and do whatever you feel like. If you're not a Green Beret, you're not happy, right?"

Oh, now *that* was a direct hit.

"Hey," he turned to face her. "You gotta admit, this all seems a bit convenient."

"Oh my God." She pointed to the door. "Get out."

He shoved the bin back and faced her. "What?"

"I'm not doing this with you. Until you're ready to listen to me, get out. You come in here, start searching my things without my permission, which makes you no better than those creeps that came in here, and then you expect to interrogate me? Not on your life. Out!"

Jonah appeared at the doorway. "Uh, guys? Everything okay? You're freaking the customers out."

Brynne spun on her for-once reasonably sized heel. "Everything is fine, Jonah. But I've asked your brother to leave. Please get him out of here."

Brynne left the shop. Just walked right out the back door up to her apartment. Jules and Val could handle it and, well, if she stood in Reid's presence another second she might have to kill him. Just make him a bloody stump.

What the hell was wrong with her, constantly gravitating to the wrong men?

She pounded on her head with both palms. *Idiot, idiot, idiot.*

Forget him.

For now, anyway.

She unlocked her apartment door, tossed her keys and purse on the counter, marched straight to the living room, and looked out the front window. On the sidewalk, right in front of her shop, stood Reid and Jonah.

The damned man was everywhere.

Of course, he'd planted his feet, folded his massive arms, and thrown his shoulders back. Ready for battle. That was him.

Always.

Damn him.

At least his big mouth wasn't moving. For once, Jonah was doing most of the talking.

She pivoted and stalked the tiny living room, all that fierce anger burning just below her skin. She reached the far wall and stalked in the other direction. Oooohhh, she needed to hit something.

She picked up a sofa cushion, slammed it to the ground, let out a few grunts. She couldn't even scream or the big ape in front of her building would come running and then she might really have to kill him.

Grabbing a second pillow, she sent it flying. This time against the corner of the bare wall.

"Brynne!"

She spun back, found Evie standing behind her. Terrific. After everything she'd been through, she forgot to lock the door. Another thing she should have learned—along with how to ignore men—by now. "Your brother is an asshole!"

Evie threw her hands up. "Hop off! He's a lot of things, but he's not an asshole. What happened? Did you two fight?"

"His mouth! That's what happened."

"Oh. Well." Evie's eyebrows lifted. "Yeah. That's usually a problem."

"He thinks Nelson was selling pot and I helped."

"Um, why?"

Brynne picked up another pillow, let it fly. "He found the guy who broke in here and that's what he told him. That Nelson's potpourri business was really for selling pot." She flapped her arms. "I don't know. But Reid had a package of weed with that damned logo—*Nelson's* logo—on it."

"Wow."

Ha. Wow. Yeah. Good one.

"Do you think..." Evie scrunched her face. "Could Nelson have been selling drugs?"

And, oh, this was unbelievable. All of it. Because now, standing here putting all the pieces together, she didn't know.

She looked down at the pillows, squatted, and picked one up, hugging it to her chest. The last days had drained her, sucked every working brain cell dry. "Evie, at this point, anything is possible."

And if Reid was right? God help her, she'd never hear the end of it.

One way to find out.

She pushed by Evie into the kitchen, scooped up her purse and keys, and headed for the door. "You have to leave."

"Why?"

"I'm going out and I need to lock up."

"Where are you going?"

"To Nelson's."

Evie's jaw dropped. "Why?"

"Because I have a key and I'm going to search every inch of his stuff. If he's been selling pot, there has to be some evidence of it."

She stood on the porch, waved Evie out. "Move it, girl. Get out."

"You can't go by yourself. Reid will have a fit."

"I don't care." She hustled down the stairs. "I swear, Evie, if he was in front of me right now, I'd strangle him."

"I totally get *that*. Still, you can't go by yourself."

"I'll be fine. I'm so mad right now, if anyone tries to bother me, I'll tear him apart. Maybe I'll call Maggie. Have her come with me."

It would be the smart thing. For sure. But Brynne needed answers. For herself. For the memory of her friend. If Nelson had been dealing drugs, she needed to know first. To absorb it and process the fact that another man, one she'd known most of her life, had duped her. Horribly.

Men.

How could one woman be so colossally bad at picking them?

"I'll come with you," Evie said. "For moral support. Besides, if two of us search, it'll go faster. And you won't be alone."

Evie breezed by her, waited for Brynne to lock up. She shouldn't involve Evie. Not any more than she had already.

"Evie, I love you, but stay out of it."

"No. You're my friend. This is what friends do. Now shut up about it."

Huh. These Steeles. Every one of them was obstinate.

"Safety in numbers, Brynne. That's all I'm saying."

Good point.

At the bottom of the stairs, Brynne swung back. "Are you sure you want to do this? Your brother will go insane. I don't care if he screams at me, but he's your brother. He's in your life forever."

Forever.

Which meant...no. Not going there. She refused to acknowledge the twinge in her chest. The implication that Evie was stuck with him while Brynne wasn't.

Evie waved that off. "Pfft. I'm not afraid of him. Let's do this. Maybe we'll find something important."

Reid stood on the sidewalk, arms folded in a piss-poor attempt not to put hands on his baby brother.

"Dude," Jonah said, "you've got to chill."

Chill? The guy whose biggest problem was dreaming up video games, wanted him to *chill?*

"Jonah, are you out of your freaking mind?"

An older woman window-shopping and holding the hand of a toddler shot him a look. "Pardon me!"

Great. Now he was offending random tourists. "Sorry, ma'am." He waited for the woman to pass, then went back to the billionaire. "We've got two murders and one of the dead guys could be dealing drugs. In our town! If ever there was a time *not* to chill, it'd be now."

"You're gonna tell me you're all jacked up because of the two murders and not Brynne?"

Hell, yes, he was pissed about Brynne. About the fact that she could be a scheming witch—crap on a cracker, he didn't want to believe that—who'd totally played him into thinking she was innocent in this whole thing. After all, she'd been right there in the middle when all this had gone down. The shooting, giving him the potpourri—which, hey, could be weed. He'd have to check that. Then there were the thugs searching her shop, and Dexter.

Yep. Brynne. Right smack in the middle.

"Of course it's about Brynne, jackass. Things aren't adding up and I'm pissed. Sue me."

"Maybe if you didn't act like an animal and tear up her stockroom, she'd have been more open to conversation."

Oh, Mr. Fucking Brilliant.

Reid did his best to puff up his chest and get in Jonah's grill, moving into his personal space, staring down at him since he had a mere inch on his baby brother. "You about done playing shrink?"

Jonah shoved a finger into his chest and pushed, knocking him back a step. "Calling it like I see it, bro. Get your shit together." He pointed at the shop's door. "Get your ass in there and talk to her like you're human.

Apologize for tearing through her stuff and, for once in your goddamned stubborn life, listen."

"Hey!" Randi yelled from the doorway of the Triple B. "Knock it off, you two. Whatever you're arguing about, take it off the street. You're distracting my customers!"

Great. Now they had an audience. Well, too bad. "Fuck you, Jonah."

"Excellent response. That response tells me you don't have a solid argument against what I've said. If you did, because, hey, you're a heck of a debater when you want to be, you'd come up with something a lot more intelligent than *Fuck. You.*"

Reid unfolded his arms and let his hands dangle at his sides while he weighed his options.

Pop Jonah.

Pop Jonah

Or pop Jonah.

He inched closer, almost touching Jonah's nose, ready to push every one of the Baby Billionaire's buttons.

Years of the two of them trading punches had perfected their routine.

The corner of Jonah's mouth lifted. Oh, he knew what was coming. He was waiting for it. The attack.

What the hell am I doing?

Harsh sunlight fried the back of Reid's neck and he set his hand over the hot skin. None of this was right. The standing on the sidewalk screaming at each other, him going at Brynne; it all sucked.

All because he was afraid of getting too attached. To Brynne and to the home he'd spent years running from. Now a woman, one in the Ridge of all places, had finally reduced the hotshot Green Beret to a sniveling wimp. How fucking fitting that he wasn't man enough to deal with it. Instead, he'd lashed out like a five-year-old, screaming at the people he loved most.

And, yeah, he could include Brynne in that. Way too soon to know if it would be love, solid, down-deep love like Grif and Carlie Beth, but it was more than casual.

More than a quick lay.

Reid knew that, understood it on an emotional level he'd never reached before. One that terrified him. That level meant commitment and staying put in Steele Ridge.

For a woman.

God, save me.

New territory for sure and probably why he blew his top. When it came to fight-or-flight instincts, he fought. Every time.

"I'm sorry," he said. "You're right."

Jonah's head snapped back as if disbelief hijacked his body.

Reid burst out laughing. "Yeah, douchebag, I said it. Happy now?"

Jonah blew out a breath. "Could you repeat that? So I know I heard it right."

At that, Reid flipped him off.

"What are you two doing?"

Jesus. Reid angled back, spotted Britt lumbering toward them. He'd been cooling his jets in the Triple B while Reid waited on Brynne.

But big brother apparently got tired of waiting. First Jonah and now Britt. Could this get any worse?

Jonah cuffed him on the arm. "Reid just admitted I was right about something."

Britt's eyebrows drew in. "No shit?"

"Everyone," Reid said, "shut the fuck up."

A horn honked and Grif's—yep, just got worse—minivan rolled to a stop in the middle of Main Street. He'd never get used to his slick sports agent brother driving a mom-mobile. More evidence of his life going down the crapper.

Grif rolled his window down. "What are you d-bags doing?"

Stevie Ray Vaughan's "Little Sister" blurted from Reid's phone. Saved by a text from Evie.

Jonah jerked a thumb at Brynne's shop. "Reid's about to get his ass in there and apologize to Brynne."

"No shit," Grif said.

Reid finished reading Evie's text and fought for his last bit of control.

"Too late," he said. "She's not in there."

"Where is she?"

He fired a text to Evie and shoved his phone in his back pocket. "On her way to Nelson's. With Brynne. Let's go."

"Where?"

"To *Nelson's*. Where I will ask your baby sister and Brynne just what the fuck they're thinking."

After parking in Nelson's driveway and ringing the bell to make sure Mr. and Mrs. Marsh weren't inside, Brynne unlocked the front door and led Evie in.

The pungent aroma of neroli oil slammed her. That damned potpourri. He'd put it in every room and now simply stepping into Nelson's house unleashed a wave of sadness that sliced into her.

Grief was a fickle thing. No doubt. But she didn't have time for it right now. "I think we should start in the basement. I went through the house with Maggie the other day and didn't see anything on the upper floors. We didn't spend a lot of time in the basement."

"Is it finished?"

"Partially. There's drywall, but he never painted or put in carpeting. He hadn't gotten that far. It's mostly storage down there." Brynne pointed toward the back of the house. "This way."

She walked through the kitchen to the door tucked in the back corner. At the top of the stairs, she peered down to where sunlight streamed through a side window and lit the bottom landing. She flipped the switch, lighting the remainder of the stairwell. "These steps are narrow. Don't fall."

At the base of the steps, she smacked at another set of switches that lit up the entire basement. Stacks of boxes sat in one corner and adjacent to the boxes an exercise bike. He'd even mounted a television on the wall.

Brynne tilted her head.

Television.

Behind the exercise bike.

She hadn't noticed that little detail the other day when she'd shown Maggie this space.

"That's weird."

Evie set her hands on her hips and looked around. "What?"

"The television. Why would he have that *behind* the bike? If you were exercising, wouldn't you put it where you could see it?"

"Maybe he moved the bike."

"Maybe."

But Brynne wasn't buying that. Not completely. Nelson never did anything without a reason.

She stepped away from Evie, positioned herself across from the television and looked down at the cement floor. Why, why, *why* did he have that television there? Plus, he'd run cable. Obviously, he'd spent time down here.

In a partially finished basement.

She peered at the wall behind her where he'd wainscoted the right-hand portion and the memory of watching home improvement shows with him brought a fresh wave of sadness. On the night he'd decided to wainscot down here, they'd watched an episode on how to build a secret storage room door.

Using wainscoting.

She measured the distance between where she stood and the television. If he'd been down here working on the remodel, it wasn't unreasonable to think he'd want the television on while he worked.

A gap between the edge of the wainscoting and trim caught her eye. She moved closer, squatted, and found a seam running from floor to ceiling. In the middle of a section.

What the heck? That made no sense. Being the perfectionist he was, Nelson would make sure the seam was closer to the corner.

Unless...

Secret door.

"Evie?"

"Yeah?"

"I think there's something behind this wall."

CHAPTER NINETEEN

"GET OUT OF TOWN," EVIE said.

"I'm serious."

Brynne put her hand against the wall and pushed. A door-sized hunk of the wainscoting swung open.

"Whoa." Evie rushed over.

"We saw this on television one night. I didn't know he'd actually done it."

Brynne poked her head into the opening. Behind the wall was a long, narrow workspace that lined the right side of the house.

"Looks like a workshop," Evie said.

Sure did.

They moved into the room, where folding tables had been set up on one side. On top of the tables were spray bottles and large cookie sheets. Overhead, Nelson had hung a row of wire shelves. The first shelf held four clear plastic boxes.

"Huh," Evie said. "Maybe he did his potpourri stuff down here."

"Maybe."

But he'd never mentioned it. In fact, he'd told her he'd experimented with the potpourri in the kitchen where he could spread out on the large rectangular table.

"Don't touch anything."

"Why?"

"Because I have no idea what this is and your brother just told me he thought Nelson was selling pot."

At the end of the second long table was a chair and next to it Nelson had flipped over two milk crates that held his missing laptop.

And a phone.

Dammit. That had to be the phone her intruders were looking for.

Oh, Nelson, what did you do?

Curiosity getting the best of her, Brynne ignored her own warning to not touch anything and picked up the phone.

Dead battery. Of course. He must have left it on and then…never came home.

Evie trailed along behind her. "Brynne?"

She turned back, found Evie eying the bottom of the plastic bins through the wire shelving. "Yes?"

"These bins are labeled on the bottom." Evie met her gaze. "All drug names."

"What?"

She pointed to the bins. "All of them have powder in them." Evie pulled her gaze from the boxes to the spray bottles on the table. "The spray bottles."

"What about them?"

"Oh, wow." She put her hands out. "I could be wrong. I hope I am, but we talked about this in my human anatomy class the other day." She looked over at Brynne. "It was the day that kid from Asheville died. The one who smoked synthetic pot."

"Synthetic pot?"

"Yeah. It's crazy. Dealers buy drugs online—mostly from China. They dilute the drug and spray it on grass or whatever dried plants they can get their hands on. The worst part is, my professor said it's technically not illegal."

"Oh come on! How is that not illegal? They're making homemade pot."

"It's the drugs. The DEA can't keep up with the

different drug compounds. Every time they discover a new compound and put it on the controlled substance list, the drug manufacturers tweak the compound. They may mix in five different drugs. The boy that died last week? His friend smoked the same stuff and he got wasted, but that was it. It's nasty stuff. Basically the killer combo of a methamphetamine, LSD, and PCP."

"Oh, my God."

"Yep. Once the compound is tweaked though, it's technically not—" Evie made air quotes "—illegal. It's basically a new recipe. At least until the DEA discovers it and the government adds it to the list."

Nelson's recent spending popped into Brynne's mind. He'd said he'd gotten a raise. "But the people selling this stuff have to know they're riding the edge."

"Of course they know. To protect themselves, they put a label on the packaging that it's not for human consumption. The people buying the stuff know how to use it to get high, though, and the manufacturers are making millions."

Evie's phone rang. "Uh-oh. It's Reid." She tapped the screen. "I'll call him back. After we figure out what we're doing here. He's going to freak over this."

Brynne looked up at the bins on the shelf, then cut her gaze to the spray bottle. Could Nelson have been doing this? Using his potpourri business as a front to manufacture and sell synthetic pot?

Vomit lurched up her throat. How could she not have known?

"I'll take that."

Brynne and Evie swung back. Standing in the makeshift doorway behind Evie was a man. An extremely large man the size of Reid, but dressed in slacks and an Oxford shirt.

And he had them blocked in.

"Who are *you*?" Evie said in a voice that was more Reid than Evie.

The man pointed to the laptop and phone sitting on the upended milk crates. "I'm the one looking for that fucking phone and the *recipes* that belong to me. Thought I'd spin by here and see if I could find it."

Frying panic started at Brynne's core and exploded outward. Her fingers twitched. She closed and opened them—*close, open, close, open.*

The man took two steps forward and Brynne slid in front of Evie. The guy's hands were at his sides, but he could have been armed, the gun in a holster at his back or something.

And Evie was an innocent in all of this.

"Whatever you want," Brynne said, "just take it. Take it and go."

A slow smile lifted one side of his mouth. "I was planning on it, sweetheart."

"Just let us go."

He stepped closer, then stopped. "Can't do that. Now that you know about this side business, you've"—he circled one hand as if searching for the words—"become a liability."

"We don't even know who you are. Just take the laptop and phone and go."

Footsteps above them, in the kitchen by the back door, drew everyone's gazes up and Brynne's slamming pulse eased a bit.

"Oh, crap," Evie said.

The creep reached behind him and whipped out a gun—a giant one that looked like a single bullet could shred its victim.

He pointed the gun at Evie. "Who's that?"

"I...don't know," she said. "But my brother just called me. If it's him, you're in a butt load of trouble."

If that was Reid up there, this thing was about to get crazier. *Please let it be Reid.*

A muffled voice came through the floor, followed by a second, louder one. Definitely Reid. And Jonah maybe. But more footsteps sounded. More than two people.

"You two," the guy said, "move." Using his free hand he pointed to the secret door leading to the main part of the basement. "Out there. But you—" He poked the gun at Brynne. "Grab that phone and computer."

She glanced at the laptop, then went back to the giant gun. Dammit. Trying anything in such close quarters would be risky, and if anything happened to Evie...

No way.

"Grab the phone, too."

Fingers trembling, she stuck the phone in her back pocket and picked up the laptop, holding it lengthwise. She squeezed her fingers around it and gently tested its weight while the man glanced up at the ceiling again.

If she could get close enough, she could slam him with the laptop—pow—right over the head. It might not knock him out, but it could give them a second to run.

To escape.

If they didn't get shot first.

Brynne eyed Evie. *Get her out.* Breathing in, she faced the intruder. "Let Evie go. She can walk upstairs and tell her brother—who by the way is a badass—that she's the only one here. He'll believe that. Evie and Nelson were dating."

Hopefully Evie would catch on to the lie and play along.

"Yes," Evie said. "I came here a lot by myself. I'd wait for Nelson to come home. My brother is probably checking on me."

The guy shifted his gaze to Evie. "How come Nelson never talked about you?"

That one set Brynne back and another chip flew off her already broken heart. This guy was close enough to Nelson to know his dating habits. And Brynne had no idea who he was.

So much she didn't know about her best friend.

"They were keeping it quiet," Brynne said. "Evie is still in school. Her family didn't want her distracted by a boyfriend at home."

Worst excuse ever. Wait. The idiot nodded. Maybe he'd bought it. Or maybe he didn't care. Who knew?

"Brynne!" Reid's voice. Still upstairs. "Where are you?"

And, oh, that last bit of panic vanished. With Reid here, they had an even better chance of escaping.

The intruder's shoulders flew back and he gestured at Evie with the gun. "You. Go first. We're all going." He aimed the gun at Brynne. "Or she dies."

Evie swung back to Brynne, eyes bulging. Still holding the laptop, Brynne focused on her friend and made direct eye contact. "Listen to me. No one is dying here. Just do what he says."

A strangled noise came from Evie's throat and she scrambled through the doorway. Brynne and the intruder fell in behind her, but Brynne wanted her out of here. Away from the gun. She had to try. "Why not just let—"

"Shut up," the guy said. "Stupid bitch. You've been in the way for days. I wanted that fucking recipe and Nelson wouldn't give it up. Fucking pansy. One kid has a bad reaction and he pisses himself. And *then* Dexter and Reggie fucked the whole thing up. All they were supposed to do was scare him. Then his asshole friend had to go to."

"What?"

"Shut up."

At the base of the stairs, Evie stopped. "What now?"

"Go up."

"Brynne!" Reid hollered again.

Evie started up the stairs, her hands now visibly shaking. "S-s-s-s...someone has to say something. He knows we're here."

At the base of the stairs, the guy poked Brynne in the back with the gun, and a fresh wave of panic exploded, just swarmed her body in one violent rush. With all that had gone on, if this jerk was the leader, he wouldn't have an issue killing her.

Or even the troop of people in the house right now. He could wipe out the Steele siblings. All because of her.

That couldn't happen.

"Get out!" she yelled. "He's got a gun! Evie, run!"

She swung back, blocking his aim as Evie charged up the stairs. *Don't let him shoot. Stop him.*

He slid his finger to the trigger and her vision tunneled, blocking out everything but the gun, and a loud *whooshing* drowned out any coherent thought. *Stop him.*

His finger started to move. A slight twitch. On the trigger.

No.

Using the laptop as a weapon, Brynne whacked at his arm. He squeezed the trigger. *Boom!* The shot went wide, blasting through a hunk of trim along the ceiling.

From somewhere above, Evie let out a terrified scream and Brynne's head spun from the chaos and the panic raging at her. She glanced up to check on Evie and the basement door flew open. It smacked against the wall, but no one was there, just an empty space. Someone must have pulled the door open but taken cover.

Evie ran right through, disappearing into the kitchen, and a mix of relief and added fear hit Brynne.

Now she was alone.

And then everything went quiet. The screaming and pounding footsteps vanished, giving the house an eerie, charged feel.

The intruder aimed the gun at her, but—*crash*— something flew through the half-sized basement window lining the staircase. Glass flew and Brynne swiveled away, shielding her face and eyes. Something thumped on the steps. A brick. One of the brothers had thrown a brick through the window.

Capitalizing on the distraction, she glanced up, spotted Reid charging down the stairs into the firing line of the gun and Brynne's mind went crazy with visions of a bullet tearing into his chest. Just like Nelson.

Not happening. She gripped the computer in both hands, pivoted, and blasted it down on the intruder's hand. The force of the blow knocked the gun free and sent it to the floor. She kicked it and sent it skittering.

"Bitch!" the man seethed.

She looked back at Reid, now on the fourth step.

"Move!" he barked.

She leaped clear just as he braced his hands on the stair rails, swung his legs up and punched his giant feet into the intruder's chest, slamming him back into the wall.

Somehow, the man didn't go down. Dammit, what would it take?

He bounced off the wall and charged, his hands out, ready to strike.

Reid came off the stairs, straightened his arms and swung them in an arc—*whap*—deflecting the man's blows, and sidestepped as his attacker rushed forward. He shot one hand up over the guy's face, pivoted behind him, brought up his other hand to wrap around the back of the head, and locked his fingers. From there it was the work of seconds to yank the guy backward and spin him in midair. He landed on his stomach, winded and defenseless. Reid pounced, shoving his knee into the attacker's back, holding him in place.

That fast. Seconds.

And, day-am, it was *hot.*

Grif and Britt stood on the steps watching their brother and Reid looked up.

"Buttheads, you gonna stand there or call Mags?"

"On it," Grif said, shaking his head. "Jesus, Reid, the gossip mill will be busy today. All those goddamned busybodies'll flood into town. Do you know what kind of traffic jam this'll create on Main Street?"

That's what he was worried about? Brynne let out a horrified laugh, thankful for the stress relief.

The guy on the ground lifted his head. "Get off me!"

Having had enough of him, Brynne *nudged* him on the ankle with her foot.

"Ow," the guy said.

So, maybe it was more than a nudge, but too bad.

"Hey," she said, "be grateful that's the worst you got. And don't say I didn't warn you. I *told* you he was a badass."

An hour later, Brynne sat in the passenger seat of Grif's van, the sun streaming through the windshield and warming her post-adrenaline-fatigued body. After this, she'd sleep for a month.

On the front lawn, Maggie directed a county crime scene tech into the house. The creep had already been hauled off to jail by one of Steele Ridge's deputies and Brynne was thankful not to have to look at him.

What a mess.

Reid stepped up to the open window, hooked his big hands around the frame, and squatted a bit so he could see her. And, God, it hurt to look at him. Every emotion churned. He'd rushed in like the superhero he was and literally saved her. That alone should be enough to make her love him. After these past days and all he'd done for her, part of her already did.

But he'd hurt her. He hadn't trusted her. He'd *doubted* her. And for someone determined not to let a man's opinions influence how she lived her life, she couldn't accept that.

"Are you all right?" he asked.

Hardly. "I'm good." She met his gaze, that electric blue that always drew her in. "Thank you. If you hadn't shown up…"

"You'd have handled it."

Not like he had. Reid Steele was a rock star.

"I was worried about Evie," she said.

"She's fine. A little spooked, but otherwise intact."

Thank God.

"Um," Reid said. "Mags is gonna have some questions for you. You can hold off if you're tired. I can take you back to my mom's to rest. Mags'll come by later."

She couldn't do that. Couldn't pretend like nothing had changed since this morning.

"I'd like to go home."

"Sure. I'll take you."

He made a move to stand, but she shook her head. "My home. My apartment."

His lips dipped into a frown and she knew him well enough to know an argument would ensue. "Reid, I'm going home. Whether you take me or not. I *need* to get back to my life."

"Hey, I get that, but let's at least wait until Maggie rounds up the rest of this guy's crew."

"I'll be fine. Their boss just got arrested. I don't think they're going to be coming anywhere near Steele Ridge. Besides, Maggie told me she'd assign a deputy to the alley behind my shop tonight. Maybe tomorrow, too."

If he had a rebuttal, he kept it to himself. Good. Because every second of looking into his eyes chipped away at her determination.

Finally, she lifted her hand, set it on top of his. "Thank you. For everything. You've been amazing. You're amazing."

"Then why aren't you coming home with me?"

"I need a little space." She shook her head. "I'm confused. About you. About that fight we had. You just took over, came to your own conclusions without including me, and I've already lived my life that way. I'm not doing it again."

He let out a sigh. "Here we go. Did it occur to you that maybe I was trying to figure this shit out?"

"I know you were. The problem is, you didn't bother to ask for my input. You just started searching my store. And that wasn't fair. Now I need to go home, grieve for my friend, and get my life back together."

Maggie appeared next to Reid and he finally stood.

"Okay," Maggie said. "We're under control here. Brynne, I'll have some questions for you and Evie, but if you want to head home, I'll have a deputy take you."

Brynne looked up at Reid, whose face was a whole lot of tortured control. At least his mouth wasn't running.

As tired as she was, if he'd argued enough, she'd have given in. *Can't have that.* "That would be great, Maggie. Thank you." She slid her gaze to Reid. "I think I need some time by myself now."

CHAPTER TWENTY

REID WAS HAVING A BAD day.

At four that morning one of his army buddies called with the epically sucky news that Gage Barber, the Intelligence and Operations sergeant from Reid's old detachment, had gotten shot by a paranoid villager in Mozambique and was now fighting for his life.

As much as Reid loved the military, he'd been the lucky bastard who'd managed to stay alive. Now he'd spent the last three hours wondering if Gage would also be that lucky.

All he wanted was to call Brynne. To head into town and put himself in her orbit. Remind himself that good things could happen in this world.

In Steele Ridge.

But, oh, right, Brynne was ignoring him. Of course she was. *Well, screw that.* Reid had shit to do—sure he did—and he wasn't about to sit around having some kind of lame-ass pity party.

Shit to do.

He'd gotten up, once again noted the lack of calls, texts, or e-mails from Brynne, and hopped on his four-wheeler. Rather than mope around and worry after his friend, he'd outline the proposed area for the outdoor shooting range. The layout for the range bugged him and he needed to get a visual of where the targets might lie.

Ear buds firmly in place, his iPod churning some vintage Merle Haggard, he paced off what he thought was about 250 yards and marked it with the flags he'd bought at the hardware store the day before. Being productive meant ridding his thoughts of Brynne.

Brynne. Brynne. Brynne.

Dammit.

He tipped his head back, tugged his ear buds loose and stared up at the sky where the morning sun broke through a cloud. He breathed in the fresh air, focusing on the chirping birds, the sound of the hundred-year-old tree branches swaying in the breeze and the...peace. He gave it a solid ten seconds. All his body could stand of doing nothing. Each day he'd been practicing, training himself to be still. All of it part of his indoctrination to civilian life.

Behind him, the growl of another four-wheeler sounded and Jonah flew over the small hill, the ATV literally leaving the ground and Reid had to smile. One thing the Steele boys loved was fast living. But it must have been important if little brother was moving this early in the day.

Jonah whipped into a spin and skidded to a stop.

"If Mom sees you riding like that, she'll skin you."

Jonah yanked his helmet off—at least he'd worn it—and hooked it on the handlebars. "You gonna tell her?"

"Not me, little brother."

"What are you doing? I've been calling you."

"Sorry. I've been"—he waved one hand to all the flags he'd placed—"busy. We got problems with the berms."

"Berms?"

"Those seriously important mounds of dirt behind shooting stands that stop bullets from going any farther and leaving the range."

Jonah swung off the ATV, revealing a T-shirt that

read "I'm not good at empathy. Will you accept sarcasm?" Lord, if that couldn't be their family slogan.

Reid tucked his ear buds in his pocket as his brother approached.

"I know what berms are," Jonah said. "What's the problem?"

"They're a pain in the ass to place. We can't have anything behind the range. A bullet could deflect and skip over the berm. Best place for them is in front of dense woods or a field that's open for miles. I thought this was the spot with the woods right behind it, but with the way the trees circle around, I think it's gonna be an issue for the hotel. Which is why I just laid out the whole thing for the last three hours."

"But the hotel is all the way on the other side. It's parallel to this."

"Yeah, but if you got families there, a kid could wander into the woods and if a bullet deflects, who the hell knows what direction it'll go. Think about when we were little. All we did was run into the woods and climb. And if we're out here shooting and a bullet goes astray…"

"Shit," Jonah said.

"Yeah. I was thinking we could put berms over there." Reid pointed to the far corner of the proposed range. "But the back entrance road curves and would run headlong toward the range for a few hundred yards."

"Damn. What do you want to do?"

"I have to see it on paper, but I think we can move the hotel over by the main building. Closer to the front entrance and classrooms. It'll also keep civilians away from the training area."

Jonah scrubbed his hands over his face. "Good catch, big brother. Holy shit, that could have been bad."

For the first time in two days, Reid grinned. "That's what you pay me the big bucks for."

"Speaking of." Jonah whipped an envelope out of his back pocket. "Here's the contract we talked about. It's exactly what you asked for. Temporary gig with a hard stop date."

The contract. The one Reid had suggested after Maggie told him to set boundaries.

Reid stared down at the envelope, but left it in his brother's grip. If he signed that contract, he'd have to decline the job in Georgia.

"Shit, Reid, don't even tell me you're bailing."

Was he? Bailing? "No, it's not…"

Jonah waved the envelope. "What's your problem? You've been pissy for days now. I'm guessing this is about Brynne, since she's suddenly scarce."

Sure was. "I've been thinking."

"Always dangerous."

Funny man. "Hey, fuck off. Listen, with the experience I have, the weapons I've used, this training center is a no-brainer for me."

"Exactly what I said."

"Yada, yada. But I'm not an admin guy. I'm boots on the ground. All that administrative crap. *Paperwork?* I'd put a bullet in my head."

"And?"

If he said it, it would happen. He knew that. Jonah wouldn't mess around.

"Christ sakes, Reid, what?"

Reid cleared his throat. "What if…you know…we hired an admin guy and I do the fun stuff? I could come up with a syllabus for each training class. Figure out what kinds of advanced training would benefit law enforcement. I'll get Mags to give me the basics from the police academy and then layer on from there. I did some research and there's a SWAT academy out West. State-of-the-art. How cool would it be to offer training like that right here? Not SWAT, but super slick, seriously advanced courses for local police officers to keep their skills sharp. Or that individual law enforcement folks— or even former military, like me—can come to on their own. I'm telling you, it'd be a slam-dunk. Assuming the budget allowed for it, I bet Mags would send the deputies in a heartbeat. And if it's not in the budget, I'd find a way to make it work. Maybe if they pay for it on their own, it gets them a bump in pay grade. I don't know. But I think there's a market there."

Jonah pursed his lips, squinted a little. "You'd be willing to stay on? *Permanently?*"

"If you hire an admin and stay the heck out of it, I think so. I don't want this coming between us."

After a few seconds, Jonah cocked his head. "Here's the deal. You promise me you'll take this beast off my back and I'll make you a full partner in the training center. Fifty-fifty, dude."

Now they were talking.

The idea of owning part of a business and, assuming its success, the financial security that could come with it would give Reid something to do all day. And if things really got rolling, he could take off every now and again in search of the latest-greatest training options.

But that meant staying put—in Steele Ridge—the rest of the time. Did he want that?

He focused on his little brother, his family. Getting adjusted to being home hadn't been easy, but there were moments—family dinners, paintball wars, and ripping on each other—he couldn't find anywhere but here.

And Brynne. Brynne was here. Even if she wasn't talking to him right now, he could work on it. A little at a time, he'd concentrate on winning her over.

Home. Finally, the running from his hometown could stop. Everything he needed—and wanted—was right here.

Reid held his hand out. "Brother, you got a deal."

Reid whipped into town and cruised by La Belle

Style, hoping for a glimpse of Brynne, but no luck. Figured.

The lights in the shop were still dark and his hopeful mood nosedived.

For two days, she'd been blowing him off and just generally sending the silent message that she was done with him.

So he'd hauled himself into town thinking he'd *accidentally* run into her before she opened the shop. This was what his life had come to.

Accident schmaccident. He'd do this Reid style and just knock on her apartment door.

He snagged a parking space on Main Street and once again contemplated his options. Knocking on her door meant her possibly not answering.

Or he could wait until the shop opened. Then she couldn't ignore him or slam the door in his face.

At least he didn't think so.

He banged his head against the steering wheel. Clusterfuck. All of it.

Someone knocked on the passenger side window and he lifted his head. Mags.

He popped the lock on the door and she slid in, holding a coffee she'd just bought at the Triple B.

Mags handed him the cup. "Looks like you need this more than I do. It's black. No sugar."

Perfect. He took a sip, let the hot brew scald his tongue and took another. "I love you, Mags."

"I know. Why are you sitting out here alone?"

"Operation planning."

Mags laughed. "I'm afraid to ask."

"Relax. This one is personal. I'm trying to figure out how best to throw myself on Brynne's mercy."

"Ah. She's still mad at you, huh?"

"Apparently I'm a jerk."

"You're not a *jerk.*" Mags stared out the windshield, her sheriff's gaze scanning the sidewalk. "Reid, I adore you. Still, you might be the biggest dope I've ever met."

"Well, hell, Mags, don't hold back."

Mags lowered the window, hollered at little Tommy Perkins to pick up the gum he'd just spit out on the sidewalk. "Damn kids. What's a four-year-old doing chewing gum anyway? But back to Brynne. I was just with her. Giving her an update on Nelson."

Reid slid a glance her way, forced himself not to pry. The new Reid. The one who didn't insert himself into his cousin's investigations. If he'd learned anything over the past week, it was that butting into criminal investigations could get his loved ones hurt.

Or worse.

Maggie's lips spread into a wide smile. "Oh, my goodness. You are seriously not going to ask."

"Nope. Not my business."

"Wow."

"But, hey, if you wanted to share, I wouldn't mind."

"Atta boy. You scared me for a second there. Thought the Reid I knew and loved had vanished."

Now she was a comedian? The women in his life. Ballbreakers. All of them.

He drilled her with a look and she held her hands up. "Sorry. Couldn't resist. Anyway, Nelson bought the drugs Brynne found in the basement online, from China. He'd mix them, then dilute them and spray the mix on dried plants. Voila...synthetic weed. It's also called a designer drug."

How nuts was this? "What the hell? Brynne said he was a straight arrow."

"He was. Except he liked to smoke a little pot every now and again. Having this fascination with potpourri, he figured he could make his own synthetic weed. Then he realized how much cash he could make selling his concoction to other recreational smokers. Somehow he got hooked up with Marty, the guy from the basement."

"And Marty is involved how?"

"Marty runs the drug ring. He has people like Nelson making synthetic weed in ten states. He's even got a fleet of trucks for delivering the stuff. He sells it to convenience stores and in some areas, like here, local gangs. He's been making millions on it."

"Jesus," Reid said. "All in our little town. What about the other murder? Ed Wayne?"

"Nelson talked to Ed, who he apparently knew through work somehow. Ed does graphic design and created all the packaging. As near as I can tell, he wasn't directly involved. All he did was create the designs."

"But the gang thought he was a partner?"

Maggie nodded. "Looks like it. We went through Nelson's laptop. There was a note on there to Brynne. A kid from Asheville had smoked his weed and had a stroke."

"I saw that on the news. That was Nelson's weed?"

"Yeah. And he freaked. I honestly think he thought the stuff was harmless. It's weed, right? What's the big deal? Except the kid dies, Nelson panics and tells old Marty that's he's done. He didn't sign on for this. But Nelson had his recipes and all his drug manufacturer contacts and refused to share."

"And Marty got pissed."

Mags jerked her head. "And Marty got pissed. He assumed Ed Wayne and Nelson were partners and told the drug ring members to get them to give up the recipe. That's where Dexter Sweet and Reggie come in. Dexter has been selling drugs for the gang, but wasn't a member yet. They were basically giving him a trial run with getting the recipe from Nelson. When that didn't work, Marty got pissed and someone went to Ed Wayne. Could have been Marty himself. We don't know yet."

Reid looked out the windshield at Brynne's shop, imagined all that could have gone wrong for her. "My guess is Wayne told them he wasn't involved and they figured he was being cagey and popped him."

"In her statement, Brynne said something about Marty ranting about Dexter and Reggie fucking the whole thing up. They were only supposed to scare

Nelson. They then tried to get the recipe from Ed and when he couldn't give them anything, they were afraid he'd squeal so they killed him. We picked up Reggie the other night, but he's not talking. As soon as all these idiots start turning on each other, we'll know who did what. Either way, Nelson was scared. He knew Marty was looking for him. And with that teenager dying, since Nelson made the drugs, he figured a murder charge was in order and he wasn't sticking around for that."

"He was gonna run?"

"According to the note on his laptop. He had enough cash to last him awhile and apologized for his"—she made air quotes—"sins."

"And then Marty's boys caught up with him at Brynne's shop and figured he'd hid the phone there."

"Yep."

Reid let out a grunt. That shit was probably being sold in Steele Ridge. "You gotta shut that ring down, Mags."

"I know. The DEA is on it. I'm going to scare the pants off of everyone in this town. If I find that crap around here, people are going to jail. I don't care how old they are."

"Good." He glanced back at Brynne's shop. "You just told her all this?"

"About an hour ago. I think she's okay. Sad. Bewildered, I guess, but after the last few days, I'm not sure much else could shock her."

"I need to talk to her. Get her to forgive me for being an asshole."

Mags patted his arm. "Start by apologizing. Tell her you have this issue with being bossy and point out that sometimes, the fact that you're an alpha is a good thing."

"Huh?"

"I'm a female. I'm also an *alpha* female. Here's the thing I've come to understand about alpha males. As women, a lot of us like a strong man who is willing to take charge of a situation, one who wants to be the first to kick in the door. The problem is, a lot of those types of guys aren't really romantics. I don't see you reading her poetry, right?"

Ew. "Hell, no."

"Exactly. You wouldn't be any good at it. Some men are. You? You're a caveman."

Jeez with the insults. "Again, don't hold back."

She waved him off. "What I'm saying is it's unreasonable for women to expect a guy like you to be the whole package. To be the tough alpha *and* the romantic with a squishy underbelly. You're not built that way. If it could happen, well, that's a world-class jackpot, but being an alpha woman, I understand that and I choose the men I date carefully. In my case, I'm okay with a well-intentioned dope who occasionally puts his foot in his mouth because I know, I *know*, when it comes down to it, he'll be the first to kick in the door to protect me. And something tells me that as much as Brynne wants her independence, she wants a guy—like you—who'll stand beside her, who'll help her through the rough stuff, but who is willing to admit when he screwed up."

Like every other time Maggie had talked him through a life lesson, Reid took it all in. Processed it. She was right. He'd never be the poetry guy. Sure, he liked looking up at the stars, but that might be as romantic as he got.

What he needed to do was play up the positive parts. The protective parts, the parts of him that would fight any battle on Brynne's behalf, or that would dismantle any enemy who came for her. That, he could do.

"Okay," he said.

"Okay?"

"Yep. I know what I have to do. Thank you. You always know what to say. Kinda like Brynne. She gets me. When you two talk, it makes sense."

The lights in La Belle Style flicked on, but the closed sign was still on the door.

Mags pointed. "Looks like she's in there. I'd figure out a way to weasel in." She opened the truck door. "And for the love of God, be nice. Try not to talk too much."

His cousin laughed and Reid had to smile. Making people laugh might be the best cure for a pissy mood.

"I'm going," she said. "And I'm proud of you."

"For what?"

"For not asking about the investigation. Last week you'd have been bugging me about it."

"Well," he said, "I'm preoccupied with figuring out my life."

She slid out of the truck. "Go get her, champ."

By his way of thinking, Reid had one shot at this. With that in mind, he hopped from the truck into the morning sunshine, stretched his legs, noted the lack of twinge in his knee and figured it was a good sign.

Yep, he'd go with that and march into the shop to throw himself on Brynne's mercy.

He walked toward the door, ready to launch into his spiel about intending to help, but being a screw-up and an egomaniac who sometimes has trouble sticking his opinions on hold and allowing people to explain.

With that self-examination, why would anyone want him?

He thought about what Mags said, let it bolster him.

I've got this.

He grabbed the door handle and pulled.

Locked.

Shit.

Brynne stood behind the counter and must have heard the jiggle of the door because she looked up, stared at him through the glass for a solid twenty seconds.

At least she hadn't screamed at him to go away.

When she didn't move from her spot it became obvious, he'd have to yell through the door.

Excellent. Nothing like making an ass of himself on the damned sidewalk.

But, hell, he'd always thought part of his charm was

his ability to look like an idiot, yet get shit done.

He waved one hand in greeting. "I know you're pissed at me. Can we talk?"

"Ah, Christ," Mr. Greene said as he made his way toward the Triple B for his daily breakfast. "Hang on, Reid. Let me get my coffee so I can watch this."

Reid gave him a look. "All due respect, Mr. Greene, zip it. A man's gotta do what a man's gotta do. And if begging helps, I'm up for it."

On his way by, Mr. Greene patted him on the arm. "You're a good kid."

The snick of a lock sounded and Reid snapped his gaze back to the door where Brynne stood on the other side. And, God help him, she wore jeans, a pair of flat leopard-print shoes, and a ribbed top that hugged her curves. The added bonus of her seriously toned-down makeup kicked his desperation to another level. And she had her hair in a long braid that hung over one shoulder. Damn, she looked amazing.

She stepped back and opened the door for him.

"Since I know you well enough to know you won't go away, you might as well come in."

"Thank you. I think." Good gravy on a Tuesday, she might have just insulted him. "I'll say what I have to and then if you throw me out, I'll go. I promise. Is that a deal?"

She eyed him, twisting her lips one way, then the other. "Fine. But I swear, if you say one moronic thing, I'll club you."

One moronic thing. Only one?

That might be asking a lot.

Reid wanted to talk.

Well, *she* wanted one normal day. To open her shop, have some quiet, but with enough customers to keep her mind occupied on making a living and...well...*surviving*.

On her own.

But damn him for playing the superhero and making her want him. For two days she'd been picturing him storming that basement, rushing down there and bringing that guy down in seconds.

Extraordinary. Yep, that was Reid.

Except when he opened his mouth.

As much as she loved that badass-nothing-is-impossible attitude of his, she couldn't be with a man who wouldn't treat her as an equal. Who wouldn't listen when she spoke or thought he could decide how she should live her life.

She locked the door behind him, walked to the loveseat and sat. "I think we *should* talk. Have a seat."

"Good," he said, "that's good." He slid into the loveseat, turned to face her and when he reached a hand out, maybe to touch her face or her hair, she backed away.

Allowing him to touch her wouldn't make this easier. He paused and his mouth dipped into a pouty frown. He dropped his hand.

"I'm sorry," he said. "For all of it. For searching your stockroom, for doubting whether you were being straight with me—"

"You thought I lied. Big difference."

"There you're wrong. I did *not* think you lied. I wasn't sure you'd told me everything."

Semantics. All of it. "Stop with the word games. You didn't trust me."

"I trusted you until I found Nelson's potpourri in Dexter's house. That threw me. Especially after you'd given me some to take to my mother. And, hello, you'd just spent the night in bed with me, so yeah, I got stupid there. Then I couldn't get a hold of you and all my questions ate away at me. By the time I got back to town, my mind was blown. I didn't know what I was doing."

"You didn't let me explain."

"No, I didn't. I'm sorry."

She believed him. As mad as she wanted to stay at him, Reid didn't say things he didn't mean. "I accept your apology."

"Why do I think there's a but?"

Strength here was key. If he sensed any weakness, he'd exploit it and she couldn't fall back into the old Brynne. Ignoring her shattered heart, she looked him straight in the eye. "We're not good for each other."

For a second, he narrowed his eyes. "I don't believe that. Not after everything that's happened between us."

Don't give in. She pushed her shoulders back, tilted her chin up. Strong Brynne. In control Brynne. "In a lot of ways, we're great together. But when you get dug in, that's it. You're stubborn and you see things in a linear way. You get so locked on it's like tunnel vision and the only way is yours. For me, on an emotional level, that's not good."

"I get that. I do. I'm working on it."

"I've tried to become an independent woman who won't always give in to what others need. All my life I've been a pleaser, putting myself behind everyone else. I can't do that anymore. And you're strong-willed and charming enough—in your own sick way—to make me fall into old habits. I'm sorry, Reid, I can't do it. I am who I am. You helped me see that I don't need a ton of makeup and fancy clothes. That I can be myself. But my looks, my opinions, the way I live my life, which is here in Steele Ridge, it all has to be enough for you. You want things your way. And you'll always want more than this town. It's who you are. I can't spend my life worrying about the day the Green Beret in you will pop up, say it's not enough and you're moving to Georgia. I've already had one husband tell me I wasn't good enough. Now, Steele Ridge and I have to be enough."

"I won't leave. I'm done with that."

She set her hand on his and squeezed. "You want to believe that."

"No. I'm serious, I'm done. Georgia is off the table. I called the guy on my way over here."

Wait. What? No, no, no. She couldn't let that sway her. Couldn't let that bit of hope change her mind. "You did?"

Dammit. So much for staying strong.

"I did."

"Because of your knee?"

He thought about that for a second. "No. The knee is the excuse. I don't want the job. Yeah, I want to be able to travel some, but not constantly. I thought I wanted the action, but then my buddy got hurt yesterday and I realized it's not the action. It's the adrenaline rush I crave. I can get that other ways. I also kinda like being around my family. And I definitely like being around you."

He reached into his back pocket, pulled out a folded document, and handed it to her.

"What's this?"

"A contract."

"For?"

"It needs some tweaks, but I'm staying in Steele Ridge and I'm running the training center. Jonah promised me he'd hire an admin guy to handle the day-to-day stuff. I get to design all the training classes and teach. I'm the hands-on one."

She glanced down at the document and that flicker of hope sparked in her chest. He was *not* serious.

"Reid Steele, don't you tease me."

He nudged the paper at her. "I'm not. Look at it."

She unfolded the document, scanned it.

"You crossed out the end date."

He flashed a smile. "Caught that, did you?"

That flicker morphed into an inferno and she knew, dammit, as sure as she was sitting in front of him, she'd give in. "You're serious about this? You, the world traveler. You're going to stay in Steele Ridge and settle down? Why?"

"Because, well, my family makes me nuts, but the

other day? Playing paintball with my brothers, that was amazing. But then watching you and Evie held hostage—" He closed his eyes a second, cleared his throat before opening them again. "And my buddy getting hurt last night? I guess it hit me that I'm lucky. As much as washing out sucked, I was able to walk away. I've lost friends. Good friends. I've watched them get blown away in firefights and have limbs torn away by IEDs. I've watched that."

"I know. I'm so sorry."

"Seeing my family in danger puts things into perspective. I know how precious life is, but before coming back here, I'd never considered losing my family. It scares me. Makes me realize how much I've missed all these years. Now, I want some peace, well, as much peace as I can get with the Steeles, but that's what I want. To spend time with my loved ones. To spend time with you. And to remind myself how lucky I am."

And, oh, no. There was that boyish charm that terrified her. Not two minutes ago she'd told him she was afraid of that charm and here she was with a full-blown burn in her chest and her body begging to lean in, to fold herself into the crook of his arm.

"Damn you, Reid Steele."

He perked up. "Is that a good *damn you* or a bad one?"

She laughed. "Both!"

"That's good. I can work with that. Just give me a chance, Brynnie. I don't want to steal your independence or who you are. To me, who you are is what makes you so amazing. What I want is time. With you. I don't know where we go from here, but I promise you, if you give me a chance, I'll do better."

This time, when he reached out to touch her, she let him. He dragged one finger down her cheek and clucked his tongue. "Progress."

"You're an idiot."

"I know. I think part of you likes that about me."

He was right about that.

But then he stood, stretched his long legs. "You need to open soon, so I'm gonna go. Let you get your work done. Just think about it. If you decide we can give this another go, I'd like to take you to dinner one night. Any night. Just like the first time I hit on you at the B."

Damn him. So well played. Here they were, back at the beginning. A clean start.

He bent over, kissed the top of her head. "I miss you, Brynnie."

She didn't move. Sat there, half-stunned by a humbled Reid Steele. And yet he still had the inherent strength and sense of purpose that had wrapped around her.

She inhaled the musky scent of his soap and her mind flashed back to him loving her under a sky full of brilliant stars.

She let out a breath, let her shoulders drop.

Then he was gone, moving away, heading for the door and—*stop, stop, stop.*

"Reid?"

He pulled the door open, but looked back over his shoulder. "Yeah?"

"I'll close the shop early today. Pick me up at seven."

Enjoy an excerpt from Tracey Devlyn's *Loving DEEP*,
Book Four in the Steele Ridge series:

BY TRACEY DEVLYN

HELPLESS ANGER BLURRED BRITT'S VISION. He
pushed it back and concentrated on diluting their
conversation down to a cold-blooded business
transaction. No emotion, nothing to lose. "If I add my
savings, cabin, property, business, and truck to the
money the bank is willing to lend me, I'll be close—"

"Your cabin and truck? Your business?" she asked,
horrified. "Why would you give up everything of value
to save Mom's property? I don't understand."

"Because I made her a promise." *And because I am the
wolves' last hope.*

"No promise is worth the kind of sacrifice you're
suggesting."

"Normally, I would agree with you. But, in this case,
it is."

"I can't do 'close,' Britt."

He bolted from his chair, startling her. At the
moment, he didn't care. She was one comment away
from leaving, and he couldn't think of a way to stop her.

His mind sparked in a thousand different directions. Staring out the picture window, he saw nothing of the towering cluster of trees or the dilapidated shed. He saw only his reflection, his failure.

If he'd been Grif, he could have charmed her over to his side. Jonah could have waved a wad of cash to win her over. Reid could have...God only knew how, but the devil would have managed the situation. Britt had— nothing. Not a single special quality he could employ.

A light touch on his sleeve brought his attention around to an insanely beautiful pair of green eyes. How many times had he lost himself in their depths? Had wanted her to see him as a man and not just a patron? Had wanted to gather her into his arms and kiss her until they clawed at each other for release?

"There's something more going on here than a mere promise," she said in a tone one reserved for wild animals. "Tell me."

His gaze dipped to her mouth for an aching second before returning to the outdoors. Complete darkness had set in, making their reflection even more pronounced. Impenetrable.

Could he trust her with his most valuable secret?

Could he afford not to at this point?

Barbara hadn't done so. Wouldn't a mother confide in her only daughter?

Probably not, given their estrangement.

Dammit, he didn't want to make an irrevocable mistake. So much rode on the wolves remaining invisible.

He sought her gaze in their reflection. The glass barrier could not disguise her compassion, her strength, her honor. Trust budded through his veins, strengthening with every inch traveled until his spine snapped straight with his resolve.

He took a Mount St. Helens-sized leap of faith.

"An endangered species lives on the property."

"Plant or animal?"

"Isn't it enough to know one exists?"

"No. North Carolina has nearly fifty species of plants and animals listed as endangered. Due to its pristine nature, I don't doubt the property contains one or more on the list."

"If you know this, why consider selling to someone else?"

"Part of the buyer's mission is wildlife conservation. Seems a good fit to me."

"There are many levels of wildlife conservation. Many of which your mother did not approve."

"Then she should have willed the property to you. But she didn't, so it's left to me to figure out the best course of action."

A nugget of hope rattled the cage of Britt's hopelessness. Not many people could recite the number of endangered species in their state. Hell, he only knew because of the research he'd been doing in the last year. So, why would Randi—someone who'd shunned the environment for more than a decade—know such a thing?

"In 1980, the U.S. Fish and Wildlife Service declared the species extinct in the wild. Through a successful reintroduction program, the species has made a small comeback, but none have been known to exist this far west since the late nineties. Until now."

Randi sucked in a sharp breath. "A canid?"

"Yes."

"Red wolf." Awe wove between the two short words. She didn't ask him to confirm or doubt her answer. "A breeding pair?"

"And a litter this year."

She covered her mouth with shaking hands, then lifted her wonder-filled gaze to his. "Show me."

ACKNOWLEDGMENTS

There are projects that seem to take on a life of their own. The Steele Ridge series would be one of them. It's taken two years for the series to be released and if I'd known how complicated three authors writing the same characters in the same world would get, I probably would have run screaming. Thankfully, that didn't happen. As always, my pals Tracey and Kelsey were amazing wingwomen. Two years, multiple spreadsheets, and many invaluable lessons later, I'm looking back on this project and I'm smiling over how lucky I am to have experienced it. So thank you to Tracey and Kelsey for taking this journey with me and helping me get Reid Steele on the page. Much like Vic Andrews from *Man Law*, Reid is one of those characters who never shuts up. He's always in my head, chattering at me, but I loved writing his story. As happy as I am that the book is finished and in readers' hands, I'm also sad that the writing part of Reid's book is over. Without Tracey and Kelsey and our amazing plotting sessions, Reid's story wouldn't have existed.

For research with every book I have a list of go-to people who make my writing life so much fun. Thank you to Milton Grasle, who, no matter what scenario I throw at him, helps me figure out how to make an action scene work. To Scott Silverii, there are not enough ways to say thank you. This time is even more meaningful since you saved me from a major problem when, during *final* edits, I thought my plot might be derailed over search and seizure laws. Thank you, my friend! Thank you, Misty Evans, my writing partner and all-around great friend for the plotting help on Reid's book. You always know just what I need to break through a wall.

A big shout-out to Brandi Knight-Prazak for not laughing at my medical questions and managing to decipher what it was I actually needed to make my scenario work.

Thank you also to Laurie Shulman, one of my earliest readers, and her husband Bill. Your military experience helped me create a career for Reid to love and I'm so grateful. This character has a special place in my heart and your insight let me dig a little deeper into what moves him. To my friend Janet Pepsin, thank you for coming up with the perfect name for Brynne's shop. The smaller yet important details always make me a little crazy and naming the shop was one of them. Muhwah! To Dangerous Darling Crystal Andrews, thank you for playing along with the name game and suggesting Dexter "Dex" Sweet as a character name. It's a great fit.

I would be remiss if I didn't thank our amazing editors, Gina Bernal, Deb Nemeth, and Martha Trachtenberg. Personally, I think you're all insane for taking on this beast of a project, but I'm so grateful you did. This has been an amazing experience for me and I'm thrilled to have worked with all of you on it.

Blazing appreciation to my readers who give me a reason to get back to my desk every day. I've said it before, but without you, I don't have a job and I'm incredibly grateful that you allow my work into your lives. Thanks also to my review crew and the Dangerous Darlings for all the support and being part of my writer-girl life.

And finally, as usual, thank you to my guys for all the love, laughter, and support. I love you.

ADRIENNE GIORDANO is a *USA Today* bestselling author of over twenty romantic suspense and mystery novels. She is a Jersey girl at heart, but now lives in the Midwest with her workaholic husband, sports-obsessed son and Buddy the Wheaten Terrorist (Terrier). She is a cofounder of Romance University blog and Lady Jane's Salon-Naperville, a reading series dedicated to romantic fiction.

www.AdrienneGiordano.com

11851671R00176